Dear Reader,

When I worked as a features writer for the newspaper, I did a story about a sheepherder and his "tender" who'd spent three months back in the Beartooths—only them and a huge band of sheep.

It was the tender, a young man whose job it was to keep camp, that gave me the idea for *Forsaken*. The teen was so glad to be out of the mountains and told harrowing stories about his summer that included grizzly bears, storms and rough dangerous terrain.

What would it take to send a young man like that racing out of those mountains in absolute terror? And what about the widowed sheep rancher who must go into the remote area to check on not only her sheep—but her sheepherder? That was when my story was born.

I hope you enjoy the trip back into the Absaroka-Beartooth Mountains.

B.J. Daniels

FORSAKEN

This book is dedicated to the Western ranchers, sheepherders and tenders who used to trail sheep to summer pastures in the "Beartooths."

In 2003, after three months and 150 miles, the last band of sheep made the round trip for summer range in Montana's Absaroka-Beartooth mountains, ending an era that dates back to the late 19th century.

CHAPTER ONE

THE HORSE STUMBLED under him as he plunged down the steep mountainside, but he spurred on the mare. Around him, the dark pines swayed and sighed in the wind as he crashed down through them, his only thought to reach the ranch alive.

Terror quilled the hair on the back of his neck, but he didn't dare turn around. Fighting to stay in the saddle, he raced along the creek before charging into the fast-running stream. The clear water showered up in an icy wave that soaked him to the skin and stole his breath.

His horse bolted up the other side, forcing him to cling to the saddle horn to stay on his mount. A pine bough caught him in the face, a sharp twig scraping across his cheek and cutting into his flesh.

Behind him, he heard a familiar sound over the roar of his pulse and the howling wind and the thundering hooves of his horse echoing through the timber. Behind him was that unearthly silence that had chased him out of the Beartooth Mountains.

Even as he rode the horse harder, he knew he'd never be able to outrun it—or the smell of death lingering on his skin.

Deputy Sheriff Bentley Jamison was the only one in the office when the call came in.

"That you, Frank?" a grating elderly male voice asked when the dispatcher put the call through.

"Sheriff Frank Curry is out of the office. This is Deputy Sheriff Bentley Jamison. What can I do for you?"

"*Bentley* Jamison? Never heard of you."

Jamison must have said the next words a dozen times a day since he'd recently joined the force. "I'm new."

"Huh," the man said with a chuckle. "Bet you ain't from around here, either."

That was a bet the man would win. At least he hadn't asked what most people did on meeting the new deputy. "What the devil are you doing way out here?"

"What can I do for you?" Jamison asked.

"Well, this is Fuzz Carpenter. You don't know me, but I just run across a kid comin' out of the Beartooths. He was a-ridin' hell-bent for leather like the devil was chasin' him. Had blood all over him. I flagged him down to try to find out what was wrong, but he wasn't makin' an ounce of sense. All I could get out of him was that he worked for the Diamond C sheep ranch. That's 'bout all I can tell ya, exceptin' I didn't like the look in his eyes. Somethin' bad happened back up in those mountains, sure as hell."

Jamison wrote the words *Diamond C Ranch* on the pad next to his phone. "How long ago was this and where exactly?"

"Not ten minutes ago up the Boulder Road. He was

a-headin' back to the ranch, I'm supposing, since he was ridin' in that direction last I saw of him."

"Thanks for letting me know. I'll check it out."

The man grunted in response and hung up.

Jamison asked directions to the Diamond C from the dispatcher then climbed into his patrol SUV and headed toward what the locals called the Boulder. It was actually the Boulder River valley. As he left Big Timber, Montana, he followed the river, the tall thick cottonwoods only giving him glimpses of the clear, green water.

The valley was wide, broken up by plowed fields and creeks that ran down to the river in a winding trail of pines and cottonwoods. With breathtaking beauty, mountains soared up around him, snowcapped and covered in dark pines.

The nearer he got to the Diamond C, the more the valley narrowed. Sheer rock cliffs towered a thousand feet over the two-lane paved road, and ranches became fewer and farther between.

He passed the Natural Bridge and waterfalls up into the Absaroka mountain range, or the Beartooths as locals called them because of one jagged crag that looked like a bear's tooth.

Not far after that, the pavement ran out and he found himself in a tight canyon with nothing but the roaring river still full from spring runoff and high mountains hemming him in.

The Diamond C was snuggled in a coulee back off an even narrower dirt road and across a private rickety bridge spanning the river. It was early June in Montana and the snow-fed creeks were all running high.

As he came over a small rise, he saw the house and low sheep barns. Wind buffeted his patrol SUV, letting out a low howl. Nearer to the house, he saw a lone wooden weather-grayed rocker teetering back and forth in the blustery wind at the edge of a wide porch. Freshly hung sheets billowed and snapped on the clothesline nearby.

He'd had his share of premonitions before. Several of them had saved his life. But none had ever been as strong as the feeling of dread that washed over him as he drove toward the white clapboard two-story farmhouse.

MADISON "MADDIE" CONNER felt the change in the air just a moment before she heard the vehicle approaching. The wind had been blowing all night and morning, screaming down out of the mountains, sending anything not nailed down cartwheeling across the yard.

She'd awakened in the middle of the night when one of the big metal garbage cans had taken off, banging across the wide expanse between house and barn before crashing into the side of the shed. It had been difficult getting back to sleep. Everything was always darkest at that hour—especially her worrying thoughts.

Since rising, she'd kept busy. But a feeling of unease had burrowed under her skin like a splinter, festering as the day progressed. Finally at midmorning and unable to shake off her dismal mood, she'd tried to reach her sheepherder by radio. So far she hadn't been able to raise him or his tender, who were both back in the mountains.

Branch Murdock often purposely forgot to take his radio with him when he was out checking the sheep. He refused to carry a cell phone, not that she blamed him. There was little coverage back in the mountains anyway. She'd told herself she'd try him later.

Stepping out on the porch now, she leaned against the railing and watched the patrol SUV pull to a stop in front of the house. She'd expected to see Sheriff Frank Curry, a handsome fiftysomething big man with a drooping handlebar mustache, climb out.

The man who emerged after the dust settled wasn't Frank—but he was as large and broad-shouldered.

Maddie squinted with both curiosity and an inkling of concern as a man in what she estimated as his thirties tilted back his Stetson on his thick head of brown hair to look in her direction. His eyes were pale and hooded. She could make out enough of his features under the shaded brim of his cowboy hat to realize she'd never seen him before.

He wore the entire sheriff's deputy uniform from the tan shirt to the creased-front slacks and dress boots. She'd never seen any of the local law enforcement in anything but the tan shirt, jeans and well-worn cowboy boots.

Even before he opened his mouth, she knew he wasn't from anywhere around here.

"Good morning, ma'am," he said in a voice that was surprisingly low and soft. The accent, though, was all

"back East." He removed his hat and turned the brim
in his fingers, and she got her first good look at him.
His face was more lined than she'd originally thought,
and his hair was graying at his temples. She realized
he was closer to her own age, mid-forties.

His eyes were a haunting pale gray. It reminded her
of the wolves that had been reintroduced just over the
mountains in Yellowstone Park. The wolves that often
killed her sheep.

"I'm Deputy Sheriff Bentley Jamison and I'm looking for Madison Conner," he said, squinting up at her.

"Well, you found her." She saw his surprise and
couldn't help smiling to herself. He wasn't the first
man who had just assumed the ranch owner was male.

"I'm here about one of your employees," he said. "A
neighbor of yours saw a young man come out of the
mountains a little while ago…. The man who called
thought your employee might have been in trouble."

His words brought back the full force of the unease
she'd awakened with last night. "What kind of trouble?
I don't know anything about—" She took a step to the
edge of the porch stairs then stopped as her gaze slid
past him to the faded red barn in need of fresh paint.

Her breath caught as she recognized the lathered-up
horse standing next to it. The horse was still saddled,
but there was no sign of its rider. Even from the distance
she could see that the mare needed tending to at once.

She shoved off the porch steps and sprinted toward
the barn. When she got hold of Dewey Putman she'd
tan his hide for treating a horse like that. Even as she

thought it, though, she felt that sliver of worry dig in deeper.

What was her tender doing back at the ranch? And what had a neighbor seen that would make him call a deputy instead of her?

Maddie reached the horse, her heart breaking at the shape it was in. The mare had been ridden hard. Her fingers brushed over a four-inch cut along one flank, and she saw that the mare was favoring one leg.

She dug her cell phone from her jeans pocket and tapped in the veterinarian's number, then shoved open the barn door and called Dewey's name.

Behind her, she was only vaguely aware that the sheriff's deputy had followed her. In the dim light of the barn, dust motes twirled in the early-morning light as she called Dewey's name again before the vet came on the line.

"I've got a horse that needs attention right away," she said into the phone. "If you can't come out…" She let out a relieved sigh. "Thanks, Doc. I appreciate it."

As she disconnected, she heard a rustling sound deeper in the barn, then a whimper and what sounded like sobbing. She felt her chest tighten. Stuffing her cell phone back into her jeans pocket, she grabbed up a pitchfork as she followed the sound to a back stall.

A few feet from the muffled noise she felt the deputy's large hand drop to her shoulder. He'd unsnapped his weapon and now motioned for her to stand back and let him handle it.

As a groan came from inside the stall, Maddie gave

a shake of her head and banged the stall door open with the pitchfork.

"What the hell is wrong with you, Dewey Putman?" she demanded then froze as she saw her sheep tender cowering in the corner. Her gaze took in his blood-stained clothing, the scratches on his face and the terror in his eyes before he dropped his head into his folded arms again and wept.

"Come out of there, son," the deputy said as he pushed past her.

She let out the breath that had caught in her throat at the sight of Dewey like this and slowly lowered the pitchfork. "You heard him. Come out."

Dewey looked up. A lock of his dark hair had fallen over one bloodshot brown eye. She felt her stomach roil.

"Come on," she said, gentling her voice the way she would have for a spooked horse. She dropped the pitch-fork over the partial wall into the next stall and held out her hand.

But before Dewey could take it, the deputy stepped between them.

"I'm going to have to handle this," he said to her then turned to Dewey. "What's your name?"

"His name is Dewey Putman. He's my sheep ten-der." Then turning to Dewey, she said, "What I need to know is what you're doing here, and where are Branch and my sheep?"

The deputy shot her a look that said he'd prefer to do this his way.

Before she could remind him that he was on her

ranch or that she had two thousand sheep and possibly no herder, he said, "Could you please make some tea?"

Bristling, Maddie raised a brow. *"Tea?"*

"Or coffee if you prefer. Something to warm him up. Also, he'll need a change of clothing. His clothes are soaked. If he isn't suffering from hypothermia, he will be."

Ready to do what came naturally and take care of things herself, she had to bite her tongue as she shot another look at Dewey. He was trembling like a dog cornered by a grizzly and in as bad shape or worse than his horse.

Something had happened in the sheep camp back in the Beartooth Mountains. Even before she'd seen the blood on his clothing, she'd known by the look in the young man's eyes that he was in trouble. The deputy knew it, too.

Dewey was her employee, her responsibility. While her first instinct was to help him, she knew from the warning look the deputy had given her that Dewey's welfare was now out of her hands.

"I'll see to his horse," she said. "There's a pot of coffee on the stove. Help yourself."

CHAPTER TWO

DEPUTY SHERIFF BENTLEY JAMISON watched the ranch woman stride off, before turning back to the young man cowering in the corner of the stall. He'd seen his share of young men with blood on their hands. None, though, had looked as terrified as this one.

"Son, I'm going to have to ask you to stand up now," he said.

As Dewey Putman stumbled to his feet, Jamison searched him for a weapon or any sign of an injury that could account for the blood on the boy's clothing. The tender was little more than a kid, late teens at most. He had no weapon and had no visible wounds. So there was a good chance the blood on his clothing wasn't his.

"Let's go up to the house," Jamison said. "I'm going to need to call your parents. Can you tell me that number?"

The boy shook his head.

He figured Mrs. Conner must have it as he led the young man through the dimly lit barn.

As they neared the open barn door, Dewey balked. He shook his head, hugging himself and moaning under his breath as he looked toward the bright daylight outside.

It was one of those beautiful early June days in southwest Montana. A blinding sun hung in a cloudless blue sky. The breeze smelled of spring, but its cold bite was a reminder that summer in these parts was weeks off.

"It's all right," he told the boy. "It's not that far to the house. I won't let anything happen to you." Still, he had to take Dewey's trembling arm to get him to cross the patch of sunlit earth to the house. What, he wondered as an icy chill settled over him, had frightened this kid so badly?

At his patrol SUV, he took out the investigation kit he'd been given when he'd started as deputy. So far, he'd had no use for it. Crime in this part of the world was barking dogs, an occasional barroom brawl and traffic control when a semi blew over on the pass. It was a far cry from his job as a homicide detective in New York City.

On the porch, he had the boy strip off his wet, soiled clothing down to his underwear. He led him into the house and was looking for the bathroom when he heard Madison Conner come up the porch steps.

"Don't touch those," he said through the screen door as she knelt to pick up the boy's dirty clothing.

She rose with an indignant sigh, took one glance at her half-naked tender then pulled open the screen door and walked past them. "The bathroom is the second door on the left," she said, pointing down a short hallway without turning to look at them.

"I need to contact this boy's parents or guardian," he said to her retreating back.

"You're looking at his guardian," she said before disappearing into the kitchen.

In the green-and-white-tiled 1950s-style bathroom, Jamison turned on the shower and quickly ran the necessary forensics tests, scraping under the boy's fingernails and swabbing his hands and wrists for gunshot residue, before he let him climb into the hot shower.

He left Dewey long enough to bag the boy's clothing and load it and the specimens he'd taken into the patrol SUV before he returned to the house.

When he walked in, he found Madison Conner putting clothing outside the bathroom door. She gave him a look that made it clear she didn't like him interfering with what she considered her business.

Since arriving in the state a few weeks ago, Jamison had learned how independent Montanans were—especially ranch women. Behind the often weathered suntanned skin he'd glimpsed an iron-strong will. He'd never seen more capable women.

Whether hauling trucks loaded with ranch supplies, feeding dozens of ranchers at brandings or jumping in to help with every chore on the spread, there was little these women didn't know how to do—and well.

This was the first ranch woman, though, that he was about to butt heads with.

He took note of Maddie Conner's clothing from her loose-fitting large flannel shirt and jeans. Her boots were as worn as her hands, and both were a sign of a hardworking rancher. There were fine lines around her cornflower-blue eyes. The set of her jaw bespoke of a stubbornness born of living in a man's world. But while she might hide her femininity under a lot of attitude and loose clothing, there was kindness in her face that the years and her lifestyle hadn't yet eroded.

As she straightened the stack of clothing she'd left for the boy he glimpsed a deep sadness in her expression, which she quickly masked. She made a swipe at an errant lock of her hair. It was long, the dark red of cherrywood with a few streaks of silver woven through. It surprised him to realize she was probably close to his own age.

As if sensing him watching her, she checked her expression and gathered up her thick mane. With nimble fingers she trapped it again in the large clip that held her hair off her neck. He couldn't help noticing how pale and soft the exposed skin appeared.

"Yes?" she asked, irritation in her tone as her gaze met his.

"I need to ask you a few questions," he said, embarrassed that she'd caught him staring at her. "You're Dewey's legal guardian?"

She gave him a grave nod. "Come into the kitchen," she said, turning her back on him. She appeared reconciled to the questions and his being there, but definitely not happy about it. "The sooner you get your answers, the sooner I can see to my shepherd and flock."

Jamison followed her into a sunlit yellow kitchen that looked as if it, like the bathroom, hadn't been remodeled since the early fifties. The table was large and long with curved metal legs and a yellow checked top that matched the counter. The cabinets were knotty pine and the floor was a familiar linoleum pattern reminiscent of another era.

"How do you take your coffee?" she asked as she pulled down several mugs from the cabinet.

"Black." He heard the shower shut off. "You said your *tender's* name is Dewey Putman?" he asked as he produced his notebook and pen.

Maddie could tell by the way he said "tender" that he had no idea what that was. She put a cup of hot coffee in front of him. A pot was always on at most ranches. Hers was no different since she never knew who might stop by. Not that she got much company anymore. Her own fault for being so contrary, her husband would have said and would have been right.

She was too worried to sit, so she leaned against the counter, cradling her coffee mug, soaking in its warmth. She tried to remember the deputy's name—something odd, she thought. All she could recall was his last name. Jamison.

"Dewey worked as the tender," she said. "His job was to take care of the camp while Branch, that's my sheepherder, took care of the sheep up in the high country for three months this summer."

"The high country?"

"Back in the Beartooth Mountains—that's where I graze a couple thousand sheep. The tender moves camp as needed. He cooks, comes down for supplies when they run low—"

"Would they have been running low?"

She shook her head. "Branch just took the sheep up to the grazing area four days ago."

"And that's where this boy has been?"

She nodded.

"When was the last time you heard from your sheepherder?"

"Four days ago when I helped take the sheep up. That was the last time I saw either of them until…" An image of Dewey's horse, then the boy flashed into her mind. She gripped her mug tighter as she lifted it to her lips.

"Your sheepherder is named Branch?"

"Branch Murdock."

Jamison looked up from his notebook. "His parents named him Branch?"

She gave a shrug. "That's the name I've been putting on his paycheck for almost twenty-five years. Before that my mother wrote the checks."

"Did everything appear normal when you left them up in the mountains?"

Maddie hated to admit she'd had misgivings about giving the boy the job. "Dewey's a little green, I'll admit, but I figured he'd learn well enough from Branch."

"So the boy hadn't been a tender before?"

"No."

"How old is he?"

"Sixteen." She saw the deputy's eyes widen. "Plenty of men his age are doing a lot harder ranch work than being a sheep tender." She knew she sounded defensive, but the deputy unnerved her with his intent silver gaze.

"If you're his legal guardian, then where are his parents?"

"Divorced. I don't know where his mother is off to. His father works odd jobs that take him north to the Bakken oil fields for long periods of time. That's why Chester asked me to give the boy a job and made me his guardian."

The deputy studied her for a long moment before he asked, "Has Dewey been in trouble before?"

"Who says he's in trouble *now?*" she snapped, and looked away, angry with herself, Dewey and the situation. If this man would just let her talk to Dewey and find out what had happened up in those mountains, she could get this cleared up before Deputy Jamison jumped to the wrong conclusion.

"You might as well tell me if the boy's been in trouble," Jamison said. "I'll find out soon enough."

Silence stretched between them until she finally broke it. "Dewey got into some dustup at school. His father thought spending the summer in the mountains, away from his friends…"

"What kind of…dustup?"

"Boy stuff, I would imagine." She glanced toward the sound of footfalls in the hallway. "I don't really know," she said quietly then turned as Dewey filled the open kitchen doorway. "Come have some coffee," she called, moving to get him a mug.

Dewey came meekly into the kitchen, wearing her son's clothing. He looked enough like her Matthew that it felt like being kicked by a horse. She already felt sick at heart as it was for Dewey, for his horse, for whatever had frightened him and maybe worse, whatever he might have done.

"Sit," she ordered, and turned away to cut the chocolate cake she'd made only that morning. She'd planned to take the cake to the stock-growers' meeting she had later in the afternoon, but all her plans would change now.

Dewey pulled out a chair at the end of the table, and she placed a slice of cake and a mug of coffee in front of him. She automatically reached for the sugar and cream because that was the way Matthew had always taken his coffee. Dewey ignored both and began to slurp up the hot coffee as if dying of thirst.

The deputy was watching the boy closely. She felt her chest tighten at the thought of what kind of trouble Dewey might be in. "Dewey—"

Jamison cut her off. "That cake looks awfully good, Mrs. Conner. Mind if I have a piece?"

Maddie tried to still her impatience as she sliced the deputy a large portion and topped off his coffee even though he hadn't touched it. She desperately needed to know what had happened and what she was going to have to do about it.

"Mrs. Conner here was just telling me—"

"Maddie," she interrupted.

Jamison shot her an annoyed look before turning back to the boy again. "*Maddie* was just telling me you were hired on as the sheepherder's tender."

Dewey nodded but kept his eyes on the cake he was

in the process of devouring. He acted as if he hadn't eaten in days. She realized with a start that Branch wouldn't have let the boy go hungry—that was, if he'd been able to take care of the two of them.

Did that mean something had happened to Branch? Her stomach dropped at the thought. What of her sheep? She'd been hanging on to the ranch by a thread for so long…

"Son, can you tell me what happened?" the deputy asked.

The fork froze in Dewey's hand, and then slowly he began to scrape the crumbs from the plate, never taking his eyes off the table, before dropping his fork and washing the cake down with the rest of his coffee.

"How about we start at the beginning?" Jamison said. "For the past four days, you've been up in the mountains with the sheepherder, is that right?"

Dewey nodded.

"Where is Branch now?" Maddie asked, ignoring the warning look the deputy shot her.

"I don't know," the boy said, dropping his voice and his head.

The deputy cleared his throat. "When did you last see him?"

"Just before bed last night. He said he'd been having trouble sleeping. The noises were keeping him up."

"The noises? You mean the sheep?" the deputy asked.

Dewey lifted his head and frowned at the silly question. "Branch was used to the sheep. He said he could tell if they were happy or scared just by the sounds they made at night."

"Then what was keeping him up at night?" the deputy asked.

"The strange sounds..." Dewey glanced back down at the table "...the...crying."

Maddie couldn't help herself. *"Crying?"*

"I'm not making it up," the boy said, lifting his head to plead his case with her. Tears filled his eyes, and he began to tremble again. "I swear. We heard awful... crying on the wind."

"You have heard the sound of wind or a coyote calling at night, haven't you?" Maddie asked in exasperation.

"It weren't no coyote," the boy snapped. "It weren't just the wind, either. It was...something else. Even old Branch was spooked by it."

"Are you sure Branch didn't just wander off?" the deputy asked.

"Maybe. His horse was missing this morning. I called for him and looked all over."

Maddie doubted Dewey had done much searching for the sheepherder given how scared he was.

"How did you get the blood on you?" the deputy asked.

The boy wagged his head without looking down. "One of the lambs. She was hurt. I tried to help her." He was close to tears again. Maddie remembered her son at that age, so tough and yet so tender, a boy on the edge of manhood doing his best to measure up. If only Matthew was here now, she thought with that unbearable grip at her heart.

"How did you and Branch get along?" Jamison asked.

"Fine," he said to his empty plate.

Maddie took the plate and cut him another slice of cake. She could feel the deputy's irritation with her, not that she gave a damn as she slid the second slice of cake in front of Dewey and refilled his mug. She noticed the deputy had hardly touched his cake *or* his coffee.

"I would imagine with only the two of you up there all alone, you might have had disagreements on occasion," the deputy asked.

Dewey said nothing as he dived into the cake and coffee she'd set before him. She felt torn between wanting to shake the truth out of Dewey and wanting to protect him. All her instincts told her that the boy needed protecting.

"Branch hard to get along with, was he?" Jamison asked.

"Meaner than a rabid dog when he drank." The kid, realizing he'd just spilled the beans, shot Maddie an alarmed look and quickly gulped out, "Not that he drank usually."

Maddie groaned.

"If you had something to do with Branch going missing up there—"

"I didn't!" he cried. "I swear. I don't know what happened to him."

She felt her stomach go tight with fear as a thought

hit her. "Where's Branch's dog, Lucy? That dog would never have let him out of her sight."

Dewey shook his head and began to cry.

"Son," the deputy pressed. "If you know something, you have to tell me."

"I don't know. I'm telling you. I…I don't know anything."

"I've had enough of this," Maddie said as she shoved off the kitchen counter.

Dewey looked up, startled, as if he thought she planned to beat it out of him.

"I have two thousand sheep up in those mountains, and I can't be sure anyone is watching them," she said to Jamison.

"Right now, I have bigger concerns than your sheep," he said, getting to his feet. "I'm going to have to hold the boy until I know what happened up there. I'm afraid this warrants investigating."

"Then you see to your investigation, Deputy. I'm going to check on my sheep." What she couldn't bring herself to say, let alone admit to this Easterner, was that the future of her ranch was riding on this year's sheep production.

Not that she wasn't even more scared out of her wits that something bad had happened to Branch. He wasn't just her sheepherder. He was as close to a grandfather as she'd ever had. He was also her closest friend.

But if she had tried to explain it to the deputy she would have been fighting tears. And she never cried. She'd done all her crying a long time ago.

As she started down the hallway toward her bedroom, she heard him coming after her. "Mrs. Conner—"

"Maddie," she snapped without turning around. She had no idea what had happened back in those mountains, but she was scared, sick over the pain she saw in that boy sitting in her kitchen and worried as the devil about Branch, as well as her sheep.

She didn't have the time or patience to deal with the law right now.

Jamison caught up to her halfway down the hall and grabbed her arm, forcing her to stop and face him. "*Maddie,* I can't let you go up there alone."

"No offense, but a greenhorn like you would just slow me down."

"I'll do my best not to," he said. "But I'm going with you." His gaze softened as he seemed to notice the tears in her eyes. She wiped at them, as angry with herself as she was with him for noticing.

"Right now I'm concerned about my sheepherder. Branch has been with my family for years. He wouldn't leave the sheep unattended. Either Dewey is wrong or—"

"Or your sheepherder met with some kind of accident."

She connected with his gaze. "He's *my* responsibility. I really don't need your help."

"Did you notice the kid's knuckles?"

Maddie started. She hadn't.

"He's been in a recent fistfight. And that cut over

his eye? He didn't get that from falling down. On top of that, he's lying about something."

"You don't know—"

"I might be a greenhorn in Montana, but I know when a suspect is lying. Before I took the job as deputy here, I was a homicide detective."

A dark, cold lump formed in her chest. *A suspect? Homicide?*

"I'm sorry, Mrs.—Maddie, but I'm afraid under the circumstances, neither of us has a choice right now. You have a missing sheepherder and sheep you need to see to. But I can't let you go up there alone and destroy what I suspect is going to be a crime scene."

CHAPTER THREE

NOTHING MOVED FASTER in the near ghost town of Beartooth, Montana, than gossip. Even the powerful, fearful winds that blew down out of the Crazy Mountains were no match for the wagging tongues.

This morning the gossip was about Maddie Conner and the Diamond C Ranch's young tender.

Every morning Lynette "Nettie" Benton crossed the street from her store to the Branding Iron Café to get a cinnamon roll and coffee and the latest gossip. She could always depend on the regulars to dish up tasty tidbits of news or scandal.

In fact, she prided herself on knowing everything that was going on in town. She spent much of her day at the front window of the Beartooth General Store watching the world go by. True, the world passed more like a glacier in Beartooth.

The town, in the shadow of the "Crazies," as the locals called the Crazy Mountain range, had once been quite the wild mining town back in the late eighteen hundreds. Now, though, other than a bunch of deserted old buildings, there was only her general store, the post office, the Range Rider Bar, a community church and the café, which suited most folks in the area just fine since the larger town of Big Timber was only twenty-some miles away.

In Montana traveling twenty miles was nothing. Many traveled much farther and often on dirt roads just to get to a store—let alone to catch a flight or shop at a big-box store.

Nettie liked to say that she knew more about the people in the area than they did about themselves. And she'd never been shy about spreading what she knew, either, which was why she'd become known as the county's worst gossip.

She didn't mind. Let them say what they would. Most days, the tidbits she picked up weren't all that exciting. This morning, though, she'd hit the mother lode when she'd overheard Fuzz Carpenter.

Fuzz was sitting at the front table at the Branding Iron Café with the rest of the ranchers who gathered there every morning when she heard him mention the woman sheep rancher and her young tender.

Historically sheep ranchers, in what had originally been cattle country, weren't all that popular. While cattle and sheep ranchers now got along, it was still rare for a woman to be running a sheep ranch. Not to mention the fact that Maddie Conner didn't take any guff off anyone—especially male ranchers who thought she needed their advice.

"Covered with blood," Fuzz was saying. "Didn't take more than a look in that boy's eyes. Somethin' bad happened back in those mountains. Mark my words."

Nettie's first thought was to call Sheriff Frank Curry

and find out what was going on. But then she heard Fuzz say that he'd talked to some new deputy because the sheriff was out of town.

"*Bentley* Jamison," Fuzz mocked with the worst impression of a New York accent Nettie had ever heard. "What the hell kind of name is that?" The ranchers all laughed. "Wait until he meets Maddie Conner." That brought on more laughter. "*I* wouldn't even want to take *her* on."

Nettie was thinking about the sheriff being out of town. No doubt Frank was visiting his daughter, she thought with a chill.

SHERIFF FRANK CURRY nervously turned the brim of his Stetson in his fingers as he waited. He was a big man, a throwback from another era with his thick handlebar mustache and longish hair. He could have been a sheriff from a hundred years ago.

The nurse had told him to sit down in one of the chairs in the glassed-in solarium, but he could no more sit than he could fly. He stood at the window, looking out at the rolling land and counting his regrets. They'd been few—before a seventeen-year-old young woman named Tiffany Chandler had shown up at his door. Actually the first time they'd met, he'd caught her in his house going through his bureau drawers as brazen as any thief he'd run across.

Now, at the sound of footfalls behind him, he braced himself and turned to see his daughter and a nurse come into the room.

"Hi, sweetheart," he said.

Tiffany looked paler than he remembered, thinner, too. She'd cut her long blond hair, hacking it short and choppy with a pair of scissors she'd somehow gotten her hands on.

"How the hell does a mental patient get hold of scissors?" he'd demanded when he'd received the call from the hospital.

"Your daughter is a very…determined young woman," the nurse had told him. The woman meant sneaky, cunning, shrewd, manipulative—deadly. *Determined* was a kindness to him that sounded more like pity.

Frank knew what extremes Tiffany would go to once she set her mind to something. She'd almost killed him, after killing something he'd loved.

Looking at her now, he could see there was still a lot of hate and anger in her. He knew that defiant, hurt look too well and liked to believe it masked fear rather than soulless hatred.

Tiffany glared at him with huge blue eyes that dominated her waiflike features. She had refused to let anyone repair the damage she'd done to her hairdo. He'd always noticed a fragility about her, but now it was heightened.

He felt desperate to take her in his arms and protect her—just as he had last February when he'd learned who she was. Until then, he hadn't known he had a daughter. Still didn't, actually.

After she'd tried to kill him, the county attorney had sent her for a mental evaluation to see if she could stand trial. The state had also insisted on running a paternity test to see if the teenager actually was Frank's birth daughter.

The report had come in a large brown envelope, but Frank had never opened it. He felt Tiffany was his responsibility no matter what blood ran through her veins because she was the creation of his vindictive ex-wife.

When he thought of his ex-wife, Pam, he often thought of killing her. That thought only lasted an instant because he wasn't a killer—and because he had created Pam, just as she had created Tiffany. Pam had kept the pregnancy from him, raising the girl alone and programming her to ultimately take revenge against the man they both now hated.

"How are you doing?" he asked Tiffany, gripping the brim of his hat when he wanted more than anything to hold this poor child. But the nurse had warned him not to try.

"How do you *think* I'm doing in this crazy bin?" Tiffany spat.

Better than prison, he wanted to tell her. But he couldn't be sure that prison wasn't still in her future. It would be up to the state eventually. Right now, he was fighting to keep her from going before a judge on attempted-murder charges against an officer of the law. He feared she would be tried as an adult, and he couldn't bear the thought of her in prison.

"Is there anything you need, anything I can get for you?" he asked.

"You've done quite enough. If that's all..." She started to turn away.

"Tiffany, the doctor said you haven't been cooperating."

She raised one very pale blond brow at him as she let her blue eyes return to him.

"If you get well—"

"Is that what you're telling them?" She crossed her skinny arms over her skinny chest. "That I'm *unwell? Crazy? A lunatic just like my mother?*" The nurse put a hand on her shoulder, but Tiffany shook it off. "I'm just *fine.* And so was my mother before she met *you.*"

He hated that she wouldn't take responsibility for what she'd done any more than her mother had the one time he'd talked to her after he'd found out about Tiffany.

"You tried to kill me," he said to the girl now.

Her eyes glittered an instant before she gave him a slow smile. "I'm just sorry I failed."

"It's talk like that that will end you up in prison. Don't you understand I'm trying to help you?"

"By pressing charges against me?"

"That was the state because I am a county sheriff." And Tiffany *was* dangerous, no matter how much he might want to argue otherwise. He sighed, his heart breaking with frustration. He wanted to help her. Why couldn't she see that?

"Tiffany, I love you. You're my daughter. I want time to make up for the past since I didn't even know you existed. Give us that time by working with the doctor so you can get out of here."

Tears suddenly filled her eyes. "You turned my mother against me."

His fury at his ex-wife boiled to the surface. She'd sent her only child to seek revenge in the most deadly, destructive way for both him and Tiffany. And now she'd washed her hands of the girl. What mother could do such a thing?

Pam was the one who needed to be in a mental institution, he thought, tamping down his murderous rage. "You know I have no control over your mother. She wants to hurt us both. By making you think I'm responsible, it's just another way for her to drive us apart."

Tiffany shook her head, tears now streaming down her face. "She said you would blame her."

Frank balled his fists at his sides. He didn't know where Pam was, afraid sometimes of what he would do if he found her. He unclenched his fists, not wanting to give his daughter any more ammunition against him.

"This is your fault," Tiffany cried. "If you had loved my mother and not that horrible Nettie Benton…"

Frank felt his heart clinch at his former lover's name on his daughter's lips. There was only one other person Tiffany and her mother hated more than him.

"None of this has anything to do with Lynette," he said, using the name he'd always called Nettie. "She was married to Bob when your mother and I were together, and there was nothing going on between us."

"Mother said you never got over the bitch."

He would have loved arguing that, but he couldn't. His daughter would have seen the truth. "I married your mother because I loved her." That much at least was true. Pam's jealousy had destroyed the marriage, but Tiffany wouldn't believe that. He hated even thinking about those dark days, never knowing what mood Pam would be in when he returned home.

"Mother said you never tried to get her back."

They'd had this discussion too many times, and nothing he could say weakened the venom Pam had injected into their daughter's veins.

"I can't change the past. Had I known about you, I would have gone after your mother and brought you both back. She never gave me that chance."

The girl shook her head, her big blue eyes filling with tears. "If I had known that Nettie Benton was the woman you were in love with…" She didn't have to continue. He knew. Tiffany had come to Beartooth with a gun and a heart full of hate.

She knew where to find him, but she'd been looking for Lynette Johnson. That had been Lynette's name when the two of them were in their early twenties and lovers. Tiffany hadn't known that Lynette went by the name Nettie Benton.

Frank wished more than anything that he and Lynette had married and had children of their own. Instead Lynette had married Bob Benton. And years later, he'd foolishly married Pam Chandler. Their marriage had been short and far from sweet.

It wasn't enough that Pam and Tiffany had brought

him to his knees. But he lived in fear that Tiffany, if released, would go after Lynette, the woman he'd loved and lost years ago and still loved now.

Or that Pam, realizing her daughter might never be free again, might decide to take matters into her own hands.

JAMISON CALLED HIS office in Big Timber and discussed the situation with the undersheriff in charge. They both agreed he should go up into the mountains with Mrs. Conner.

"At this point, it doesn't warrant sending search and rescue up there," Undersheriff Dillon Lawson said. "We don't know that a crime has been committed or even if the sheepherder is actually missing."

They wouldn't know about the blood on the boy's coat until the forensics came back from the state lab, and who knew how long that would take?

"The boy's been in a fight," Jamison said. "*Something* happened up there. Something bad enough that the boy is terrified. But you're right—there's no smoking gun." Not yet anyway.

"Okay. This could take you a few days, though. You're scheduled off this weekend. If this case runs over…"

"I doubt it will. If it does, it isn't a problem."

"Let me know what you find—if you can get cellphone coverage from one of the higher peaks up there, call me. Coverage up there is sketchy at best. If it becomes a rescue operation or worse, we can send in a helicopter once we have the location. So it is just going to be you and Maddie Conner going up there?"

"She's not keen on my going along."

Dillon chuckled. "I'll just bet. Good luck."

Jamison hung up and went to check on Dewey Putman. He got the feeling that the undersheriff thought his going up into the mountains would be good for him. Knock some of the back-East off of him. Apparently Maddie's reputation had also preceded her since the undersheriff found some humor in his going with her.

In the kitchen, he saw that Dewey had finished his cake and coffee, shoved his dirty dishes away and, with his head cradled on his arms, had fallen into an exhausted sleep on the table.

He knew Maddie Conner was holding out hope that Dewey hadn't done anything wrong and that they would find nothing out of the ordinary back in her summer sheep camp. He wished he could share her optimism.

"For all you know that *is* lamb blood on that boy's jacket, just like he said," she'd argued before he'd gone out to make the call to the office.

"Maybe. I think you should call the boy's father. Meanwhile, I'm afraid he'll have to be held in custody at the jail since his guardian will be in the mountains with me."

"I already called the oil company and left a message for his father. Since there is no one else, I guess that's the best we can do for now."

"We shouldn't be gone that long," Jamison had said.

She'd given him a disbelieving smile. "There is only

one way to get back where we need to go, Deputy, and that's by horseback, so it's going to take a while. You ever ridden a horse? Never mind. I'll saddle you a gentle one. But you're going to need some boots and some practical clothes. I think some of my husband's will fit you."

Before he'd been able to ask about her husband, she'd disappeared down the hall. He remembered the way Maddie had been looking at the kid earlier, so much heartbreak in her eyes. It had made him wonder where she'd gotten the clothing she'd given Dewey. Did she have a son of her own?

Leaving the sleeping boy, he stepped back in the living room and looked for family photographs. While he waited for Maddie, he couldn't help being curious. To his surprise, he found no family photographs. That seemed strange. She'd mentioned a husband and she'd produced boys' clothing, but there was no sign anyone lived here but her.

"I put some clothes out for you," she said from behind, startling him. As he turned, she gave him an irritated look as if she knew he'd been snooping. "I put them in a room down the hall. I'll get what we'll need together and go load the horses." Without another word, she disappeared out the front door.

Jamison found a flannel shirt, canvas jacket, a yellow slicker, jeans and several pairs of heavy socks along with a pair of cowboy boots waiting for him in what appeared to be a spare bedroom. He was surprised when everything fit fairly well.

Having changed quickly, he came out of the bedroom and listened for a moment to make sure Maddie had left the house before sticking his head in the other rooms. He found Maddie's bedroom and the family photos he'd been looking for. In a wedding-day photograph, he studied an innocent-looking young Maddie standing next to a handsome young man.

She'd been beautiful. So fresh and sweet looking. She'd had that "I'm ready to conquer the world" look in those blue eyes of hers. She'd looked...happy.

There were later photos of the husband and Maddie and finally some of a son. So where were this son and husband now?

Stepping back out of the room, Jamison went into the kitchen to check on Dewey again. The boy still slept as if he hadn't so much as dozed in days. In the living room, Jamison put in a call to the sheriff's office again.

Lucille Brown, a good-natured older woman, was working dispatch today. She'd put through the earlier call from Fuzz Carpenter and had given him directions to the Diamond C.

"Can you provide me with some background information on Madison Conner?" he asked. Through the window, he could see Maddie talking to a man he suspected was the veterinarian she'd called earlier about Dewey's horse.

"Maddie? What do you want to know? She raises sheep. She still sends her flock up into the high country every summer. Last of the ranches to do that. Gotta hand it to her. She's tough as any woman I've ever met."

Jamison could sure as hell attest to that. He'd probably met a more stubborn, headstrong woman in his life, but he couldn't recall one.

"Does she have a son?" he asked just as Maddie turned and started back toward the house.

"Matthew. Lost him and her husband in a tragic accident four summers ago. Everyone thought she'd sell out and leave after that. But not Maddie. It's her family's place, but word around town is that it might not be for long. She's had some tough breaks. If Fuzz is right and something has happened to Branch…"

"We don't know that," he said.

Just as Maddie reached the porch steps, a Sweetgrass County patrol car pulled in. "I've got to go," Jamison told Lucille, and disconnected as Maddie came through the door.

"Ready?" She had a resigned look on her face as if braced for not only being forced to allow him to go along, but also for whatever she had to face up in those mountains.

Jamison had noticed the tall antenna on the roof when he was walking Dewey back to the house from the barn. He assumed it was for a radio and now saw the base unit on a table in the corner of the living room.

"Have you heard anything from Branch?" he asked, motioning to the two-way radio receiver.

"I haven't talked to either of them since I left them four days ago. I already told you that."

"But you tried to reach them." She'd left an earlier coffee mug by the base unit. He was betting that the coffee was cold from this morning. So she had been worried, just as he suspected.

She swallowed and let out a sigh before she answered. "I tried to raise Branch this morning."

"You couldn't?"

"It doesn't mean anything. He doesn't like carrying the radio, so he often leaves it in camp." She sounded defensive and not for the first time today.

"Why did you try to reach him this morning?"

"I was just checking—"

"You were worried because of Dewey."

Her gaze came back to his, as determined as the set of her shoulders. "Are you trying to put words into my mouth, Deputy?"

"Sorry. What were you checking on?"

"Just to make sure they were doing all right."

"You do that often?" He wondered if she'd lie and was glad when she didn't.

"No. I was concerned that Dewey might be…homesick. His father was determined that sheep camp was just what his son needed. He wanted Dewey away from his friends, and with his father gone so much of the time…"

"But you had your doubts."

She gave him an impatient look. "Not everyone can spend that much time alone."

"But Branch was with him."

She let out an amused snort. "Branch isn't much of a talker. He could go for days without a single word, so yes, Dewey would have had a lot of time to himself.

Just because he got scared and came out of the mountains, doesn't mean—"

"Please try to reach Branch," he said, motioning to the radio.

She did as he asked, though with apparently the same result as she'd had earlier. "Like I said, he probably doesn't have the radio with him."

"Or he's unable to answer. Does he have a cell phone with him?"

"No, but they aren't worth a hill of beans back where we're going. Not really anywhere to plug it in, either, when it runs out of juice." She turned and started out the door, clearly over his interrogation.

"So where exactly are we going?" he asked as he went after her. Even with his longer legs, he had to walk fast to keep up with her.

"Up there," she said without slowing down as she descended the porch steps and strode across the yard toward the barn. She waved a hand past the low sheep barns to the snowcapped mountains rising to dizzying heights in the distance. "It's a good day's ride." She shot him a look, assessing him, as he caught up to her. He could see that he came up lacking in her estimation.

"A whole day?" That surprised him. He looked again to the mountains. He'd come out here wanting to lose himself in this wild remote country, but he hadn't meant literally.

"We're getting a late start," she said as if his questions were slowing them down even more. "We'll be lucky to reach camp in two."

Jamison had looked at a map of the area before he'd left New York and had been in awe at the way the mountains to the south of Big Timber ran all the way to Yellowstone Park with the only access from this area by foot or horseback.

As he stared at the snowcapped peaks, he couldn't imagine what it must be like way back in such an isolated place, let alone how difficult it would be to survive in such unforgiving, wild country. It had to mess with a person's mind. He wondered what it had done to Dewey Putman.

CHAPTER FOUR

THE PICKUP RATTLED up the road, the horse trailer with two horses inside knocking along behind it. As Maddie drove, the road narrowed until it was little more than two ruts. They followed the Boulder River through a tight canyon of rock and pines, the road winding deeper into the mountains.

Jamison looked over at the ranch woman. She had a tight grip on the wheel, her eyes on the road ahead and a determined set to her jaw. He wanted to ask about her husband and son as well as how far they would drive before they would unload the horses and head up into the mountains.

But he held his tongue, sensing the last thing she wanted to do right now was talk to him, especially about her husband and son.

So he focused on the road ahead and tried not to let his thoughts get too far ahead of him—or behind him for that matter. When he'd left New York for Montana, he'd promised himself that he wasn't going to belabor that former life with thoughts of *if only*.

But he couldn't help thinking about Maddie's ranch house with its 1950s decor and its family photos in her bedroom—and the high-dollar, high-rise apartment he'd shared with his now ex-wife and the complete lack of family photographs anywhere in it.

Lana had insisted on a professional decorator who had assured her that family photographs on the mantel were tacky.

He'd given her free rein, not caring at the time. He'd just wanted Lana to be happy.

"So have you always done this?" Jamison asked, needing to break the silence and avoid thoughts of his ex-wife and that other life.

Maddie shot him a glance. "Driven a truck with a horse trailer on the back?"

"Raised sheep."

"It's my family's ranch, so yes, five generations worth of sheep ranchers. You know anything about sheep?" She continued before he could answer. "Sheep don't like to walk in water or move through narrow openings. They prefer to move into the wind and uphill rather than downwind or downhill. They see in color but have poor depth perception. That's why they avoid shadows and always move toward the light. They have excellent hearing, so they're more sensitive to high-frequency sounds. Loud noises scare them. They're actually quite timid, easily frightened and defenseless against predators. A sheep falls on its back? It can't right itself. It will die right there if someone isn't watching over it."

"I...I didn't know—"

"Sheep are nothing like cows," she said as if he hadn't spoken. "Cattle need to be fenced in or handled by a bunch of cowboys on horseback. With sheep, all it takes is one experienced sheepherder. He can handle over a thousand head of sheep alone with no fence, no night corrals, just him, his horse and his dog."

"Why are you—"

"Because you don't know anything about sheep or where we're headed. I'm willing to bet you've never been in country like this. It's rugged and wild, isolated and unforgiving—not the kind of place to take a greenhorn. So it's not too late to change your mind," she said.

"Change my mind?"

"About going with me. I'd be happy to let you know what I find."

He shook his head. "I'll be fine."

She scoffed at that. "When was the last time you spent two days on horseback at over ten thousand feet above sea level?"

"I'll try not to be a bother to you."

She sighed. "If you can't keep up, I'll leave you behind." She shot him a look. "I'm serious. I need to get to the sheep camp and check on my sheepherder. I won't *let* you slow me down."

"Agreed." He glanced at the .357 Magnum pistol strapped on her hip. "As long as it isn't your policy to shoot stragglers."

"Best not find out," she said, slowing the pickup. Ahead he saw a wide spot next to the river. Beyond that was a Jeep trail that rose abruptly, and beyond that was nothing but towering pine-covered mountains.

"This is where we leave the truck," she said and climbed out.

NETTIE BENTON HATED to think of Frank up at the state mental hospital visiting his daughter. She'd known right from the start that there was something wrong with Tiffany when she'd rented her the apartment over the store. But it wasn't until she'd seen the girl's demonized drawings of Sheriff Frank Curry that she'd realized Tiffany was dangerous.

She shook her head, remembering how that girl had almost killed him. Just the memory made her heart pound. Poor Frank. Nettie had tried to warn him, but Frank being Frank had thought the girl harmless. Tiffany and her horrible mother had put him through the wringer, and they weren't through with him yet.

"Don't be jealous of my daughter," Frank had said when she'd tried to talk to him about Tiffany.

"You don't even know if she's really your daughter."

"Lynette—"

"Frank, she tried to kill you!"

He'd just shaken his head and given her one of his patient smiles. "I have to try to help her. Please try to understand."

She understood that he'd been scarce as hen's teeth since the girl showed up in town and worse now that Tiffany was locked up miles away at the state mental hospital.

Nettie missed him stopping into the store for his usual: an orange soda and a candy bar. She'd always thought he dropped by as an excuse to see her. She'd even thought they might have a second chance together—after her husband, Bob, had left for good, after deciding he wanted to live in Arizona, and before Frank's daughter had come into his life. If she even was his daughter.

Nettie shoved away the heartbreaking thought that maybe she and Frank had missed their chance for happiness a second time as she listened to the men in the café speculate on what could have happened to Maddie's young sheep tender.

Sensing there was nothing more to be gained this morning at the café, Nettie made her way back across the street to the two-story Beartooth General Store. She'd married the store, choosing Bob instead of Frank at her mother's encouragement. She regretted the Bob part, but the store was her life. Especially now that her husband—soon to be ex—had deserted her for a trailer in an Arizona desert. Running the store had kept her mind off her unfulfilled marriage and the regret that had eaten away at her for almost thirty years.

The only bright spot in her day had been Sheriff Frank Curry's occasional visits. With those few and far between lately, Nettie felt at loose ends. Even the latest gossip about Maddie Conner's tender couldn't lift her mood.

As she neared the store, she saw a customer waiting for her in the shade of the wide store porch that ran the width of the building.

"If you'd read the sign on the door, it would have told you to come over to the café to get me." She squinted against the bright spring day and did a double take as she recognized the man waiting for her. "J.D.?"

J. D. West stepped out of the shadow of the Beartooth General Store porch, a grin on his handsome face. In his mid-fifties, J.D. was one of those men who only got better looking with age—much like Sheriff Frank Curry, Nettie thought.

"How ya doin', sweetheart?" He had dark hair and eyes and a grin that had made many a young woman drop her panties before he'd left town.

She couldn't have been more surprised to see him. It had been years since he'd left on the run after a row with his older brother, Taylor, and the law hot on his trail.

Nettie had heard J.D. had gotten caught and done some jail time over in Miles City, Montana. Rumors had circulated about him over the years, and alleged sightings all over the West had been reported. Most everyone either thought J. D. West was in prison somewhere or dead.

"You look like you've just seen a ghost," he said with a laugh.

His laugh took Nettie back, and for a moment they were both teenagers again. She'd always liked J.D. even though she'd never succumbed to his charm.

You like men who live on the edge. It was Bob's voice in her head. *That's why you've been carrying a torch for Frank Curry all these years.* She would be so glad when she could shut Bob up for good.

"What are you doing here?" she blurted out.

He laughed again. "Here as in Beartooth? Or here as in standing on your porch waiting for you?" He didn't give her a chance to answer. "I decided to pay a visit to my old stompin' grounds. When I saw your sign in the window…" He grinned.

For a moment, she didn't know which sign in the window he was referring to. But glancing past him, she saw her apartment-for-rent sign. The apartment over the store had been empty since Tiffany Chandler had been arrested and taken away.

"You want to rent my apartment?"

"I sure do. That is, if you'll rent it to me for a week to start. Then we'll see after that."

She wasn't surprised he had no plans to stay with his brother, Taylor, out at the West Ranch. As far as she knew, the trouble between the two had never been reconciled. The two brothers couldn't have been more different. Taylor was a family man who'd never been in trouble in his life. J.D. had been in trouble almost since the day he was born.

"I'll pay in cash," he said, seeing her hesitation.

She couldn't say no. Not to J.D. Also, she hadn't had any other takers for the apartment. She had hesitated more out of surprise than anything else.

"Of course I'll rent it to you," she said as she climbed the steps to the porch. "Come inside and I'll show it to you. It's nothing fancy, mind you."

"Not looking for fancy, but I'll bet it is real nice."

She turned to look back at him as she entered the store. "Have you been out to the ranch yet?"

J.D. chuckled. "Not yet. I'm getting up my courage. Not expecting a brass band, but even a lukewarm welcome would be appreciated."

"I hope it goes well," she said. She opened the inside door to the apartment and climbed the stairs.

"That is real sweet of you, Nettie."

It wasn't every day that a man told her she was sweet.

"Damn you look good," J.D. said, grinning when they reached the apartment.

She felt herself flush. "You always were the worst liar." Her hand went to her new hairdo. She patted her out-of-the-bottle red curls, pleased.

He shook his head, his gaze softening as it met hers. "I mean it, Nettie. You're a sight for sore eyes. I can't tell you how much I've missed you and Beartooth. So fill me in on everything that's been going on," he said as he moved through the apartment.

She loved nothing better than telling him what she knew about Beartooth. He was especially interested in the latest about Maddie Conner and her tender, and Fuzz Carpenter's speculation that Branch Murdock was dead—murdered—up in the Beartooths.

"I didn't know anyone was still running sheep up there," J.D. said distractedly as he moved to the front window and glanced out.

"Maddie's the last, and if Branch is dead, well, this will probably be her final year. So what do you think of the apartment?"

J.D. turned to smile at her. "I love it."

As she watched him pull out money for a week's rent, Nettie couldn't help but wonder what he was *really* doing back in town. J. D. West wasn't the kind of man who got homesick. He was the kind who'd put Beartooth in his rearview mirror years ago—and never looked back.

To MADDIE'S SURPRISE, the deputy offered to saddle his own horse. *"You ride?"*

"Before I moved to the city, my family had horses."

She raised a brow. "What kind of horses?"

He hesitated just long enough that she knew they'd been fancy, expensive horses. "Thoroughbreds."

She chuckled. Didn't he realize how obvious it was that he came from wealth? Apparently not. How interesting that he wanted to play it down.

"Did your family race them?" she asked as she hefted her saddle up onto the horse's back.

"No. My sister was involved in some jumping competitions. I preferred to just ride the horses."

As if that made him less of an elitist. She could hear the Ivy League education behind his words. "Harvard? Princeton?"

"Harvard," he said as he clinched up his saddle. "Law school. I was an attorney at my wife's father's firm for ten years before becoming a cop." He chuckled and looked up at her. "Aren't you going to ask how I ended up a deputy sheriff in Big Timber, Montana?"

She'd noticed the pale line on his ring finger and the way he nervously touched the spot when he thought she wasn't looking. The missing wedding band was like a phantom limb, she thought. It was still there in a way he couldn't seem to get past. She assumed its loss was too fresh. Which she'd bet explained what he was doing in Montana.

"Nope, that's sufficient information," she said.

He laughed. "It seems only fair you tell me something about you."

She shook her head. "I only asked you those things because I just needed to know if you could ride a horse and were smart enough to stay out of my way," she said as she swung up into the saddle. "Ready?"

"I'm ready if you are," he said as he mounted the horse.

"I hope so," she said, glancing over at him. "We have a long ride ahead of us." She had no idea how far they would have to go. It would depend on where Branch had last made camp with the sheep. She knew where they *should* be, but she wasn't betting on anything at this point.

Just as she doubted the deputy was any more ready for what was ahead of them than she was. But it was clear that neither of them was turning back.

"Who was that?"

On the porch of the general store just after lunch, Nettie turned in surprise to see Sheriff Frank Curry standing behind her. She hadn't heard him drive up. For a moment she was so happy to see him that she didn't even register the disapproval in his tone.

"Don't tell me that was who I think it was," he said, sounding upset.

"Well, if you think it was J. D. West, then you're

right." J.D. had professed to love the apartment, paid in cash for a week and told her again how wonderful she looked.

Then he'd bought her lunch, bringing sandwiches over from the café so the two of them could sit on the store porch and eat them. Just moments before the sheriff had appeared, she'd been watching J.D. drive away, warmed by his return to Beartooth.

"What's *he* doing in town?" Frank demanded, frowning after J.D.'s pickup.

She definitely didn't like his tone. "Visiting his family."

"How long is he staying?"

"As long as he wants to." Her hands went to her hips. "What's with all the questions?"

He blinked before turning his frown on her. "He's trouble."

"You haven't seen him in years. Maybe he's changed."

Frank scoffed at that.

It had been weeks since she'd seen Frank. This wasn't how she'd hoped things would go when he stopped by the store again.

"Well, I'm willing to give him the benefit of the doubt," she said, feeling her indignation as well as her temper rise.

"Of course *you* are."

He was making her mad now. "What does *that* mean?"

"It means, Lynette, that you have always had a soft spot for J.D." Frank was the only one who called her by her given name. Normally just the sound of it on his lips would have made her day.

"Frank Curry, that's not true! That was more than thirty years ago, but you were always the one who—" She caught herself before she said, "—I was soft on."

"You can bet he's here for more than a visit." Frank's gaze narrowed at her. "What did he want with you?"

She bristled. "Maybe he just stopped in to say hello or buy something."

Frank shook his head. "He's a lot cagier than that. Believe me, he wanted something." He shoved back his Stetson, his gaze on her face. "What did he want?" Clearly he was determined to wait her out. She realized he must have overheard J.D. saying he would be back.

"You'll find out soon enough anyway, I guess," she said with a sigh. "He asked about renting my apartment."

"I hope to hell you didn't rent it to him."

"As a matter of fact, I did."

Frank swore again. "What were you thinking, Lynette?"

"That maybe he deserves a second chance? People change, you know." She knew this was aimed more at herself and Frank and had little to do with J.D. It was she and Frank who deserved a second chance. Why couldn't he see that?

He eyed her warily. "What are you getting so mad about?"

"*You.* I haven't seen you in weeks, and you suddenly show up and…" She choked on the words, unable to say more for fear she would cry. She couldn't remember the last time she'd been brought to tears, but standing out here on the store porch, the spring air warm and scented with pines, wasn't going to be one of them.

"I want you to stay clear of him."

She stared at Frank in disbelief. "If I didn't know better I'd think you were...jealous."

"*Jealous?* Isn't it possible that I worry about you? That I don't want to see you make an even bigger mistake?"

"I'm sorry, but what was the first big mistake you're referring to?"

He pulled his Stetson off and slammed it against his leg as if to knock off invisible dust. He had to know he'd stepped in it this time.

"Well, Frank? Surely it wasn't me not marrying *you*."

He stuffed his hat back on his thick, blond-and-only-slightly-graying hair. If only he wasn't so good-looking.

"Sometimes, Lynette," he said and, without another word, turned and strode across the street toward the Branding Iron.

Nettie watched him go, wanting to call him back and start over. She realized she should have asked about Tiffany. She also shouldn't have gotten mad and said what she had. More than anything she wanted him to have been as happy to see her as she'd been to see him.

It wasn't like him to let someone like J.D. upset him like that. Frank hadn't been himself for months now. She worried about him—when she wasn't furious with him. How long was it going to take for him to come to his senses and ask her out? They'd both be ninety with one foot in the grave by the time he finally got around to it. If he ever did.

"Stubborn damned fool," she said under her breath, all the time hoping he would look back before he disappeared into the café. He didn't.

THE FIRST THING Deputy Jamison noticed after they left the truck and horse trailer behind and rode into the mountains was the quiet. It hung in the dark, dense pines. The sound of the horses climbing the mountain seemed small and isolated as if nothing could truly disrupt the mountains' eerie silence.

Just when he thought he would give anything to break that quiet, the wind came up. A dust devil spun off to his right, appearing to come out of nowhere, and then it was all around them. The wind blowing off the snowy peaks was icy cold and unforgiving. It quickly became a dull roar that was as grating as the silence had been.

As they rode deeper into the mountains, the gale shrieked. It lay over the tall grass and whipped the pine boughs. He caught glimpses of the terrain ahead, a tableau of sheer rock cliffs and grassy bowls above the tree line.

With a start, he realized he'd never been this far from civilization before. He could feel the temperature dropping as they ascended the mountain. The day wore on with the gentle rocking of the horse and creaking of his saddle.

He didn't know how far they had ridden, only that the air had gotten colder as the weak spring sun inched its way to the west and finally dissolved behind the farthest peak.

While he'd ridden a horse before, never had he ridden one for this long. He was growing weary of being in the saddle, when Maddie reined in ahead of him. As she dismounted, he glanced at his watch. There was still at least an hour of daylight. "Why are we stopping?"

"This is where we spend the night," she said without looking at him.

He glanced around. She'd stopped at the edge of a stand of pines under a sheer rock face. Ahead there was nothing but wide-open windswept country and more mountain peaks as far as the eye could see.

"I was hoping we might get far enough that we could see the sheepherder's camp before dark," he said.

"In the first place, we don't know where that is," she said, still not looking at him as she began to untie her saddlebag. "Second, this is where we make camp for the night."

He couldn't help himself. "There isn't a better place to camp?"

Maddie finally turned to look at him. "This is where we make camp," she repeated. "Why don't you make yourself useful and scare up some wood for the fire."

"Yes, ma'am," he said and slid down from his horse. The ground felt good beneath his feet. His posterior ached from the hours in the saddle, but he wasn't about to mention that to the woman. Nor did he let himself limp in her presence until he could stretch out his legs again.

"Don't go too far," she said, reaching for his reins. "There are grizzlies up here with heads the size of semi steering wheels."

"Are you trying to scare me, Mrs. Conner?"

She chuckled as she led the horses down a small slope that ended in a spot below the rock cliff. Looking closer, he made out what appeared to be a lean-to deep in the pines out of the wind. Closer, the pines at the edge of the stand had been twisted from years of wind and bad weather into grotesque forms.

Jamison set about gathering firewood. By the time he joined her down by the lean-to, she had unpacked their gear and the food she'd brought.

This close to the cliff, the wind was no longer buffeting him. It felt good to get out of it for a while, even though he could hear it in the tops of the pines overhead. The boughs moaned and swayed back and forth in a sky that was losing light fast.

He felt the cold chill of the upcoming night and looked to the mountains ahead, wondering where the sheepherder would be spending it. Or if he was in any shape to care.

CHAPTER FIVE

"I SUPPOSE YOU don't know how to make a fire," Maddie said as the deputy dropped his load of firewood next to the ring of charred rocks. The ground inside the ring was blackened from other fires. Jamison wondered how many times she'd made camp here, how many fires had burned to ashes to the sound of the wind overhead.

"Actually, I do know how to build a fire," he said, kneeling next to the fire ring.

She glanced at him, pretending surprise. "They taught that at the fancy summer camps you went to?"

"You don't like me much, do you?" he said as he set about getting a fire started.

"It's nothing personal."

He chuckled at that. "I shouldn't take you calling me a greenhorn personally? Or that you make fun of the way I was brought up?"

"You *are* a greenhorn and you *were* privileged."

"But it's more than that," he said, looking up at her.

Her eyes were the deep blue of the sky they'd ridden under all afternoon. Her expression softened. He could see the fear even before she voiced it.

"I don't like you coming up here to make a case against Dewey."

"If Dewey is innocent—"

"You're already convinced he's not."

"I have my doubts about his story, yes." He lit the small kindling under the larger logs. The flames licked at the dry wood and began to crackle. "I don't make assumptions. What I know is that Dewey's lying about something and he's terrified, not to mention his clothing was covered in blood. Also, according to Dewey, your sheepherder is apparently missing."

"Once we find Branch…" Maddie looked past the fire to the peaks in the distance "…I'm sure he'll clear this all up."

Jamison heard the hope and saw the worry. It mirrored his own.

Maddie cooked a simple meal that they ate around the fire, both quiet, both lost apparently in their own thoughts. The only sound was wind high in the pines and the soft crackle of the fire as darkness seemed to drop over them without warning.

Jamison had never seen such blackness. Up here in these mountains the dark appeared to have a life of its own. It became a hulking beast crouched just beyond the glow of the campfire.

While it made him uneasy not knowing what was out there—maybe whatever had scared Dewey Putman so badly?—Maddie seemed content here. Jamison had little fear of the animals. It was humans and what they were capable of that kept him awake at night.

The fire flickered, casting golden light on Maddie's face, and he glimpsed the beautiful woman she'd been when she was younger. It was nothing like the quiet beauty she had now, though. There was a tranquil magnificence in her that sneaked up on him. That she was capable and self-assured only added to that beauty.

She brushed back an errant strand of hair as if she felt him watching her. He saw irritation in the movement. She was a woman used to spending most of her days alone, he realized. She wasn't used to a man looking at her—maybe especially the way he was. He found her intriguing equally in her strength—*and* her vulnerability.

"I really would like to know more about you," he said as the silence stretched taut between them.

She glanced up at him, pretending to be surprised to find him sitting across from her. "Are you asking as a deputy?"

"No, I just thought since we're going to be spending time together—"

She rose abruptly, dusting her hands off on her jeans. "Then I can't imagine why you'd have any interest in me. We leave at daybreak. I'd suggest you get some sleep."

He watched her walk over and pick up the saddlebags with the food she'd brought. As she moved to tie them to a rope hanging from a nearby tree, he got up to help her.

"You're putting our food in a tree?" he asked as he reached to help hoist the bundle higher.

She refused to relinquish the rope, forcing him to step back as she finished tying it. "Bears," she said as if he should have known that.

He glanced at their sleeping bags stretched out beside the small campfire.

"Grizzlies," she said, and he saw the first hint of mischief in those blue eyes.

"Seems a little silly tying up a small amount of food when the bears will have us to eat."

"I'm not worried," she said, stepping past him toward the fire. "They'll be full by the time they finish with you."

He smiled as she walked over and climbed fully clothed into the sleeping bag on the other side of the fire. She lay down, her back to him.

"The woman has a sense of humor after all," he said loud enough he was sure she could hear. He considered sitting on the overturned stump by the fire until the blaze burned out. He felt antsy, certainly not ready to go to sleep this early.

Looking up, he caught a glimpse of stars through the swaying pine boughs. The sky seemed alive with them. He stepped out of the trees so he could see the amazing sight. It was magnificent. He gaped at the ceiling of darkness and light in awe. He'd never seen so many stars. Nor had he ever seen such an expansive sky. It arced between the horizons, a midnight-blue canopy bespeckled with millions of twinkling stars.

Away from the fire, though, he was instantly cold. Even standing by it, only the parts of his body near the flames were warm. He walked back, but the fire had died to only a few glowing embers that gave off little heat.

Maddie hadn't made a peep. He wondered if she was asleep. He thought about looking for more wood for the fire, but changed his mind.

He'd never slept in his clothing in his entire life. Even as cold as it was up here, he slipped out of the canvas coat she'd lent him, then the flannel shirt down to his T-shirt. Goose bumps rippled across his skin. He considered taking off the jeans she'd provided for him, but one glance around and he decided he might have to get up in a hurry, and would be better off at least partially dressed.

The lining of the sleeping bag was ice-cold against his bare arms, and it took him a moment to warm up. He rolled up his coat and shirt for a pillow then curled on his side to watch what was left of the fire die away. He thought about what they might find tomorrow and how he would handle it.

It kept his mind off everything but Maddie Conner.

SHERIFF FRANK CURRY couldn't help being mad at himself on so many levels. Right now, though, it was the way he'd handled things with Lynette.

After their run-in, he'd gotten something to eat at the café, half hoping Lynette would come over and join him. She hadn't. Too upset to go to his empty house, he'd driven over to Bozeman and gone to a movie. Now, on the way home, he couldn't even remember what it was about.

Driving through the darkness toward his ranch east of Beartooth, he mentally kicked himself for not calling

Lynette. He could have patched things up by asking her to the movie. What would it have hurt? He could have called her, apologized... But what did he have to apologize for? She was the one who'd rented her apartment over the store to J. D. West and thought nothing of it.

His chest ached at the thought of J.D. pulling the wool over her eyes. Why was Lynette so blind when it came to men?

"So what are you going to do about it?" he demanded of himself as he drove down the narrow dirt road toward home. What *could* he do?

Nothing right now. He felt like a single parent. He knew that was silly. But he now had all the responsibilities that came with being a single parent. Tiffany needed him since Pam had deserted her daughter. He was all the girl had now. So when he wasn't working, he went up to the state hospital to see her.

But that wasn't the only reason he'd stayed away from Lynette. He was afraid for her because of Pam and Tiffany. He thought that if he put distance between them, then maybe it would keep her safe.

So the situation frustrated the hell out of him when he was around her. He wanted Lynette, needed her, but right now the best thing he could do was give her a wide berth. Who knew what would happen with Tiffany's case? What if she did get out of this?

He couldn't forget that Tiffany was a danger to Lynette. And Pam...well, who knew how dangerous she was to them all?

When he'd found out about Tiffany, he'd tried to find

Pam. Apparently she hadn't wanted to be found, which shouldn't have come as a surprise after what she'd done.

He'd hired a private investigator to get her number for him. He'd talked to her once—for all the good it had done. She had pretended not to know what he was talking about when he'd accused her of poisoning Tiffany against him, programming the child to kill him.

Months later he'd called again and found the line had been disconnected. Which was just as well, he told himself. He was afraid of what he would do if he knew where she was.

He figured she'd probably taken off. Done her damage to him and Tiffany and then gone off, her mission over. But to add fuel to the fire, she'd managed to tell Tiffany that the reason she was running away was because she was afraid of him. Tiffany, unfortunately, believed her mother's lies.

Sometimes in the middle of the night when he couldn't sleep he thought about how to find her. The fantasy—he had to think of it as that—always ended the same. It ended with him murdering Pam with his bare hands.

It was those dark thoughts that plagued him, that and worry over Tiffany. Worry also about Lynette.

"With good reason," he muttered under his breath as he turned into his ranch. Lynette had proven she had terrible taste in men when she'd married Bob thirty years ago instead of him. Now she'd rented her apartment to J. D. West? Worse, she thought the man deserved a second chance?

He felt himself getting upset again. J.D. had gotten more chances than he deserved before he had even left Beartooth all those years ago. To think Lynette might be taken in by him upset him more than he wanted to admit.

And she thought he was merely being jealous? He let out a curse as he neared his house.

Automatically he slowed. Not that long ago, he would have been anxious to return home. He liked his small house, his few animals, the wide-open spaces the ranch provided him.

Back then he'd had a family of sorts waiting for him. A family of crows had taken up residency in his yard. He'd come to think of them as his own and had spent years studying them, intrigued how much they were like humans.

They would always be waiting for him as he drove in and would caw a welcome. He'd gotten where he could tell them apart by their greetings.

Now, though, the telephone line was empty, just like the clothesline and the ridge on the barn. Tiffany had killed one of them to get back at him. Crows, being very intelligent birds, had left. He'd learned from studying them that they would warn other crows about the danger at his house. They wouldn't be back nor would others come if they felt threatened.

With a heavy heart, he pulled in and climbed out. The night was dark here in the valley with clouds shrouding the stars. He stood for a moment, staring up at the empty telephone wire, feeling the terrible weight of all his losses.

The sudden sound of glass breaking somewhere inside his house startled him from his dark thoughts. Drawing his gun, he sprinted toward the open front door.

MADDIE LISTENED TO the wind whipping the tops of the pines. Closer, the fire crackled softly as it burned down. The familiar sounds were comforting—unlike the sound of the deputy across the fire from her. He moved restlessly in his sleeping bag. She'd bet this was the first time he'd slept under the stars—let alone in the middle of nowhere on the side of a mountain.

She could have erected the tent that was kept here along with a few supplies. It hadn't been all orneriness that had made her dismiss the idea. True, she hadn't wanted to take the time to put up the tent. Nor had she wanted to expend the energy, and she'd figured the deputy would have been no help.

But those weren't the real reasons. If she was being honest, she hadn't wanted to be in the close confines of a tent with her worries—or the deputy. Not tonight.

She mentally cursed herself. What was she doing here with such a city slicker? He didn't know the country. Worse, he didn't know how dangerous it could be. What was he doing in Montana, anyway?

It irritated her that she'd had to bring him. But her other choice was letting him look for the sheep camp alone. Better to take him up here to alleviate his concerns. She desperately wanted to prove him wrong.

Jamison was the least of her problems and she knew it. She closed her eyes against the fears that had haunted her from the instant she'd seen Dewey in the back of that stall.

What had happened? She clung to the hope that when they reached the camp, they would find Branch sitting outside his sheepherder wagon whittling on a piece of pine, his dog, Lucy, at his feet, and all two thousand sheep in a grassy meadow behind him, safe and growing fatter.

It was conceivable that the boy had gotten scared when he couldn't find Branch. When he found a dying lamb, just as he'd said, he would have foolishly thought he could save it. Failing that, he'd panicked and hightailed it out of there. It could have happened just that way, she told herself.

Which meant that when they reached the sheep camp, Branch would give her hell for hiring Dewey, something she had to admit she deserved. She'd take the deputy back down out of the mountains and get Branch a new tender, someone older, someone with experience.

Even as she thought it, she knew how hard it was going to be to find a tender. No one wanted to spend three months back in the wilds. Even sheepherders were hard to find, for that matter. Good thing Branch enjoyed it, but he was getting old—just a few months short of his sixty-eighth birthday. It wouldn't be long before he couldn't make the trek, she thought, refusing to let herself accept that this might be his last year—no matter what they found back in the mountains.

All good reasons to give up herding the sheep to high grazing pasture each summer season, she told herself.

She heard the deputy roll over again and felt a stab of guilt. She shouldn't have mentioned grizzlies, but smiled even as she chastised herself for purposely trying to scare him. He was probably worried about bears and wouldn't get a wink of sleep.

Maddie thought about telling him that she had her shotgun as well as her .357 Magnum pistol within reach. Also, she could mention that with two thousand sheep not far away, the grizzlies would rather have lamb than either one of them.

But a moment later, Jamison seemed to settle down, and as he did, she heard him snoring softly.

Irritated he could fall asleep so quickly, she snuggled down in her sleeping bag and prayed. It had been so long since any of her prayers had been answered, though, that she didn't have much hope these would be, either.

FRANK KNEW HE should call for backup, but the last time he'd caught someone going through his things it had turned out to be his daughter.

He moved cautiously up onto the porch. The front door was ajar. He hadn't noticed when he'd driven up because he'd been grieving for the loss of his crows.

But now he was paying attention. He glanced back over his shoulder. Where had the intruder parked? Not by the barn or he would have seen the vehicle when he drove in. Whoever it was must have used the back road, parked behind the house and sneaked around to the front to get inside.

That meant the person knew about the back way into the property. It was no leap to assume whoever was inside his house knew him and knew he never locked the front door.

Standing to one side, Frank eased the door all the way open. The living room was dark, but a light was on down the hall. It cast a faint yellow glow that weakened as it reached the living room. But it was enough light to see that the place had been ransacked.

A thief would have gone straight for the guns in his den or the television and stereo, even the old laptop he kept on the small desk in the spare room. A thief wouldn't have bothered tearing up the living room, which was only sparsely furnished and clearly had nothing of any real value.

As Frank stepped in, he was pretty sure he wasn't dealing with a thief—but a vandal with a grudge. He'd made enemies as sheriff, but not that many in his career. Avoiding the floorboards that creaked, he moved through the house toward the sound of the racket going on in his bedroom. He could hear his vandal destroying everything within reach.

Frank had never gotten very attached to things, so he had little regard for the furnishings in his home. All were replaceable. Maybe his intruder didn't know that about him. Or care. It sounded as if the person was working out some anger issues on his house. As he moved closer to the open door to his bedroom, he was anxious to know just who it was.

Nearer the open door, he stopped. He listened to things breaking for a moment. Then cautiously, he peered around the doorframe.

Frank almost dropped the gun in his hand. As it was, he hadn't been able to hold back the shocked sound that escaped his lips.

His intruder turned. In the single light glowing overhead in the room, a woman stood holding a baseball bat. He felt his knees go weak as he stared in shock at his ex-wife.

He hadn't seen Pamela Chandler in almost twenty years. Nor had he given any thought to her—until February when he'd found out they had possibly conceived a daughter she hadn't mentioned. Since then, whenever he did think of Pam, it was only with one desire: to kill her.

He stared at her as if seeing an apparition. When they'd married, she'd been fifteen years younger. She'd been too young for him, too young period. He felt he'd since grown into his age. He couldn't say the same for Pam.

The past two decades hadn't been kind to her. She looked stringy thin, her pale skin stretched over her facial bones. Her hair had grayed without her putting up a fight with a dye job. But the eyes were the same—a fiercely bright brittle blue—much like her daughter's.

She stood with the baseball bat in both hands, caught in a backswing after smashing his bedside lamp to smithereens. She didn't look surprised to see him. Hell, she was even smiling. It was that smile he'd thought of most recently and how he would wipe it off her face once he had his hands clamped around her throat.

"Hello, Frank." She said it as if she'd merely seen him in passing on the street and not standing in the middle of his bedroom surrounded by the destruction she'd caused. She said it as if they were old friends—not like a woman who'd poisoned her own child with her lies and bitterness.

When he finally spoke, his voice didn't sound like his own. "What the hell, Pam?"

"Isn't it obvious?"

He shook his head, shaken by how surreal this felt. He'd dreamed of finding Pam, of catching her off guard and cornering her somewhere, stopping her from terrorizing Tiffany. Of making sure she never hurt anyone again.

Late at night, he would plan her murder, her disappearance. He'd been in law enforcement long enough that he knew how to get rid of her for good. No one would ever know what had happened to her. She would just be…gone.

Four strides. That was all it would take to reach her and take that baseball bat away from her and—

"What's the matter, Frank? Can't pull the trigger?"

He'd forgotten he was holding his gun. It hung at his side, his hand having dropped with his shock at seeing his ex-wife vandalizing his house.

Still smiling, Pam took a step toward him. She clutched

the baseball bat in her hands, evil intent glowing in those blue eyes as hot as the hell she brought with her. Her smile dared him to lift the gun and shoot her.

In his fantasy of murder, Pam was always afraid. Maybe even a little sorry. Not like the woman now moving toward him.

Frank felt his hand slowly rise until the barrel of his weapon was pointed at her heart. She kept coming, the baseball bat cocked back, ready to swing.

He saw himself emptying the gun into her. But even as he envisioned it, he wondered if it wouldn't take a wooden stake to put this woman down.

"Well, Frank?"

He realized he was shaking his head. "Don't," he heard himself say as she kept moving toward him. He felt his finger on the trigger. Another step and—

The blow caught him in the back of the head. Until that moment, he'd been too surprised to think clearly. But in that instant, he realized his mistake. If he'd been acting like a sheriff, he would have figured out that Pam wouldn't have come here alone. Pam was too calculating—and knew him too well.

He felt his body go slack from the brain-numbing blow. His legs buckled, his thoughts scattering like dried fall leaves blown across his yard.

As he dropped to his knees, his gaze met hers. He'd never seen so much hatred, so much anger, so much evil—and absolutely no fear.

"You really didn't think I was done with you, did you?" she said and swung the baseball bat.

CHAPTER SIX

MADDIE WOKE TO the sound of fire crackling in the pit next to her, the smell of bacon and daylight. She rolled over quickly, shoving the bag down as she attempted to climb out. She was surprised she'd slept so soundly. It had taken her a long time to fall asleep last night, her thoughts and the deputy keeping her up. She'd finally drifted off long after the campfire had burned out.

She blinked at the day's brightness, momentarily confused as to where she was. But the moment she spotted Jamison, it all came back to her.

Deputy Jamison stood next to the creek, his broad naked back to her. He'd stripped down to nothing but his jeans and boots and now washed himself in the icy cold stream. The sun shone on the water on his back, making it glisten.

A ripple of need shot through her so sharp and shocking that it hurt. She hadn't felt anything close to it in years. Maybe never. Its fierce intensity made her weak with a wanting she'd thought she'd put behind her. Until that moment, she realized, she hadn't thought of herself as a woman for a very long time.

She quickly turned away, shaken and upset by the alien feelings. She told herself that her reaction was normal given that all she'd seen in Deputy Jamison before that moment was a lawman butting into her life and her livelihood. It didn't matter that he had a badge.

Now she saw the man and had to grudgingly admit he was nice looking if you liked that type. Still, he was nothing like the men she'd known all her life, although he was smart, that went without saying, and not as much of a greenhorn as she'd feared.

When she turned back around, she found herself staring at his bare chest as he walked back toward the fire. It was broad and muscled like his back. Light brown hair formed a V that continued past the top button of his jeans.

"Good morning," he said cheerfully and pulled on his shirt. "I didn't realize you were up."

She nodded and turned to roll up her sleeping bag. A groan rose in her throat. She'd seen half-naked men before. So why was she acting like a schoolgirl? It was enough to make her furious with herself.

"I thought we should have breakfast before we head out," he said behind her. "I hope you don't mind. I took the food down from the tree. It will only take me a moment to finish cooking it."

The last thing she wanted was breakfast—let alone for the deputy to cook it for her.

"I don't really want—"

"I'm not all that hungry, either, but I figured we might need it before the day is over," he said, cutting off her protest.

She hated what she'd heard in those words. It bespoke his fear of what they were going to find up ahead of them. With a start, though, she realized that wasn't why he'd cooked.

He'd made breakfast for her because he suspected she was the one who would need all the strength she could muster today. She couldn't remember the last time a man had done something so thoughtful just for her. She didn't want to be touched by his kindness. But she was.

He also expected the worst and, with a sinking heart, she feared he might be right. To think yesterday she'd been ready to face whatever had happened on this mountain by herself. Right now, she was actually glad he'd come with her.

He looked up from his cooking. "Your hair is beautiful."

His compliment knocked her off balance—and just when she was starting to accept his being here with her.

Her mop of hair had come loose in the night. She hadn't realized she'd been working her fingers through the thick strands to get the tangles out until he spoke. Now she felt self-conscious.

She glanced at the reddish locks that tumbled over her shoulder. Lately she'd noticed the spun silver intertwined with the red. It had startled her since she hadn't been aware of the passing of time or how she'd aged with it.

He looked away to tend to breakfast as if sensing her discomfort. She'd never much cared about the way she looked in the mornings—at least not since losing Hank. Nor did she want to start again.

It was another reason she dressed the way she did.
There were a couple of old widower ranchers who had
been giving her the eye. Dollars to doughnuts they just
wanted her land. It didn't matter even if they really were
attracted to her. She wasn't interested.

Jamison looked up again, and she quickly pulled her
hair up, turning her back to finish the job. She thought
she could feel the deputy's gaze warming her back as
she worked her fingers through it.

She cursed herself for letting him make her feel self-
conscious. Worse, unnerve her. Her heart pounded with
a long-forgotten pleasure from the compliment and a
flicker of her earlier desire. Both burned through her
body, igniting emotions she'd buried with her husband
and son four years ago.

For so long she hadn't let herself feel. Every day, she
rose with only work in mind. Running the ranch and
trying to keep her head above water had taken all her
energy. She'd had little time to think of anything else.

Each night she'd fallen into bed, so exhausted that
the only thing she had wanted or needed was sleep.

The last thing she needed was for a man to make
her feel, let alone want again, especially when it was
this greenhorn.

JAMISON REALIZED HE'D upset Maddie and regretted saying anything. He noticed the way her fingers trembled
as she fought her beautiful long mane into an obedient
plait that trailed down her strong back.

She seemed to take a steadying breath before she

slapped on her hat and turned back to him and the fire. Her cheeks were heightened in color, her blue eyes bright as diamonds. She ducked her head as if afraid of what he might see in those eyes.

He suspected it had been some time since anyone had complimented her on her appearance. He hadn't meant to embarrass her. The words had just come out without thinking.

"I didn't know what you liked to eat," he said as he offered her a plate of thick bread slices he'd toasted over the fire with strips of bacon, scrambled eggs and cheese tucked between them.

She took it without much enthusiasm as if no hungrier than he was. Sitting, she balanced on one of the log stumps as if she'd done it hundreds of times. She probably had. This was her country. She knew it no doubt better than anything else in her life. It sustained her sheep and a part of her as well, he thought. She was at home here, more content than his wife had ever been in their expensive high-rise apartment in New York City.

Taking a small polite bite, she chewed for a moment. Her gaze sprang up to his as she swallowed. "It's... *good.*"

She sounded so surprised it made him laugh. "Thank you for that grudging compliment," he said with a grin.

"I didn't realize you could cook."

"I'm glad I can surprise you."

"Summer camp?"

"Actually Boy Scouts."

"I'd have to see the badge to believe *that*."

He couldn't help being pleased. He'd teased a smile out of her.

"Thanks for...cooking."

He gave her a nod.

She ate quickly after that, no doubt as anxious as he was to get moving. Since he'd awakened, he'd been unnerved by the sudden quiet that had settled around them. The wind had stopped sometime during the night, and now a hush had settled over the mountainside.

"I'll get us saddled up," she said when she'd finished the breakfast sandwich. He noticed that she'd eaten it all, just as he had. Like him, she must fear she was going to need the strength later today.

As she readied the horses, he broke camp, packing up the rest of the food and putting out the fire.

"How much farther?" he asked as they swung up into their saddles.

"We should find their camp by afternoon." He could see how hard her next words were for her. She hadn't wanted him along, didn't want him interfering. Maybe more to the point, she didn't want to have to worry about him along with her other concerns. "Are you doing all right?"

He smiled. "You don't have to worry about me."

She snorted at that as she spurred her horse out of the pines and into the clear blue Montana morning.

When Sheriff Frank Curry opened his eyes, he was on his bedroom floor. He hurt all over, so at first it was impossible to know how badly he'd been injured. He couldn't even tell where all the pain was coming from.

As he tried to sit up, his head swam. His vision blurred to pinpoints, forcing him to lie down again. He lay on his back with his eyes closed and tried to make sense of what he was doing on his bedroom floor with the room in shambles around him.

What had happened? The last thing he could recall was seeing Lynette at the store, wasn't it?

As he gingerly touched his aching shoulder, his memory came back in a flash, along with the pain of being hit with a baseball bat. Pam! The pain and anger threatened to blind him. He sat up, gripping the edge of the bed for support. Pam had been in his house. She'd—

He glanced around the room, at the destruction. It made no sense. If it wasn't for the mess she'd left behind he might have thought he'd fallen, hit his head and dreamed it all.

As he started to get to his feet, he looked around for his gun. It wasn't in his holster and yet he remembered pulling it. He remembered Pam daring him to use it. He hadn't, though, had he?

No, if he had, Pam would be lying here in a puddle of blood.

So why hadn't she taken the gun and used it on him? "Why didn't you just kill me?" he bellowed even though he knew Pam was long gone, and just as he was well aware of why she hadn't used his gun on him.

Pam had no intention of going to prison for killing him. Not when she could just torment him and get away with it.

But not this time. She'd been in his house. She'd torn it up. She and whoever she'd brought with her had attacked him. She wasn't getting away with this.

He got to his feet and took a wobbly step. As he bent over to see if the gun had been kicked under the bed, everything started to go black again. He gave it a minute then looked again. No gun.

Pam must have taken it. Great. He pulled out his cell phone. It dawned on him that the first call he should make was to the hospital. His temples throbbed, and when he touched the back of his head, he could feel the crusted blood in his hair. He was sure he had a concussion. How bad of one, he didn't know. It would depend on how long he'd been out.

Through the window he could see the sun coming up. It was late when he'd come home from the movie in Bozeman and heard someone in his house. But still he'd been out for hours.

His left thigh ached, and when he touched it, he could feel that it was badly bruised. The memory of Pam swinging the baseball bat came back. He was amazed he didn't have some broken bones or that she hadn't beaten him to death once he was down.

He guessed that she'd stopped because she'd made her point. No sense in beating a dead horse, right?

As he dialed 9-1-1 and asked for an ambulance and the undersheriff, he recalled her last words.

You really didn't think I was done with you, did you?

Riding beside Maddie, Jamison crossed a wide meadow between two mountain peaks before working his way along the bottom of a sheer granite cliff that shot up to dizzying heights over them.

Sunlight traveled down through the pine boughs to bathe them in flickering golden beams. He breathed in the sweet scents of pine and new green grasses, the morning air crisp and cold. He feared the air was so clean it would intoxicate him since he had never breathed anything like it before.

The air, the altitude or Maddie Conner would be his undoing, he thought. He didn't doubt that if he couldn't keep up, she would leave him behind. Didn't they shoot animals that couldn't keep up with the herd?

Once they left the pines, the sky overhead seemed as endless as the wide-open mountain slopes in front of them. The huge expanse was a startling clear blue, no clouds on the horizon that he could see.

The wind kicked back up the higher they went. Above the tree line, it swept across the grassy slope in a blistering howl of undulating tall grasses that looked like waves rushing to shore. Water gushed from a plethora of small creeks as higher snowfields melted slowly. It was still early in the year up this high. The sun had a lot of climbing to do before summer warmth ever reached these mountains.

Still, the view was breathtaking. The land seemed alive with color from the dark silken emerald of the trees to the vibrant chartreuse of the grass. All this was in contrast to the dark rocky peaks with their cap of blinding white snow and the clear, deep blue sky overhead.

He'd heard Montana called God's country but until that moment he'd never understood it. The beauty made him ache. Just as the high altitude made him light-headed. Maddie was right about him. He was a fish out of water up here.

"How high are we?" he asked as they crossed a wind-blown ridge, the horse hooves clattering on the rocks.

"Close to ten thousand feet."

The last time he was this far above sea level, he'd been in a plane.

He didn't know how far they'd ridden. He hadn't felt the hours slip past, lulled by the gentle rocking of his body in the saddle and the mesmerizing beauty juxtaposed against the remoteness and endless isolation. It gave him an odd, alien feeling and added to his apprehension about what they would find over the next mountain.

He didn't realize anything was wrong until Maddie suddenly pulled her horse up short. "What is it?"

She didn't answer, but seemed to be listening, though he couldn't imagine what she could hear over the relentless wind.

Reining in, it took him a moment to hear anything but the deafening gale. When he finally did hear what had caught her attention, he felt the hair on his neck shoot up as goose bumps skittered over his skin.

An eerie keening sound rode the wind.

Last night, he'd heard coyotes calling in the distance.

But this was no coyote. If this sound was human, the person was in terrible pain.

"Where is it coming from?" he asked as he eased his horse up next to Maddie's.

She shook her head, still listening as if trying to pinpoint the sound. But with the wind shifting around them, he couldn't tell any more than apparently she could.

Maddie cocked her head. Her expression gave little away, but he could tell that, like him, she was shaken by the spine-chilling sound. Unlike him, though, he had a feeling she knew what it was.

"This way," she said after a moment. He glimpsed her face just before she rode off. There was more than determination etched in her expression. There was pain and regret. She had come to a sad conclusion based on what, he didn't know.

He followed, riding up along the edge of the wide basin then across another high rocky ridge. The view took his breath away and gave him vertigo. He swore he could see forever and yet he still couldn't see what was making that heart-wrenching sound.

The keening grew louder just before he and Maddie dropped off the high ridge and over a rocky rise. He could feel the wind in his face, wearing away at his skin the way it had worn away at the land.

They hadn't gone far when Maddie pulled up again.

He reined in just an instant before he saw the dog. A small Australian shepherd mix of a mutt was sitting on a rocky knob below them. Its head was thrown back, and long, mournful howls were emitting from deep within its throat.

Something was crumpled on the ground below the dog in the rocks. He caught only a glimpse of dark red plaid fabric, and then Maddie was racing down the mountainside toward the dog.

CHAPTER SEVEN

MADDIE'S HEART SANK at the mournful cry of the dog—let alone whatever was lying at the dog's feet just over the rocky ledge. She braced herself for what she would find and yet she was already fighting tears before she reached the animal.

She'd been so sure she was going to find Branch Murdock's body just below the dog on the mountainside that she was startled when the familiar red-and-black-plaid fabric just over the edge of the ridge was only that—the red-and-black plaid of the sheepherder's coat.

Maddie slid off her horse, still stunned and even more confused when she saw that the coat had been spread out like a bed for the dog.

It was what a hunter did when he lost one of his bird dogs and couldn't find the animal before dark set in. He would leave his coat with his scent on it. The dog would hopefully find it and stay there until he returned. With luck, the hunter would find the dog lying on the coat, waiting for him, the next morning.

How long had Lucy been waiting for Branch? And why would he leave his coat here for the dog? Branch and Lucy were inseparable.

As Maddie approached the dog, Lucy quit howling

for a moment, but started up again. It was the most heartbreaking sound Maddie had ever heard on that lonesome mountain ridge so far from everything.

"Where's Branch?" she whispered as she squatted down next to the dog. She remembered when Branch had adopted the puppy. Just the thought of the two of them crossing the ranch yard, Lucy still a puppy, running hard on her short legs to keep up with Branch's long stride, broke her heart.

As she put her arm around Lucy, she heard the deputy dismount and come toward them, his boots crunching on the rocky ground. Not his boots, she reminded herself. Her husband's. That thought shot like an arrow through her heart.

Her husband.

The loss often hit her out of the blue as if until that moment, she hadn't realized Hank was gone and never coming back.

She blinked back tears as she knelt by the dog. "It's all right," she whispered to Lucy, even though she suspected it was far from it.

Picking up Branch's coat from the ground, she held it close. The coarse wool smelled of a strong mixture of tobacco, campfire smoke, sheep and dog. She breathed in the familiar scents that would always remind her of Branch as she looked out across the mountain—just as Lucy was doing. There was no sign of her sheepherder—or her sheep.

"May I see that?" Jamison asked and held out his hand for the coat.

She hesitated, feeling protective and afraid, but grudgingly she handed it over to him and watched as he went through the pockets then checked the fabric. For bloodstains? Bullet holes?

He didn't seem to find anything of interest, she saw with relief. She watched him sniff one of the pockets, then the other one.

"He took his tobacco with him and whatever tool he carried in his other pocket," the deputy said.

"A knife. He always carried a pocketknife." She watched as he shook out several flakes of loose tobacco from the one pocket. The wind caught the stray tobacco leaves and sent them whirling off over the side of the mountain on a downdraft.

Jamison turned the other pocket inside out to show her where the pocketknife had worn a hole in the fabric. "Why would your sheepherder leave his coat here and take everything else with him?" he asked as he eyed the dog.

She hadn't noticed until then that Lucy had a rope tied around her neck, a couple feet of it still attached. The end was frayed as if it had been chewed off. She swallowed down the lump that had risen in her throat at the sight. Branch would never tie up Lucy, would he?

"He must have gotten separated from his dog," she said, surprised that her voice sounded almost normal. "He knew Lucy would find his coat." Or he'd wanted the dog to stay here for some reason and not follow him?

"Why would the dog wait here instead of return to camp?"

"Lucy's probably already checked camp several times." As she shoved to her feet she wondered if that was where they would find the other end of the rope that had been tied around the dog's neck. "She would stay with his coat the rest of the time because Branch's scent would be the strongest on it."

Reaching for her reins, she swung up into the saddle and called softly to Lucy. The dog looked reluctant to follow. But the deputy had Branch's coat, and as the two of them started down the ridge, Lucy finally trailed after them.

Maddie noticed the way the dog had her head down, though, looking like an animal that had been mistreated. Branch would never have laid a hand on Lucy. Nor was there any sign of abuse on the dog that she could see. What scared her was that Lucy reminded her of Dewey. He'd had that same awful look in his eyes.

"PAM HAS AN ALIBI."

Sheriff Frank Curry tried to sit up in the hospital bed. The doctor had insisted on admitting him for the concussion and contusions. He would have balked, but by the time he reached the hospital, he'd been nauseous and had a blinding headache.

Now he stared at the undersheriff, not sure he'd heard him right. Undersheriff Dillon Lawson was a sandy-haired former rodeo cowboy with an easygoing smile and charm to match. But he was also smart and at thirty-six in line for Sweetgrass Sheriff when Frank retired.

"What did you say?" Frank asked.

"Pam has an alibi."

"Like hell."

"She's been staying in a guest cabin at Judge Westfall's. She claims she was in the cabin reading until long after you were attacked. Judge Westfall backs her up. He has sworn that he saw her sitting in a chair in the guesthouse reading until almost 2:00 a.m."

"He just happened to be up that entire time?"

"Apparently he has trouble sleeping."

"He's lying and so is she. And I would lay money on the judge's grandson being the one who knocked me out."

Dillon shook his head and said patiently, "There is no proof that she was even in your house or that she was the one who attacked you. She says the last time she talked to you, you threatened her and that apparently when you heard she was in town, you decided to try to frame her."

"That's a lie, too. Someone tore up my house. You saw it."

"Yep, and bashed you in the head. But not your ex-wife unless we find proof otherwise. She didn't leave any prints behind that we could find. Without evidence…"

Frank raked a hand through his hair in frustration. "She took my gun."

"We can get you another gun."

"You know that's the least of it." His head still ached and his stomach roiled at the thought of Pam getting away with this. She'd thought of everything since he didn't believe that even Judge Westfall would give her an alibi unless he *did* think he saw someone reading in the guesthouse.

"The judge has made it clear that if you go near Pam…"

"I get it," Frank said.

"I know this is hard, but turn the damage over to your insurance agent and move on. You lost this one."

Frank let out a humorless laugh. "I've lost worse with Pam. She didn't just turn our daughter against me. She programmed her to kill me." He saw Dillon make a face. "I know, I can't prove that either, and now Tiffany is going to be the one to pay the price. I have to stop this woman from doing any more damage."

The undersheriff shook his head. "I would strongly advise you against doing anything. You'd be playing right into her hands if you do."

Frank had always thought of himself as a reasonable man. He didn't do things on the spur of the moment. He thought things out, used good judgment.

"She could have killed you last night. She didn't."

He scoffed at that. "She doesn't want me *dead*. She wants me to suffer."

"Well, the doc said you should be able to go home tomorrow. If you want, I can call your insurance agent and then get the place cleaned up for you."

"It's okay."

"I think it would be best if you didn't see the mess out there."

"Afraid I'm going to go off half-cocked?" He chuckled. "Don't worry. I know more than ever what kind of evil I'm dealing with. I plan to stay as far away from Pam as possible—for her security as well as mine."

Dillon didn't look reassured. "If you see her on your property again or happen to run into her…"

"You'll be the first person I call."

"It's a little more complicated than that." Dillon took a breath and let it out slowly. "Pam's asked for a restraining order against you." He held up his hands as Frank began to swear. "She's claiming that you're dangerous, that she fears for her life. That you were physically abusive when the two of you were married and that's why she left you and didn't tell you she was pregnant."

Frank let out a string of obscenities and tried to get out of bed.

"You're not going anywhere." Dillon put a warning hand on his arm. "The doctor isn't releasing you, and you sure as the devil aren't going near Judge Westfall or Pam. The restraining order includes Westfall's ranch."

Of course the judge would be protecting Pam. When she'd first come to the area, she'd rented a place from the judge's sister and had ingratiated herself into the family.

"She's lying about all of it."

"Frank, I know you. I know she's lying. But right now, it's her word against yours, and without any proof and the judge providing her with an alibi…"

Frank lay back in the bed. He knew Dillon was right. But that didn't help the situation. "Just when I thought

she couldn't hurt me worse than she already has." He
focused again on the undersheriff. "You said there were
a couple of things I needed to know?"

"Apparently Pam is planning to stay around for a
while. My advice to you is to make sure the two of you
don't cross paths. You see her coming take off in the
other direction."

"She won't be content with that. There's only one
reason she's back here."

Dillon rubbed the back of his neck for a moment,
looking as if this was the part he really didn't want to
tell him. "You're right about her hanging out with Billy
Westfall. They've been seen together."

Frank groaned. "I hired Billy to find her when I first
learned about Tiffany." He saw Dillon's worried look.
"I merely called her and talked to her. The next time I
tried her number, it had been disconnected. So I'm not
surprised Pam would get Billy to help her. You can bet
Billy was the one who hit me from behind. I know that
bastard. He's been waiting for years to do that to me."

Dillon opened his mouth, but Frank cut him off.

"I *know.* I have no proof, so you can't go after Pam
or Billy. I'm sure Billy Westfall has an alibi, too. But
at least now I know who I'm dealing with—and how
far Pam will go."

"You're going to have to be careful, Frank. This
woman is out to get you. Don't play into her hand. If
you had just called for backup last night…"

"Yeah, I know. I might not be lying in this bed. The
problem, Dillon, is that she *knows* me," Frank said with

a groan. "She knew I wouldn't call for help." Just as she'd known he couldn't pull the trigger.

JAMISON COULDN'T WAIT to see the Diamond C ranch sheep. He scanned the open mountainside ahead, feeling the immenseness of the country around them seep into his bones. It made him feel small and insignificant and more alone than he'd felt since the day his wife walked out on him.

The relentless wind made him irritable as it howled like the dog, an incessant gale that flattened the grasses and threatened to send his Stetson flying. The wind alone, he thought, could make a person go mad in no time up on this mountainside.

He'd never been at the mercy of nature before, but then, he'd never been in such unforgiving country with its sharp jagged rocks and sheer cliffs, its wind and weather and wild animals. It gave him an odd feeling knowing there were large predators up here that could not only kill him, but eat him.

And all of that might not be what they had to fear the most.

What a hard existence for the herder spending months in this harsh, desolate environment with only a band of sheep and a dog to keep him company. The loneliest profession in the world, he mused.

As he glanced over at Maddie, he suspected she had been living an isolated and maybe equally desolate life, as well. He knew *he* had since his divorce a year ago. With Maddie, though, the loss had been so much greater. To lose your son and husband… He couldn't imagine how she had been able to keep going.

Out of sheer determination, he decided now as they rode across another high meadow. She was strong, no doubt about it. How would she handle another blow? He had to wonder because after finding the dog, he was more afraid of what they were going to find up here.

They were nearing the ridgeline when he heard it. The baaing of the sheep reached him on the wind before he saw them. The dog heard them, too. So did Maddie.

She spurred her horse up the side of a steep mountain slope, reining in on the wind-scoured ridge. As he joined her, he saw white sheep scattered for what looked like miles across the mountain. Everywhere he looked he saw dots of fluffy wool. The sheep stood out in the late-afternoon light as if lit from within.

What he didn't see was the shepherd, his horse or any sign of a camp.

As if sensing his question, Maddie said, "The camp will probably be down there." She pointed to an opening in the rocks.

There was tension in her expression, but she worked hard to hide it—just as she did her other emotions. Earlier with the dog, he'd witnessed a crack in her tough exterior. He'd caught it only once before—when she'd seen Dewey hiding in the barn stall.

Her concern for Dewey, then the dog and her sheepherder had exposed a tender side of her he could tell she kept hidden. Did she do that to protect herself? Or to hide her pain and fear from others?

It made him wonder how long she'd been alone, holding it all together so the world didn't see how vulnerable and scared she was or how much pain she was in. He recognized the open wounds and had to look away sometimes. He knew that kind of aching regret too well.

Maddie spurred her horse forward. He followed her down the ridge, their horses' hooves clattering in the loose rock. As they rode across the grassy bowl, he saw an opening in the rocks where water and snow had carved a path downward.

Riding closer, he saw the corner of a white wall tent and the charred black ring of rocks where a campfire had been built on a flat spot in front of it. No sign of a horse—or of Branch Murdock.

Jamison told himself that the man could have taken off just as Dewey had done. He could have had enough of this and just quit. Except that Branch would be smart enough not to go back to the ranch. Instead, he could be sitting in a warm bar somewhere right now out of the wind and cold and far from the sound of bleating sheep.

There was just one problem with that theory. According to Maddie, Branch Murdock wouldn't have left his dog behind. Jamison had noticed the rope noose tied around the dog's neck and the frayed end. He'd also noticed Maddie's surprise as if she couldn't imagine Branch tying up his dog.

If not Branch, then who? Dewey? It seemed more likely that the sheepherder who'd left his coat on a rocky ridge when his dog had gotten loose would do that.

"Why don't you see to your sheep," Jamison said to

Maddie. "I'll look for your sheepherder. I'd rather do it alone anyway."

She gave him a look, one that spoke volumes, before she reined her horse around. "Come on, Lucy. *Work.*" The dog looked reluctant but trotted off toward a handful of sheep huddled together against the rocks. The woman and dog began to herd the sheep toward the middle of the wide meadow.

He watched them work for a moment, fascinated how they performed as a team. Then he turned his horse toward the camp. He was pretty sure he knew why neither Maddie nor the dog was interested in checking the tent. Both seemed to know they wouldn't find Branch Murdock inside.

MADDIE THREW HERSELF into the work she'd done since she was a girl. The familiar sound of the baaing and bleating sheep was almost comforting, and the work kept her from thinking too hard. Lucy seemed to perk up some as well as they began to do what came instinctively— herding sheep.

Sheep naturally stayed in bands. But the bands had split, and some had wandered off as sheep were apt to do when left unattended. She didn't want to think about how long they'd been left to their own devices.

She found the bellwether, the male sheep that was the leader of the flock. The bell around his neck clanged, adding to the cacophony of baaing and bleating. Maddie moved as quickly as possible. She could feel the dark coming. Shadows had already moved into the hollows along the side of the mountain. She tried not to think about Branch, and yet as she gathered more sheep from hidden pockets in the bowl, she found herself looking for his body.

Instead she discovered the bodies of three sheep. She didn't have to dismount to know what had killed them. They lay on their sides with exposed dull red rib bones where the flesh had been torn away. It was usually either wolves or grizzlies. From the tracks around the dead sheep, this time it had been a grizzly. She wanted to stop and study the tracks, afraid there might be more than one feeding on her sheep.

But she was burning daylight, and any sheep that had strayed would be fair game for predators come nightfall. The best thing she could do was gather as many as she could. There really was safety in numbers, especially since she would be watching over them tonight, she thought as she touched the stock of her rifle.

"Don't forget you brought the law with you," she reminded herself. Killing grizzlies and wolves was illegal— even when they were eating her sheep. But she sure as the devil would give them a good scare tonight.

Just the thought of the deputy, though, was a painful reminder of why they were on this mountain. She'd seen no sign of Branch or his horse.

"Oh, Dewey, what happened up here?" She felt tears sting her eyes again, but quickly straightened in the saddle and called out to the sheep to keep moving toward the others.

Don't buy trouble. She could hear her husband,

Hank, saying those words. *Everything is going to be all right, Maddie.* The last words he'd said to her. The only time Hank had ever lied to her. Things hadn't been all right. They would never be all right again.

She angrily brushed at her tears, cold against her cheek, as darkness edged toward the mountains. For a woman who thought she was all cried out, she couldn't help the single sob that rose in her throat.

"Branch, where are you?"

As JAMISON RODE between the rocks and approached the tent, he was glad to be alone. He wanted to check the area without anyone else traipsing through it. All his instincts told him that Branch Murdock wasn't sitting in some warm bar right now downing a draft beer.

Dismounting a half-dozen yards away and leaving his horse ground tied, Jamison walked slowly toward the camp.

The canvas tent flapped loudly in the wind, but very little ash blew up from the burned-out fire pit. He would guess there hadn't been a fire in the crude rock ring for at least a day.

The ground was rocky except for a spot where the tent had been erected. Spring grass grew tall around the structure, and the earth looked soft.

He slowed as he neared it. Outside the tent on one side, a stake had been hammered into the ground. A piece of frayed rope was still tied to it.

On the other side was a pile of freshly split firewood. The flap that acted as the door whipped in the wind, giving him glimpses of the tent's interior. A small woodstove, a makeshift table and box with some utensils and supplies, and two cots. Several sleeping bags lay on the cots, an old blanket on the floor between them covered with dog hair.

Other than that, the tent was empty.

From what he could see, there was no sign of an altercation. No visible blood—at least not the quantity that could be seen from this distance.

As he moved closer to the tent, he slowed to study the footprints in the soft earth. He crouched down to study them more carefully, his pulse bumping up a notch as he realized what he was seeing.

Three distinct and different sets of footprints had been left in the dirt. Dewey's, he recognized from the boy's boots he'd bagged back at the ranch. One large set of worn cowboy boots, he was betting belonged to Branch Murdock.

It was the third set of fresh prints that caught his interest. They were fresher, made from the newer soles of hiking boots that left the imprint of the brand name in the soft dirt. They were larger than either Dewey's or Branch's, and from the varying indentations, it appeared the man had been limping.

The tracks also had crossed the others, which led him to believe whoever had worn the hiking boots had been here recently. Or at least after Dewey and Branch.

As Jamison photographed the tracks with the camera from his saddlebag, he considered the ramifications and felt a chill run the length of his spine. As he looked toward the sound of Maddie herding the sheep in the growing darkness, all his instincts told him that they might not be alone.

As he started to step into the tent, he looked again at the pile of split logs for the woodstove. It took him a moment to realize what he *wasn't* seeing, doubted he would find in the tent, either.

Someone had split the wood. So where was the ax?

CHAPTER EIGHT

BETHANY GATES REYNOLDS had The Worst Heartburn. She couldn't wait to get home and sprawl in Clete's old recliner, balance the remote control on her protruding abdomen and watch old movies for the rest of the night.

Eight and a half months pregnant, she'd never been so uncomfortable in her life. She could barely drive the pickup, but couldn't even reach the gas pedal of the SUV. So Clete had traded her vehicles. She hated the pickup as much as she hated the way her whole body had swollen up to the point of bursting.

She couldn't force her feet into real shoes tonight and, unable to get comfortable, had gotten up and gone to the store for ice cream in Beartooth in her slippers. Nettie Benton had given her one of her disapproving looks.

"What is it?" Nettie had asked, pointing at her belly.

"A boy."

The old gossip had actually smiled. "Clete must be happy about that."

"He is." She'd worked at her wedding band as Nettie checked her out—both her groceries and her. Her fingers were so fat they looked like little sausages, and she would never be able to get her wedding ring off now, could barely turn it on her finger.

When she'd mentioned that her ring was stuck on until the baby came, her husband had said, "That's good because you have no reason to take it off anymore."

She'd regretted even mentioning taking off her wedding band. Neither of them had to be reminded of how foolish she'd been a year ago. She'd almost destroyed her marriage and lost Clete.

But amazingly, he'd forgiven her and even gone to marriage counseling with her. He'd admitted his part although she was the one who'd strayed. He'd been so happy when months after the counseling she'd gotten pregnant—even happier when he'd found out he was having a son.

"Looks like you're due any day," Nettie had said, handing over the bag of groceries.

"Another couple of weeks."

Nettie had looked skeptical. "I doubt you'll make it that long."

As if fiftysomething Nettie knew anything about having babies. She and her husband, Bob, were childless—and now divorcing, if the Beartooth grapevine could be believed.

"The sooner the better as far as I'm concerned." All Bethany had wanted was to get home, plop down and put her feet up.

As she started to turn down the road to her house out in the middle of the valley, another vehicle came roaring out of the narrow drive. She stopped the truck just in time as the black SUV fishtailed past her, kicking up a cloud of dust. Bethany caught only a glimpse of the driver and two passengers. She didn't catch their license plates, but she had a fleeting impression of the men: not from around here.

She watched the black SUV disappear down the road behind her, wondering who they were. Her house was the only one down this road. Of course, the men could have been lost, but she had a feeling they'd been looking for her husband.

That alone would be enough to cause her concern given the hour. Clete should still be working at the bar. She would have been alone out here at the house when the men had stopped by—if she hadn't gone for ice cream.

Suddenly scared, she drove on down the road. She would call Clete as soon as she reached the house. Just in case the men came back.

But minutes later when she drove into the yard, she saw that Clete was home. Climbing out of the truck, hugging the bag with the ice cream in it to her, she wondered why he would have left work early. She was even more curious when she came in the front door of the house and found her husband pulling his backpack from the closet.

"What's going on?" she asked.

"Oh, good, you're home," he said then saw the bag she was carrying. "You didn't have to go to the store. I could have done that." He took the bag from her and headed into the kitchen.

She followed. "You got off early?"

"It was slow, so I could slip away."

"I just saw some men leaving."

Clete put the ice cream into the freezer. He never put the groceries away. Her earlier concern heightened.

"They're some friends from college," he said finally.

Bethany thought about how fast the driver had been going. The large SUV had looked new. She couldn't put her finger on why it made her uneasy that the men in the rig had been here—or how they'd known where to find her husband since he never had friends from college stop by.

"What did they want?"

"Why would you think they wanted something?" he asked too defensively.

She took a breath, placing her hand over her huge baby bump. The kid had been kicking her hard all day.

Clete noticed. "Are you all right?" He closed the distance between them, his hand joining hers. They stood like that until they felt junior kick again.

Her husband smiled, his expression softening when he raised his gaze to hers. They'd promised each other during their marriage counseling that they would always be honest with each other.

It had been a big thing for Clete to even agree to marriage counseling. No man he'd ever known had gone to marriage counseling. Bethany certainly hadn't thought she'd ever need it. When they'd married, she'd been young and quickly disillusioned. Clete hadn't been in the least romantic. So when another man had made her feel loved and desired and special…

"I want to be honest with you," her husband said now and sighed. "They weren't *friends* from college. They were on my football team. Rich kids. None of them were there on scholarships and loans." He sounded bitter. It had been tough for him trying to play football and get good grades so he didn't lose his scholarship. Maybe he wouldn't have gotten hurt and could have finished college if he hadn't had so much on his plate.

"So they just wanted to say hello."

He looked embarrassed because it was now clear they wouldn't have stopped by if they hadn't wanted something from him. She disliked them without even meeting them. Is that why she'd been concerned when she'd seen them coming from the house? Because she'd never met anyone Clete had gone to college with. So much of his time had been spent with football that the team was all he had, and they'd abandoned him after he'd gotten injured and had to quit.

"They want to take a hike up the Boulder, back into the Beartooth Wilderness over the mountains to Yellowstone Park," he said, his hand still on her stomach. "They knew that I was from around here, so…"

"So they wanted advice?" She was hoping that was all it was. Or maybe to borrow some gear. Why else would Clete have been digging out his backpack, right?

He shook his head. "They want me to guide them. It's only for a few days," he added quickly. "I've already gotten someone to cover for me at the bar."

It surprised her he'd made the decision so quickly and without talking to her about it. "If you don't like them why would you—"

He took his hand from her stomach and raked it through his thick hair. He was still the most handsome cowboy she'd ever known. Even though he now owned a bar, he was a ranch kid at heart who still liked to ride bucking horses. Clete was one of those men who was more at home on a horse than behind the wheel of a pickup.

"I did it for you and the baby. They're going to pay me to take them. It's a lot of money."

She shook her head in disbelief. "Why would they do that?"

"What do you mean?"

"There are lots of maps and guidebooks…"

"They're rich kids," he said, clearly getting more irritated. "They can afford to have someone take them. If not me, they'll hire someone else."

She wanted to say, "Let them hire someone else."

But he didn't give her a chance. "It's easy money, and you know how I love that country. I *know* it, and it's been years since I've been up there in the spring. I *want* to do this."

It was wild, remote country. She looked at it every day from her kitchen window—the horizon filled with snowcapped mountains.

"I'm having this baby soon," she said, amazed she should have to tell him that when she was standing right before his eyes.

"The doctor said not for at least two more weeks. I'll only be gone a couple of days, four at the most." He sighed. "We need the money, Bethany. Without you working…"

She reminded herself how wonderful he'd been when she'd learned she was pregnant. It had been his idea that she should quit her job waitressing at the Branding Iron and stay home with the baby.

Now, though, she heard the worry in his voice and stepped closer to cup his warm, strong jaw in her palm. She'd fallen in love with Clete Reynolds at a tender young age. She'd always known she would marry him. He'd been older, and at first he'd seen her as nothing more than a kid. When he'd gone away to college on a football scholarship, she'd been afraid he'd never come back.

As awful as it was to admit, she'd been glad when he'd gotten hurt and had dropped out of school and come home to work at the Range Rider.

Now he owned the bar, and while maybe neither of their lives had turned out the way they'd thought it would, they were together and about to have a baby they both already loved.

"Let me do this," Clete said softly, and pulled her close.

She snuggled against him as close as she could with the baby between them, and breathed in his outdoorsy, masculine scent. Clete was her cowboy. He loved the outdoors and needed time in it.

"If it's what you want to do…" she said.

"Great." He gave her the smile that had melted her heart all those years ago. At nearly thirty, she'd been in love with Clete more than half her life.

She shoved her misgivings aside, telling herself this would be good for him. He'd make some extra money, and it was the time of year that he couldn't wait to get up into the mountains.

"Go and have fun," she said.

"Fun?" He chuckled at that. "I'm sure I'll be babysitting the three of them. I'll probably end up being their pack mule."

MADDIE SAW THE DEPUTY riding toward her in the fading light and gritted her teeth. She could tell by his expression that he was going to try to keep her from doing her job. She was in no mood for this.

Worse, she'd been so sure that once they reached the sheep camp, they would find Branch alive and well. Instead she'd found herself looking for his body. The mere thought turned her blood to ice.

But she'd found no sign of him as she gathered the sheep. The fact that they were spread all over the mountainside made it clear Branch hadn't been here for the past two days—no doubt from at least the time Dewey had said he'd gone missing.

"When you're through I need you to go to the camp and tell me what's missing," Jamison said as he rode up.

"I'm not planning to go near camp until sometime tomorrow after I have my sheep together." She cut her horse in front of his to move a couple of dawdling lambs and shot him an irritated look. It was his investigation. She wanted nothing to do with it.

"Is there anything I can do?" he asked, trailing after her.

"Just stay out of my way."

"I'm going to make us both something to eat. We need to keep—"

"Yes, our strength up," she said, reining in her horse. "You'll need these." She untied the saddlebags from her horse. "Now let me tend to my sheep."

She thought he'd argue, maybe even threaten her with interfering with his investigation, although she would have scoffed at that. As far as anyone could tell Dewey had gotten separated from Branch and, panicking, had run. At least she hoped that was how this would all turn out.

As for Branch... All she knew was that he wouldn't leave his dog or the sheep—unless something had prevented him from doing his job.

All she could do today was see to her sheep. She'd looked everywhere close to camp. It was getting too late to search farther away. And why would Branch have ranged farther, anyway?

Her worry for him increased. She knew the dangers up here. Sheep often wandered off, got into trouble on some sheer rock face. Branch could easily have tried to get them down and taken a fall. But if that was the case, then where was his horse?

If he were within shouting distance, she would have been able to hear him, she assured herself as she gathered a small band of sheep and led them back to the others. If he had remembered to take his damned radio, he could have possibly called for help. Dewey would have found him.

She felt helpless and hated that feeling more than any other. Soon it would be too dark to gather more of the sheep. The sky still had a little light left in it, but pockets of darkness would soon make riding too hazardous in this rocky terrain.

Even old Branch was spooked. Dewey's words came at her like a shot from the dark.

She tried not to worry, telling herself that Branch had seen it all. Nothing could scare him. Dewey was mistaken. Either that or...or what? She'd heard ranchers joke about what might be back in these mountains.

One old sheepherder swore that he'd gotten put up a tree by what had to be Bigfoot.

"My dog's dealt with grizzlies, badgers, wolves and wolverines. Nothing scared that old dog. But that night, pitch-black, something came out of the woods that sent that old dog a-hightailin' it. I never heard such a sound coming out of whatever it was. I scrambled up that tree, clung to a limb that whole damned night. Didn't see that dog for two days. Came back with its tail between its legs."

Maddie didn't believe Branch had met up with Bigfoot. Nor did the deputy, she thought as she watched him ride back to camp. Even in the growing blackness of night, she knew he was looking for evidence of a murder, and she was praying he didn't find it.

THE SOUND OF baaing sheep and a barking dog carried on the wind as Jamison rode back to camp. When he'd seen the state Dewey was in and his skinned-up knuckles, he'd been sure he knew what had happened up in these mountains. Two men, different ages, different backgrounds, one used to this life, the other a novice with a troubled background. Of course they were going to lock horns, the older man provoking the younger one, the younger one losing his temper and doing something rash.

Jamison had expected to find the sheepherder murdered, and that blood on Dewey Putman's coat, along with whatever other evidence he could gather up here on the mountain, would lead to the boy's arrest.

But it wasn't as cut-and-dried as he'd thought it would be. He had no body—at least not yet. And it appeared there had been more than just Branch and the boy on this mountaintop.

He played back Dewey's story in his head as darkness seemed to drop like a cloak over the mountainside.

When did you last see Branch?

Just before bed last night. He said he'd been having trouble sleeping. The noises were keeping him up. It was the odd sounds...the crying.

Crying?

It was...something else. Even old Branch was spooked by it.

Are you sure Branch just didn't wander off?

I called for him and looked all over.

Jamison could feel the darkness seep into everything

around him. Earlier, the remoteness of these mountains had made him ache with loneliness. Now that he feared he and Maddie weren't alone, the remoteness and isolation made him anxious.

He told himself that the person who'd left the tracks was probably miles away by now—no matter what had happened up here. Maddie had said there were trails that crossed the mountains into Yellowstone Park. So it was conceivable that a hiker could have come through camp and then gone on his way.

But Branch and his horse were still missing. And as Jamison reached the camp, he couldn't shake the feeling that there was more going on up here than even he had considered.

Jamison felt that unease he'd experienced earlier. Whoever might be up here, he couldn't see them any better than they could see him, right? Unless that person had night-vision binoculars.

He told himself he was letting the remoteness and isolation get to him. A passing-by hiker didn't carry infrared binoculars. And why would anyone go to the trouble of spying on them? It made no sense. Wasn't that the real reason he hadn't mentioned the extra set of footprints to Maddie? Or was it because he hadn't wanted to add to her worries?

He unsaddled his horse and hobbled it next to the nearby creek, then went back into the tent. Earlier, he'd seen a kerosene lantern. He lit it. The light flickered then filled the tent with a warm golden glow that was almost welcoming.

He had hoped that Maddie would go through everything to see what might be missing, but he understood her need to see to her sheep, and he hadn't wanted to rile her any more than he already had. He couldn't be sure a crime had even happened up here, which he knew she would be quick to point out.

And yet, she was worried about her sheepherder, hoping he'd turn up. At this point, Jamison didn't see that happening. If the man was injured but still alive, then where was he? They'd both ridden the area and seen nothing.

The best thing for Branch Murdock was if he'd abandoned camp just as Dewey had. But Maddie was convinced the old sheepherder wouldn't have done that.

That left only two other alternatives. Branch Murdock was injured somewhere away from camp—or he was dead.

In which case it was Jamison's job to find out why.

CHAPTER NINE

JAMISON CHECKED THE CONTENTS of the supply box. It seemed to be very low on food given that Dewey and Branch had been on the mountain for only four days.

Inside the saddlebag Maddie had given him, he found what he needed to make them both some beans and cornbread. He started a fire in the woodstove and went to work.

Maddie might make fun of his years at summer camps, but they were certainly paying off now, he thought. If only Lana could see him now. He let out a humorous laugh, imagining the look of disgust on her face seeing him dressed like this, smelling of horse and leather and about to have beans for dinner. And just when she thought he couldn't sink any lower.

He shook his head in wonder at how ill-suited they had been for each other. Had he not been paying attention when they were dating? Or had Lana purposely hidden her true feelings from him. Probably a little of both.

Outside the tent, the wind howled mournfully. The gusts buffeted the canvas walls, making them billow in and out as if breathing. The temperature was dropping. He could feel the cold coming in through the crack around the tent door flap.

He stopped for a moment to listen. In the distance, he would hear the baaing and bleating of the flock and the clang of the bell on one of the sheep. Every once in a while, he would hear Maddie calling to the dog or the sheep. He couldn't tell which, just that it wasn't a cry for help.

The quiet inside the tent brought on a melancholy of its own. He felt it in his bones as the lantern light flickered and the fire in the woodstove crackled and hissed.

When the food was ready, he dished up two metal plates, stuck two spoons in his pocket and, shutting down the stove, filled his coat pocket with dried dog food and walked the meals out to her. He knew the food would be cold by the time he reached her, but he doubted she would care any more than he did.

Outside, the darkness was complete. He could barely make out the flock. Only a few stars had come out, and those were shrouded by a thin veil of clouds that clung to the top of the high ridge.

Over the tinny jangle of the sheep's bell, he heard singing. The song was as mournful as his earlier mood. He wondered if it was supposed to calm the sheep or Maddie herself.

She quit singing as he approached. She sat propped against a wall of rock that overlooked the wide meadow. The sheep were a pale lake of gentle ghostlike movement below her. Out of the wind, the night had taken on a peaceful quiet. The occasional baa or bleat now seemed almost restful.

"You didn't have to stop singing on my account," he

said as he handed her the plate and sat down next to her on the cold ground.

She took the metal plate without comment. He handed her a spoon and pulled one out of his coat pocket for himself. It wasn't until he began to eat that he heard her finally take a bite. She was stubborn, no doubt about that, but she was also sensible, he thought with a wry smile.

They ate in silence for a few long moments. Two strangers on a mountaintop, so far from the rest of the world that it felt as if they'd been forgotten.

"Tell me about Branch," he said without looking at her.

"What's to tell?"

"Was he always a sheepherder?"

Out of the corner of his eye, he saw her shake her head slowly as she gazed out across the meadow filled with sheep. She didn't want to talk—let alone to him.

But after a moment, she said, "He worked for my father and had since he was a boy. My father used to say that no one knew sheep better than Branch." She grew quiet for a few seconds. "His wife died about twenty years ago now. Finding sheepherders was getting harder. Branch volunteered, said he needed some time alone."

Jamison couldn't imagine a place a person could be more alone.

"Branch knew the sheep. He studied them, worried about them," she said between bites, as if warming to the subject and finding the words were coming easier. "He put up with the loneliness, the boredom, the sudden blizzards that blew in or being awakened by a grizzly or pack of wolves after the sheep." She let out a sigh that sounded close to a sob. "There is so much that can go wrong up here. He spent three months here every summer, rising at dawn, sleeping with one eye open. He noticed when a ewe was limping and knew to clean the mud out of her hooves. He knew what not to let them eat. He knew how dependent they were on him."

Jamison understood what she was saying. It was a 24/7 kind of job, one man and a dog against a dangerous world filled with all kinds of predators and two thousand defenseless sheep.

He couldn't comprehend that kind of responsibility. Not even at his former job as a homicide detective had he felt anything near that. But then, his job hadn't been to protect. It was too late for that by the time he was called in. Just like now, he showed up only to pick up the pieces, weave the threads together. Get justice if at all possible.

She'd glanced over at him. He could barely see her features in the dark shadow under her hat. But he could feel those blue eyes as penetrating as a laser beam. He couldn't imagine the emotions roiling inside her, but he could feel them coming off her in waves. He'd seen the discouragement in the sag of her shoulders when she'd found the dog waiting at the sheepherder's coat.

"He would never have left the sheep. *Never*." She finished the meal he'd cooked then put down her plate for the dog to lick.

Jamison emptied his pocket of dried dog food onto

the plate for Lucy. "I'll look for Branch again as soon as the sun comes up," he told Maddie.

She nodded and looked away. "I can't help feeling responsible for whatever happened. Dewey was so green behind the ears, and Branch…"

"We don't *know* what happened."

"No, we don't." She took a deep breath and let it out. "Thanks for the food."

He heard the dismissal in her voice. She wanted to be alone with the night and her sheep and whatever demons haunted her.

Night was the worst for him. The last thing he wanted was to be alone with his thoughts, but he was getting used to it. Often even with other people, he still felt alone. Up here on this mountainside, he knew this night could be far worse than most if he closed his eyes and tried to find oblivion in sleep.

Fortunately, he planned to stay awake. "Fire a shot if you need me," he said as he got to his feet.

"I won't need you." She said it as a simple statement of fact that made him smile.

"Occasionally we all need someone," he said and left.

His boot heels sounded loud to his ears as he scrambled back down to the sheep camp. The sheep were quiet. The night had taken on an eerie silence that was unnerving.

He realized that the wind had subsided. It made him feel as if he had gone deaf. He had leaned into it for so many hours that the absence of it now threw him off balance. His footing felt unstable without the wind's never-ending pushback. Again he worried that Dewey might be right that something was out there in the darkness, waiting to pounce.

IT WAS LATER than usual. Nettie was just closing up the store when J.D. drove up. She hadn't seen much of him since he'd moved in, but earlier today she'd noticed he was dressed up when he'd left the apartment. She'd assumed he'd been headed out to his family ranch.

From the front porch of the store, she watched him get out of his pickup. She breathed in the spring evening, hoping he wouldn't think she had been waiting for his return—even if it was true.

Nights like this needed to be cherished, their memory stored away for when the season changed and fall quickly turned into long winter months. She realized she hadn't appreciated one of them in a long time.

As she watched him open his pickup door, the dome light came on, and from the high porch, she could see inside the pickup cab. He had what looked like dirty rags on the passenger side. He quickly climbed out, closing and locking the door. She noticed, too, that his pickup was filthy. What had his brother had him doing all day, mucking out stalls?

She tried to gauge how his night had gone as he started for the outside entrance to the apartment. He looked tired and appeared distracted. "Hey, cowboy," she called. "Tough day?"

He smiled when he spotted her and changed direction, heading for the porch instead.

"How did it go?" she asked as he climbed the steps to where she was.

"Not as bad as I thought it might be," he said as he leaned against the porch railing beside her. "Seeing you here in the starlight makes it all worthwhile." He settled his gaze on her, warming her.

"Taylor must have put you to work."

He nodded. Before she could ask more, he said, "It's good to be home. I've missed this place." His eyes locked with hers. She tried to ignore the tingling feeling in her toes or the shiver that rippled over her.

She smiled and turned away to hide the sudden rush of heat just under her skin. It was clear he didn't want to talk about his day.

"Well, I'm glad it went well." She started to move toward the door to finish locking up. Her home was up on the mountain behind the store, just a small hike up through the trees. She should have locked up much earlier, but tonight she hadn't felt up to facing her empty house and she'd hoped to see J.D.

Now that he was back, though, she wasn't sure she should have waited. Frank might be right about her and her taste in men.

"Nettie." J.D. touched her arm. His hand was warm, his skin just rough enough to remind her of what a real man's hands felt like.

"Have dinner with me." When she started to decline, he quickly added, "Come on. What's wrong with old friends having dinner? Please? I hate to eat alone, so what do you say?"

She felt herself weaken.

J.D. must have sensed it as well because he said, "Good. Let me change, and I'll pick you up at your house. I'm thinking steak at the Grand in Big Timber. How's that sound?"

It sounded wonderful, and she said as much.

She finished locking up and went out the back door. There was a trail behind the store that rose sharply up the mountain to the house Bob had had built for them. She was partway up when she looked back and saw J.D. emptying something from his pickup.

The pile of dirty rags she'd seen earlier?

She stopped for a moment in the darkness of the trees to watch as he discarded the rags in her trash container at the side of the store. He stopped as if he thought better of it, then reached into the commercial trash container and pushed the rags down farther. Turning, he went back to the pickup. She saw him wipe down the passenger-side seat then clean something off the door handle.

He must have sensed her watching, because his gaze came up. She held her breath, for no reason except that she didn't want him to think she was spying on him. Standing under the pines in the dark, she didn't think he could see her.

Evidently, she'd been right because he went back to what he was doing, then closed the pickup door and headed upstairs to the apartment over the store. This time he didn't lock the pickup.

FROM HER SPOT in his old recliner, Bethany watched her husband pack. He was meeting the men early in the morning up the Boulder for the hike over the mountains into Yellowstone Park.

"How long do you think it will take you to reach Hellroaring Ranger Cabin?" she asked.

"Depends on how bad of shape these guys are in," he said without looking up.

"I still don't understand why they want to make this hike, especially this time of year. Didn't I hear there is supposed to be a storm coming in up in the mountains?"

When Clete glanced up, he was wearing his irritated expression again. "I don't really care what their reasons are. Remember? I'm not doing this for the fun of it, okay?"

She remembered. She clamped her mouth shut, nodded and was glad when he went back to his packing. He didn't need to remind her that, while the bar was doing all right, it would be harder to support them since she would no longer be working as a waitress at the Branding Iron Café. She'd been working there since she was fifteen and hoped she'd never have to go back.

"Did I tell you that my aunt is going to teach me how to sew?" He didn't answer. "I was thinking I would make all of the baby's clothes except for jeans. But he won't need those for a while."

"My son won't have to wear homemade clothes," Clete said as he swung the pack up from the floor. "I'll do whatever I have to do to make sure of it."

She hated when he got his back up like that. He hadn't been any poorer than she and her family had been. People in this part of Montana lived conservatively. If they had money, they didn't waste it or show it off. Except in the case of W. T. Grant, she thought. He'd built himself a mansion and become the laughing-stock of the community. Not to speak ill of the dead, she quickly reminded herself.

But it wasn't until Clete had gone off to college that he'd become obsessed with the haves and have-nots. Before that she didn't remember him being so sensitive about money.

"It's all going to be fine, you know," she said before he banged out of the house to go load their SUV. She tried not to worry. Clete knew those mountains. But did he really know those men he would be taking with him?

On the twenty-mile ride to Big Timber, Nettie and J.D. talked about the old days. They had the pickup windows down, the spring night blowing in. It made Nettie feel like a kid again.

At dinner at the Grand Hotel on the main drag, J.D. amused her with stories about his adventures away from Beartooth. She knew most weren't true or at least were highly exaggerated, but she didn't care. She felt as if she'd been in cold storage for years. She found herself laughing and enjoying herself for the first time in a very long while.

"I've missed you," she said after they'd ordered dessert. "Why have you stayed away so long?" It was on the tip of her tongue to ask the obvious question: *And why have you really come back now?* But she didn't.

She didn't want to spoil the moment, and she feared

that that the question would ruin the whole night. J.D. seemed determined to put his day behind him, whatever had gone on. She couldn't help thinking of the pile of dirty rags she'd seen him discard.

When she'd gotten into his pickup, there'd been an odd smell. He must have seen her expression because he'd apologized, saying he'd hit a skunk on the way back to the apartment. It didn't smell like any skunk she'd run across, but what did she know.

"So have you heard any more about that missing sheepherder?" he asked.

"Just that the new deputy has gone up there with Maddie Conner. The ranchers at the Branding Iron this morning got a good laugh out of that. The new deputy is from back East, and Maddie is a force of nature."

"There's a storm blowing in up there," J.D. said. "I would think they'd have to turn back."

Nettie shook her head and realized he was just making small talk as if a little nervous. She knew the feeling. This felt like a real date, and she couldn't remember the last one she'd been on.

"I think I heard they left right away. They should be up there by now." She took a sip of her wine, afraid it would go to her head. "So you never married. Weren't you ever tempted?"

J.D. smiled and reached across the table to cover her hand. "You were the only woman who ever tempted me."

She scoffed.

"I was crazy about you all those years ago, don't you know?"

She shook her head, but in truth, she did remember J.D. following her around, always trying to get her attention.

"I was so jealous of Frank. Everyone knew even all those years ago that he'd stolen your heart."

She laughed off his words as casually as she could, but just the mention of Frank's name made her pull back her hand. She regretted it at once. Why was she waiting around for Frank? He must think her a complete fool.

She finished her wine and felt her toes begin to tingle. The dark booth felt too intimate, the tiny twinkling lights hanging from the old tin ceiling too romantic. The place, the night, this moment felt magical as if it had captured her and taken her far away from her real life to a fantasy one where she was young again and beautiful and...desired.

"You never even gave me a chance back then," J.D. said.

"You were just a boy."

"Three years younger than you. Doesn't matter now. We're both adults."

That made her laugh. "In our fifties, I'd *say* we were adults."

"Not too late."

Nettie shook her head. "J.D.—"

"What *did* happen with you and Frank?" he asked as he poured her more wine. "That is, if you don't mind me asking."

Nothing. "I married Bob." She shrugged as if that covered it. "A while after that Frank married Pam Chandler. She wasn't from around here. The marriage didn't last." She shrugged again. "They have a teenage daughter who is…scary."

"So your husband, Bob—"

"We're in the process of getting a divorce. He lives in Arizona."

"I'm sorry."

"Don't be. Bob and I never…" She searched for the right word. "Clicked."

J.D.'s gaze softened. "You deserve some happiness, Nettie."

She felt tears blur her eyes for a moment. "What about you?" she asked to fill the uncomfortable silence. "Have you found happiness?"

"I never stayed in one place long enough to even look for it," he said with a laugh.

"But you're back now."

He nodded thoughtfully.

"You aren't staying, are you?"

His gaze met hers, and a smile turned up the corners of his lips. "I don't know yet. I'm certainly tempted."

Her heart began to beat a little faster at the look he gave her. She drew away first, feeling guilty as if she were cheating on Frank. What a joke. She couldn't even be sure Frank cared about her. He certainly hadn't made any kind of move to even ask her out.

"So was your brother surprised to see you?" she asked, determined not to let thoughts of Frank ruin this evening.

"You know Taylor. And Rylan's *married*." He shook

his head as if surprised even though she'd told him the news when he'd rented her apartment. "The last time I saw him, he was a baby. I didn't realize how much time had passed."

"Years."

J.D. suggested an after-dinner drink, but Nettie was feeling the wine and said she'd had enough for one night. She seldom drank and, as it was, she was feeling light-headed enough being in a nice restaurant with a handsome, charming man.

He walked her out to his pickup, opening the passenger-side door for her. As she climbed in, she saw a small piece of white paper that had gotten stuck between the seat and console. Retrieving it without thinking, she saw that it was a receipt of some sort. Thinking to throw it away, she balled it up and stuck it into her pocket as J.D. climbed behind the wheel.

On the way back to Beartooth, they were both quiet as if lost in their own thoughts. Or maybe J.D. was simply enjoying the spring night. Nettie hated for it to end. The wine, the wonderful meal, the companionship—it had all been so nice.

"I had a great time tonight," she said when he dropped her at her door.

"Me, too. Thanks again for renting me the apartment. Give me a holler in the morning before you open. I make a killer breakfast burrito. My salsa recipe came from a little hole-in-the-wall café in El Centro, California. I think you'll like it."

She hesitated but only for a moment. "Okay."

It wasn't until she was in the house and was taking off her coat that she remembered the receipt she'd stuffed in her pocket. She was about to toss it into the trash, when she noticed it was a gas receipt from a station in Gardiner, Montana.

She looked at the date and time stamped on the receipt. J.D. had gotten gas in Gardiner, the north entrance to Yellowstone Park, last night at 2:00 a.m.? What was he doing in Gardiner at that hour?

Nettie thought the receipt had to be wrong. Otherwise J.D. had rented her apartment then taken off in the middle of the night to go to the park.

Her head began to ache from the wine, from her misgivings. The receipt was wrong—that was the only thing that made any sense. She tossed the receipt in the trash, wishing she wasn't so nosy sometimes.

That was when she saw the blinking light on her answering machine.

She almost didn't listen to it. She'd had such a nice night she didn't want anything to spoil it. But she got so few calls that she pushed the play button.

"Nettie? This is Gladys at the hospital. I thought you'd want to know. Frank's in the hospital."

CHAPTER TEN

THE SHOT BROUGHT Jamison out of a fitful sleep. He sat up in the darkness from where he'd fallen asleep on the mountainside and grabbed for his shotgun.

He hadn't gone to the tent. Instead, he'd camped himself out against a part of the mountainside where he'd be ready if Maddie did need him. Nor had he planned to fall asleep, but clearly he had.

Overhead the seemingly endless midnight-blue sky was filled with starlight. He blinked, still caught in the remnants of a dream. He'd been holding his wife, Lana. He could still remember the feel of her in his arms. She'd been crying. He frowned, trying to remember why.

Another rifle report echoed across the mountainside. He rolled to his side, keeping his head down, confused as to where the shots were coming from and what was going on.

A dog barked, followed by another shot. This time he spotted the flare from the rifle barrel. It lit the sky just long enough for him to see the shooter.

Maddie? What the hell?

A heavy-duty flashlight beam came on, the golden sphere skittering over the flock until it lit on something large and dark. In the glow of its beam he saw the bear. The huge grizzly stopped on the side of the mountain. The dog began to bark again. The light went out. Another rifle shot filled the night, and then the flashlight beam followed the grizzly as it loped up over the ridge and disappeared.

Jamison got to his feet and rushed across the mountainside in Maddie's direction. He was breathing hard, still caught between waking to find himself up here on this mountain and being trapped back in the dream with Lana.

"I just fired warning shots, in case you thought I was trying to kill it," Maddie said when he came charging up.

He stopped to catch his breath. He remembered why Lana was crying. Of course it was because of something he had done. Or not done, which was more often the case.

"I figured that's all you were doing, since killing grizzlies is illegal," he said to Maddie as he fought to leave the dream behind.

She smiled at that. "Exactly. Didn't mean to wake you."

He couldn't miss the sarcasm. Earlier he'd said he would be around to help her if she got into trouble. "Yeah. I must have dozed off. Sorry."

"Don't be. You should sleep in the tent on a cot, though. Would be more comfortable."

"What about you?" he asked, wondering if she'd been

awake all this time or if the dog had warned her of the grizzly.

"I think I'll stay out here. It will be daylight in a few hours, and that bear will be back."

He followed her gaze toward the eastern horizon. "I don't think I've ever seen that many stars before," he said more to himself than to her.

"Not even at summer camp?"

He glanced at her again. "A woman who can joke at this hour of the night, scare off grizzlies and still look beautiful in the starlight. You really are something, Mrs. Conner." He tipped his hat to her. "I'm wide-awake now. Please, let me watch the sheep." He saw her automatically open her mouth to turn down his offer. "Bet that cot would feel like a feather bed about now. I'll wake you if I need you."

To his surprise, and maybe hers as well, she handed him her rifle. "That bear won't have gone far. Make sure it doesn't get any more of my sheep."

NETTIE WAS WELL aware that visiting hours were long over, but she had to see Frank. She had to make sure he was all right.

The hospital was like a morgue this time of the night. As she started down the deserted hallway, she was assaulted with guilt. While she was having a wonderful night with J.D., Frank had been lying in a hospital bed.

She would never forgive herself. On the way into town, she'd remembered those days when she and Frank had been in love. He'd been the most handsome man she'd ever seen. But it was the danger surrounding him that had drawn her. Life with Frank would have been an adventure. She'd known that intuitively. Just as her mother had.

She thought of her mother's pinched expression and the advice she'd given her the day Frank had come riding up on a motorcycle to their ranch yard. *Marry Bob. Stability lasts. Adventure doesn't.*

Nettie had wished a million times she hadn't listened, but in truth, she'd been scared. Frank made her heart pound too wildly. Just the look in his eyes promised things that had made her blush.

So she'd chosen Bob and regretted it ever since. Her mother had been the kind of woman who wanted security more than passion. Nettie had sacrificed passion and feared it might be too late to ever find it again.

There was no one at the nurse's station, so Nettie kept going. The doors were open on the rooms. Most were empty. It was a small hospital, and right now there wasn't a lot going on apparently.

She found Frank in the fourth room she looked in. Stepping inside, she closed the door and moved to his bed. His eyes were closed, his head bandaged. He looked terrible. What had happened to him? All her friend had been able to tell her was that he'd been attacked. She was surprised there wasn't a guard outside his door, but maybe whoever had done this had been caught. Or Frank had refused a guard. That would be just like him.

"Frank?" she whispered next to his bed. "Frank?"

His eyes opened slowly. He blinked, and she saw surprise in his expression and pleasure before he frowned. "What are you doing here?"

"I heard you were in the hospital. Frank, what happened?"

"You can't be here, Nettie," he said, glancing toward the door.

"I'm not worried about breaking the visiting rules, Frank. I had to see if you were all right."

"I'm fine."

"You don't look fine."

"Nettie, you have to leave. You shouldn't have come."

The door opened behind her. A shaft of light spilled across the floor toward her and Frank. "Excuse me?" the nurse said. "Visiting hours—"

"I know all about visiting hours," Nettie snapped at the nurse then turned back to Frank. "What's going on? I was so worried—"

"Nettie, I need you to stay clear of me, you hear me? Just keep your distance. I can't be around you."

"What are you talking about?"

"Ma'am," the nurse said. "You need to leave now."

Frank closed his eyes. "Please, Lynette. You have to leave me alone." His eyes opened, and she saw pain as well as anger in them. "You just have to leave me the hell alone."

She felt her heart snap, a break as clean and painful as a bone. "Don't worry, Frank. I won't bother you again."

CLETE REYNOLDS GLANCED at the clock and quickly reached over to turn off the alarm so it didn't wake his sleeping, pregnant wife.

Bethany lay on her side, facing him. He could see her face in the early-morning light coming in the bedroom window. To his surprise, he was reminded of the first time they'd danced. It had been at the yearly fall festival held at the local fairgrounds. He smiled at the memory of that young, innocent Bethany. She'd been so brash and confident, coming up to him and telling him she wanted him, when in truth, she was scared out of her wits.

He shook his head now as he studied her. She'd been ready to give herself to him, fool girl. And he'd been ready to let her, driving her to a spot he knew down by the creek, far enough away from the rodeo grounds that they would be alone.

But he hadn't been able to do it. She was too sweet. Too scared. He remembered the way she'd trembled when he'd kissed her. She'd told him later that day when he took her back to the festival and danced with her that she was going to marry him.

He had laughed, telling her she was too young for him, too…sweet. She was still that way, he thought as he reached under the covers and placed his hand on her swollen belly. He hadn't been a good husband and blamed himself for what had happened to them last year.

Hell, what did he know about being a husband, anyway? His old man hadn't been much of one. Or a father, for that matter. Sure, Clete had seen the way some husbands acted in television commercials and chick flicks, but no man he knew behaved like that. He was trying to give Bethany what she wanted now, though. What she needed. Because he couldn't lose her.

He waited for the baby to move, needing that reassurance especially now. Bethany had her misgivings about the men he was taking back into the wilderness. She wasn't the only one.

But they were offering him too much money not to take them up on their offer. He didn't want his son to do without anything. Or Bethany to have to make the kid's clothes.

He felt his son move inside her and smiled again, then leaning down, he gently kissed his wife's forehead. "I know I'm crap at showing it, but I love you more than life," he whispered.

Bethany sighed in her sleep. He quickly removed his hand and slipped out of bed. He didn't want to wake her. She'd been having enough trouble sleeping these days so close to delivering their baby.

In the other room, he pulled on his boots. He'd loaded everything he needed last night. But this morning there was one more item he wanted to take. He hadn't gotten it out last night because he hadn't wanted Bethany to see him take it. He hadn't wanted to worry her any more than he had.

From the gun cabinet, he pulled out his pistol and a box of ammo. He never knew what they might run into back in the mountains. And while he would never have admitted this to his wife, he didn't trust the men he was traveling with into the Beartooths.

JUST BEFORE DAYLIGHT, Maddie came riding up the mountain to where Jamison was watching her sheep. He'd never dreamed he'd ever end up on the side of the mountain protecting a couple thousand sheep. The dog had stayed at his side the rest of the night, watching both him and the sheep, leaving only long enough to get a drink from the nearby creek and go get something to eat when Maddie had called him just after daybreak. No doubt Lucy had felt the weight of the responsibility Maddie had given them—just as he had.

Maddie had been right. The grizzly *had* come back. Jamison hadn't had to fire a shot, though, one he knew would awaken Maddie. Instead he'd shone the light on the bruin, and that had been enough to send it back over the mountain.

Maddie rode up looking more energetic than he felt, that was for sure. She'd apparently washed up in the creek, because he noticed that her hair was wet around her face and she'd recently replaited it.

"I made breakfast," she announced, motioning toward the tent. "I thought we should have something to eat before we light out looking for Branch."

"Good idea," he said as he followed her down to the camp. As he walked into the tent, he saw the indentation she'd made in the cot. It still held her shape, surprising him how small it looked.

Maddie, while only about five-six, seemed bigger

than life in her strength and abilities—not to mention her determination. It amazed him to realize what a slight-framed woman she was under her oversize, bulky ranch clothing.

The tent smelled of bacon. He saw that she'd made them eggs and toast, as well. He was glad she hadn't eaten, but had waited for him.

He watched her walk to the far cot and pick up a faded flannel shirt that had been lying at the foot.

"I assume that's Branch's?" he asked.

She nodded and laid it back on the cot. "He taught me how to ride a horse, you know. My father was too busy with running the ranch and my mother didn't ride, but Branch said a Montana girl needed to know three things—how to ride a horse, how to swim and how to hold her liquor." She smiled as she looked over at him. "Branch taught me all three."

Jamison laughed as he offered her one of the plates of food.

She took it and said, "I see most of the camp supplies are gone."

He realized she planned to eat standing up and did the same. The tent, although roomy, felt cramped with the two of them in it. "Shouldn't there be more food only four days in?"

She glanced toward the cabinet and nodded. "Even if Dewey ate like he had a hollow leg, I can't imagine them going through that many supplies so quickly."

"What would Branch have done if they were running out?"

"Killed a lamb and made bread. A sheepherder can survive if he has what he needs to make bread. I see there is plenty of flour left. But he would have sent Dewey down for whatever else they needed."

She took a bite of her breakfast, her gaze taking in the contents of the tent as she chewed. She seemed to be seeing it for the first time. He figured she hadn't bothered to look around last night. She'd probably dropped down on the cot and gone right to sleep as exhausted as he knew she had to be.

"I think someone might have helped themselves to the supplies," he said as he scooped up another bite of the eggs. "I found an extra set of tracks outside the tent."

Maddie looked up in surprise. "You think someone took their food?"

"I think it's possible." He didn't mention what else he thought might be possible.

She seemed to give that thought. "I would be surprised if it was a hiker. There isn't a trail close to here, and it's pretty early in the season. Could be another rancher stopped up." She sounded doubtful.

"Other than food, I noticed something else that appears to be missing," he said. "You probably saw the split firewood outside the tent? I can't find the ax that was used to split it."

She met his gaze, hers narrowing, but she said nothing.

"Is there anything that seems out of place?" he asked.

She started to shake her head when her gaze landed on the two-way radio receiver he'd bagged. "You didn't tell me you'd found that," she said, putting down her plate to reach for it. "Did you try to raise Branch on it?"

"I'm afraid it's now evidence," he said as he took the bagged receiver from her.

"But Branch might have the other one," she argued. "If he's in trouble—"

"He couldn't have called on this one. Someone took out the batteries."

"There must be an extra set of batteries up here," she said, digging in her heels.

"I've already looked," he said. "Whoever took the batteries didn't want anyone communicating with the outside world."

She let out an irritated sigh. "So we're back to that. Why would Dewey—"

"I didn't say Dewey did it. But whoever took them out quite possibly had something to hide. Until we find Branch—"

"This other person you said was here. He could have taken the food and the batteries."

He didn't want to argue with her, although he couldn't imagine why whoever had been here would take the batteries for the two-way radio. If the man were in trouble, wouldn't he want to call for help? Especially since he'd been limping.

"We don't know what we're dealing with," Jamison said. "The man who visited the camp was wearing new hiking boots and was limping."

"You could tell all of that from a few tracks in the dirt?"

"I could from the tracks, yes."

She shook her head. "If someone had come around, Dewey would have mentioned—"

"I doubt Dewey saw anyone. That doesn't mean whoever was up here didn't purposely scare him away. Remember what he said about the 'crying' sounds he said they'd heard?"

"Of course I remember. I'm sure, if that's what they heard, then there is a logical explanation. Why would anyone try to scare them away?"

"Could it be another sheep rancher who wants to graze his sheep here?"

She shook her head. "We have a lease for this area. This isn't the old Wild West."

"Then maybe whoever it is has another reason to want to get rid of both Branch and Dewey."

Maddie shook her head. "So they could steal a little food? Take their ax? Rustle a lamb?"

He knew it sounded unbelievable especially to Maddie. She'd been born and raised around here and felt safe. Branch had probably felt safe, too.

She shook her head angrily. "You're convinced that a crime has been committed.... This isn't New York City."

"You might be right. We won't know what happened up here until we find Branch."

She sighed, picked up her plate and finished her breakfast. "We'd better find him, then," she said as she tossed her plate and fork into the pot of hot water she had on the stove. "I'll leave Lucy here with the sheep."

CLETE THOUGHT HE would have to wait, but as he came around the corner of the narrow dirt road up the Boulder, he saw Alex's big, black SUV sitting at the trailhead.

He'd never known any of the three to be early risers. If he had to guess, he'd bet they'd probably stayed up all night. The thought of them being half-drunk did nothing for his mood.

This morning he hadn't wanted to leave Bethany. Even as he was driving away he had a foreboding feeling he couldn't shake that he should call Alex, cancel and go back in and climb into bed with his wife. Common sense had forced him to keep going, though. They needed the money. As long as Bethany didn't have the baby while he was gone…or worse, have any trouble… She wasn't due for another two weeks, and first babies didn't come early, right?

He shoved those thoughts away as he pulled in next to Alex's SUV. To his surprise the three men didn't look drunk or even hungover as they climbed out of the rig. All three were blond, blue-eyed and good-looking, attributes that they had used to their advantage and he was sure still did.

Alex was the smallest of the trio. He'd played quarterback on the team in college. Tony and Geoff had both been linemen.

It surprised him that Alex still looked in pretty good shape, but then, he had always been wiry and strong for his size. Tony, who Alex said now worked for his father in some investment firm, had gone to seed. Geoff, though, looked the most fit of the bunch since apparently he'd bought a fitness franchise in California.

But as the three men walked over to him, Clete noticed that Geoff was limping. "Did you hurt yourself?" he asked him, suddenly worried that the man couldn't make the trip.

"Old football injury. It's just been bothering me," Geoff said. "Not a problem." He shot a look at Alex as if they'd already had this conversation.

"That was something we wanted to talk to you about," Alex said as he laid a hand on Clete's shoulder. "Geoff's okay, but we discussed it, and we think it would be better if we went by horseback. Your uncle has some horses up this way, right?"

Clete was taken aback for a moment at this change of plans. Also, he couldn't remember ever telling Alex about his uncle Max or his horses.

"We thought we'd ride. Just like in the Wild West," Tony said almost too cheerfully.

"Horses?" Clete had the feeling that this had been the plan all along.

"It's not too late to regroup and take horses, is it?" Alex asked, giving Clete's shoulder a friendly squeeze.

This was a difficult trip, especially this time of year. There would be snowfields to cross, and the grizzlies would be coming out of hibernation. Anything could happen. And starting off with Geoff already limping?

Clete looked toward the mountains, concerned.

"We're happy to pay whatever extra it would cost." So like Alex to up the ante.

"Why not?" he said, hating that it had been the extra money that had swayed him.

"Great. Your uncle's place is just up the road, right?" Right.

"This way we can take more supplies," Tony said and patted his stomach. "If you can't tell, I like to eat." The three laughed, but it had an odd unauthentic ring to it.

Clete hesitated again then sighed, wondering what other surprises the three would spring on him before this was over.

"Why don't you follow me to my uncle's." It still bothered him that Alex not only knew about his uncle but also where he lived. Clete couldn't remember ever telling any of them about Max. But Alex wasn't the kind of guy who gave a thought to anyone else. Maybe Clete had mentioned his uncle. It would be just like Alex to remember Uncle Max when he wanted to borrow his horses.

"We can leave the vehicles there."

"Good idea," Alex said, slapping him on the back. "This is going to work out great."

But Clete noticed the last part was directed more toward his friends. Tony looked worried. Geoff said something under his breath as he limped back toward Alex's SUV. Both men acted as if going back into the mountains was the last thing they wanted to do.

WHEN THE SUN crested the mountains it did so with splendor. Jamison was again stunned by the beauty of these mountains. The golden light washed over the rocky peaks, making them sparkle as if filled with diamonds instead of mica and quartz.

The morning was so bright and clear it was blinding. The grass was a brilliant spring-green, the snowcapped peaks a dazzling white. Fog wreathed the very top of the mountain closest to them. Wisps of it blew past as they rode up to the ridge.

As the fog cleared, the visibility on the ridge overlooking the wide meadow was breathtaking. So was the wind that had come up with the rising sun. Reining in, Jamison surveyed the mountains beyond.

"This is amazing up here," he said, sounding as in awe as he felt.

Beside him, Maddie smiled. "An old sheepherder joke is that his home is a big room—two hundred miles wide."

"I can see why a person might want to spend three months of the year up here." He felt her gaze shift to him.

"You don't think you would get lonely?"

"Maybe."

"Some sheepherders can't take it. They get what they call 'sagebrushed' or 'sheeped.' They go mad."

"Could that have happened to Branch?" he had to ask.

She shook her head. "If he was going to do that, he would have when his wife died. No, Branch is the strongest man I've ever known and the most capable."

Maybe Maddie was right and Branch hadn't gotten "sagebrushed" from living in such isolation and eating lamb and bread as his main staples three months of the year. But something had happened to him since he was nowhere to be found.

There was the chance that he'd met with an accident. However, based on what Jamison had seen so far, he still feared the old sheepherder had met with a violent end.

As if her thoughts had taken that same trail, Maddie said, "Branch is the best shot I've ever seen with a rifle or a pistol, and he carried both. He can skin a dead baby lamb in a matter of minutes with a sharp knife." She explained how the old sheepherder would put the fleece on a lamb that had lost its mother so the mother of the dead lamb would feed it as her own.

Jamison didn't doubt Branch's capabilities or his dedication to the sheep. But it didn't change the fact that the old sheepherder and his horse were missing.

Every ravine they rode along, every high ridge and open meadow, Jamison expected to see either Branch or his horse or both.

The sun moved across the sky, marking the passing of the hours as they made a wide circle around the camp, until he finally reined in.

They'd covered a large area, followed tracks that petered out and checked gullies and thick stands of pines. There was no sign of Branch Murdock.

"He wouldn't have gone this far from camp," Maddie said, reining in next to him.

"Is there somewhere else you would suggest looking for him?"

She glared out at the beautiful landscape, looking

almost angry. "I need to get back and finish gathering the rest of the sheep before moving them to fresh grass." He could tell she was as disappointed as he was that they hadn't found anything.

If Branch had met with an accident and was still alive, then they needed to find him soon. The fact that they'd covered so much ground and hadn't found a trace of him made the chance of finding him alive all that much more of a long shot.

"I'll keep looking," he said as she reined her horse around. "Unless you need my help—"

"No, Lucy and I can finish rounding up the sheep. I think we'll leave camp where it is for now. I'll just move the sheep to the meadow beyond camp."

"Are you sure you don't want me to ride back with you?"

She gave him an impatient look. "I know the way. How about you?"

"We learned tracking and navigation by the sun and stars at summer camp."

She smiled at that as she rode off.

He watched her, the woman so sure in the saddle, so convinced that they would find her sheepherder alive. He wished he shared her conviction, but all his instincts told him he was now looking for a corpse.

CHAPTER ELEVEN

CLETE SADDLED FOUR HORSES, all the time watching as Alex, Tony and Geoff stood in the distance talking among themselves. Arguing was more like it, he thought.

He wondered if this whole thing hadn't been one of Alex's crazy ideas, hatched when he was half-drunk. Geoff and Tony had always been like sheep, following Alex blindly. Is that what had happened and now they were going to have to put up or shut up?

As he finished, he called them over and told them to put what they absolutely had to have in their saddlebags. He watched for a moment, biting his tongue when he saw what they thought were absolute essentials for the horseback trip through the wilderness. They were bringing enough booze for a week instead of a few days.

Clete mentally kicked himself for agreeing to this as he turned away. He should have known their idea of a backcountry hike would involve horses and partying. He loaded his own saddlebags then tied sleeping bags and slickers behind each saddle, reminding himself it was only for a few days. He could bear with these yahoos that long.

"Are you sure you're bringing enough food," Tony complained as Clete loaded what he'd brought.

"I'm more worried about enough booze," Alex said and laughed.

"We have four days' food," Clete told them. "Of course, we can't eat it all the first night or we'll all go hungry."

"Don't talk to me like I'm a pig," Tony snapped. "I need more food than other people, okay?"

"You don't need to tell us that," Alex joked. Geoff remained quiet, looking distracted. Clete shot him a look and caught him grimacing in pain as he touched his leg.

He thought about saying something, at least asking if Geoff had seen a doctor when he'd reinjured it. He *had* reinjured it, no matter what he said. But maybe he didn't want the others to know that was the case. Why else lie that it was an old football injury?

Clete just hoped the wound didn't get infected. It would be hard enough to get these men to Yellowstone Park as it was without one of them getting too sick to ride.

"I'm going to assume the three of you have at least been on a horse before?" he asked, thinking he should have asked that before he'd saddled up.

Alex put his arm around Clete's shoulders as he said, "Don't worry about us. We'll be fine."

He sure hoped so as they mounted the horses and he led the way up the road to the trailhead. When he ventured a look back, the three were lagging behind. None of them looked happy. Nor were they looking around.

Clete thought about what Bethany had asked him. Why were they so determined to make this trip into the wilderness? The thought made him anxious.

THE DIVORCE PAPERS came in the mail late that afternoon. Nettie knew what they were the moment she saw the brown envelope, even before she saw the return address.

Bob was finally setting her free.

Frank had done the same thing last night at the hospital, but she tried not to think about that because it made her too sad. Too angry, as well. It wasn't her imagination that he'd strung her along. Well, he'd cut her loose now, hadn't he.

Her fingers trembled as she tore open the envelope. The legal document was fairly short and to the point. She got the house, the store and any belongings he'd left behind. She got everything including her freedom.

For a long time, she just stared at the papers. Bob's attorney had been so efficient that he'd included a stamped, self-addressed envelope for her to return the papers after she'd signed them.

All divorces should be so easy, she thought as she picked up a pen and signed *Lynette Ann Benton* and filled in the date. Stuffing the papers into the envelope, she quickly sealed it.

The package wouldn't go out for hours, but that didn't matter to her. She locked up the store and put out the sign saying she'd stepped out for a while, before walking the envelope across the street to the post office to put it in the box.

The moment she let go of the envelope, her eyes teared up with a ridiculous mix of crazy emotions she couldn't even name. Regret had to be at the top of the list, though. Not that she was divorcing Bob. That had been a long time coming. And how could she regret marrying him since she'd gotten the store?

The Beartooth General Store had been her anchor all these years. Her mother had at least been right about Bob giving her stability, and she felt she needed it now more than she ever had before.

Frank had broken her heart last night.

She supposed they were even finally. She'd broken his when she'd married Bob. Or at least that was what Frank had told her.

She'd done her best all day not to let her heartbreak show. As the day had worn on, she'd become sadder and finally furious at the way her life was turning out. She felt cheated!

Bob had been a lukewarm lover at best. She was on her way to sixty. It wasn't too late, she told herself, and yet a part of her knew it was. Not that long ago she'd thought Sheriff Frank Curry would save her from her passionless life. As of last night, she had no hope of that.

While she was heading back across the street, she saw J.D. coming out of the Branding Iron Café. He was laughing, his eyes bright with merriment. When he saw her, he stopped to wait for her.

Nettie prided herself on keeping her emotions walled up from the outside world. But at that moment, she knew everything she'd been feeling was written all over her face.

As she drew nearer, he must have seen how close she was to tears. J.D. strode to her, his arms coming around her without even asking what was wrong. He held her like that for long enough that the entire county would be talking.

"You need a drink," he said as he thumbed away a tear from her cheek.

"It isn't what you think," she said, drawing back to make a swipe at her face with her sleeve.

"Aw, honey, of course it is. If it doesn't have something to do with a man then I'm buying the drinks. Otherwise, you're at least buying the first one."

She couldn't help but smile. "I can't. I have to get back to the store."

"The store will be fine for a little while. Come on. Let's go down to the Range Rider and you can tell me all about it. You buy and I'll provide the strong shoulder. After that..." He grinned. "Well, let's play it by ear, shall we?"

THE FOUR HORSEBACK riders stopped a little before two beside a small creek to have lunch. Clete had chosen the trail along Copper Creek. He hoped to reach a spot on Hellroaring Creek before nightfall.

He'd made sandwiches at the house last night to simplify the lunch meal. So far the trip had been uneventful, but slow. There had been a lot of stops along the way with one or another of the men needing to take a rest, stretch his legs or relieve himself.

Alex had become impatient with his traveling companions. "Enough screwing around," he'd finally barked. "Let's keep moving."

An angry silence had fallen over the three of them that lasted through the hurried sandwich lunch, and then they were back in the saddle.

But not before Alex pulled out a map and asked where they were.

"Here," Clete said, pointing to a spot along the trail.

"Oh." He sounded disappointed. "How far do you think we'll get today?"

Clete glanced up at the sun, an old habit, then checked his watch. "It gets dark early this time of year especially in the mountains."

"But we're on horses, so it doesn't matter. We can travel at night."

"No. The terrain is too rough. I'm not chancing it with the horses," he said before Alex could argue. "Also, Geoff and Tony are struggling enough. By the time we make camp, they will have had enough hours in the saddle."

Alex clamped his lips shut, but it was clear he wasn't happy about this news.

"Enjoy the country," Clete said. "Isn't that why you're up here?"

"Yeah. I just want to get into the high country above tree line. I'm sick of seeing nothing but pine trees." He laughed as if it was a joke.

"Yeah, you must see a lot of pine trees back home," Clete said sarcastically. "Didn't you say you've been living in San Diego?"

Alex laughed. "Did I say that? Phoenix. You must have misunderstood."

"I must have," he said and wondered why Alex would bother to lie about where he'd been living. Clete was sure he'd originally said San Diego.

IN THE DIM BAR, Nettie studied J.D. He could pass for a man at least a decade younger. He had that kind of face, still boyish. The face of an angel, his mother used to say.

And the soul of the devil, Frank would add.

Looking back, Nettie could understand why the two had never gotten along. Frank had sown his share of wild oats, but he'd never gotten caught.

J.D. was a whole other story. No matter what trouble he got into, he always got caught.

But, while that had contributed to the trouble between the two men, it was Nettie who'd driven the wedge between them. A bunch of them used to hang out on a spot on the Yellowstone River. There was a huge old cottonwood, with a sturdy limb that stretched over the water.

Frank had climbed up there and tied a rope from the limb. They spent many hours swinging from the bank to sail out over the river and drop into the warm, clear water.

One afternoon when they were in their teens, Frank had caught J.D. flirting with her. J.D., being the contrary youth he was, had seen Frank coming, and before Nettie could stop him, he'd grabbed her and kissed her.

It was the same day that W. T. Grant had saved

Frank from drowning. They'd all been just kids, the boys jumping into the freezing water of the creek that early spring to show how tough they were.

J.D. had been one of the first ones to jump in. He'd always had more courage than good sense. Frank was the only one who hadn't popped right back up after jumping in. That was when W.T. had gone in to rescue him.

After all the excitement, J.D. had kissed her. Nettie had pushed him away at once, but it had been too late. The two young men had ended up in a fistfight. J.D., though three years younger, had held his own. Finally, the others had broken up the fight.

J.D. had left not long after high school, and while he came back once when Rylan was a baby, Nettie hadn't seen him since.

"All these years," Nettie said. "It's so sad. I just assumed you and your family would patch things up and you would come back."

"It's my fault. All of it. You know that." He grinned and covered her hand with his own. "It's like when I used to try to get a rise out of Frank. Maybe he was right about the devil being in me."

Nettie shook her head as he squeezed her hand and let go. "There's devilment in you, but that is part of your charm. You should have come back sooner."

He laughed and took a sip of his beer. "I thought about it, but there was nothing for me in Beartooth. I'm no rancher. Taylor's the one who took to the land.

Me, I'm a wanderer. I'm always looking over that next hill, checking out that green grass on the other side."

"You never wanted roots?" Her mother had been right about one thing. Nettie liked stability. She liked waking up to see the rocky crag of what was called the bear's tooth from her window in the morning. She liked staying in Beartooth.

"I figured you and Frank would be married, have a passel of kids…" He looked over at her. "What *really* happened?"

She shrugged. "I told you. I married Bob Benton."

"I guess that would do it," he said with a laugh. "Frank would have a terrible time forgiving you."

It surprised her that he would know that about Frank. "I just mailed my divorce papers right before I saw you."

"I wondered."

"I don't know why I got upset. It's what I wanted and yet… It's just all water under the bridge now." She turned as the back door of the bar opened and an older rancher came in. "I really should get back to the store."

"You're worried about Frank catching you with me."

She laughed at that. "He's sheriff now, you know, and he's worried about why you're back in town."

J.D. shook his head and picked up his beer again. "I'm glad I can still worry Frank Curry." He shot her a look. "Hell, maybe I can even make him jealous. He needs to put a ring on your finger, don't you think?"

"That ship has sailed," she said as she slid off the barstool. "We're too old and too much has hap—"

"Bull," J.D. snapped. "You're not too old until you're

dead. Yep, maybe the best thing that could happen is for Frank to see us together." He grinned. "Tonight. Dinner and dancing. How long do you think it will take before he hears about us through the Beartooth grapevine?"

Nettie glanced around the bar and saw a couple of older ranchers watching them. "Oh, I think it's already too late to stop it."

"Good," J.D. said with a laugh. "Then I'll see you later."

Nettie agreed. Why not have dinner and go dancing with J.D.? Frank had made it clear that he didn't want her around him. So why not have some fun with a man who made her feel good about herself?

Unfortunately, Frank had also planted a seed of worry in her. Why *was* J.D. home?

Her biggest fear, though, was that Frank wouldn't react at all to her seeing J. D. West. She couldn't bear the thought that Frank really didn't care. Or worse, hadn't for years.

It was almost dark when Jamison picked up the tracks. He looked out across the mountains in the direction the horseshoe tracks were headed. He was far from the camp—farther than Maddie had sworn her sheepherder would have ever gone.

But Branch's horse had.

Losing light fast, he knew he would have to follow the tracks at first light in the morning. He hated not continuing on the trail now, but it was getting dark. He had no choice but to turn back.

As he rode toward camp, the sunset was still burned orange at the edge of the mountains to the west. It made him think about the sunsets he and Lana used to see from their New York City apartment.

Funny, but he'd missed those sunsets more than he missed her. He'd been unhappy with their life together. They'd gone such different ways. She was involved in every charity and fundraiser under the sun. He'd quit her father's law firm to become a cop. He wanted to shed his old lifestyle, not realizing that would also mean losing Lana.

"I'm sick of black tie," he'd confessed as he'd watched her dress one night. She'd actually laughed, thinking he was joking. "I mean it, Lana," he'd said, taking hold of her arms and forcing her to look into his eyes. "I don't want to do this anymore. Remember when we used to joke about our parents and all their social obligations and how that would never be us?"

She'd frozen, an iciness moving through her until it settled in her gaze. "First you had to become a cop."

"I'm a detective." One of the youngest to ever achieve that rank so quickly. But it was just as well he hadn't said that.

"A *detective*," she'd mocked.

He hadn't realized until that moment how much she looked down on him. And it wasn't something new. That was the real revelation that night. It wasn't changing his job. She'd always looked down on him. All those years he'd worked for her father, she'd held him in contempt. He'd thought she'd wanted him working for her father, but he'd been wrong about that, too. She'd expected more out of him. How could she brag to her friends?

When had she changed and become not only her own mother, but also his, as well? "I'm sorry I disappoint you," he'd said.

She'd looked away, not even able to lie. They both knew that her disappointment had been growing and festering their whole marriage.

But she rebounded quickly. "Don't be difficult, Bentley." She'd softened her words, rubbing his shoulder for a moment and giving him one of her smiles.

Had he really been that easily placated all the years of their marriage by a smile, a kind word, a gentle touch? Apparently, because that night she had turned it off quickly enough and had finished dressing.

Was that the night everything changed for him?

No, it had taken him months of pretending nothing had changed before one day after a hard day at work he'd refused to accompany her to one of her "events."

There'd been no coddling that night.

"I'm sick to death of your attitude," she'd snapped. "I don't have to put up with this."

No, she didn't. Her father would see that she didn't go hungry. Like Jamison, she'd come from money. More money than even his family. Unlike him, she'd never worked a day in her life. Nor would she ever.

"You are so righteous about your 'job,'" she'd said before she'd finally walked out. "I have helped more people than you ever will."

"Lana," he'd said, pulling the trigger on their marriage, "did you ever ask yourself why you belong to so many charitable organizations? I think I've figured it out since you don't have a clue why you're always raising money. It's not guilt over your ultra-privileged life. I think you just like getting dressed up, hanging out with your own kind and feeling important and good about yourself because you can afford five-thousand-dollar-a-plate meals. And me? I was just the guy in the black tie sitting next to you. Any guy in a black tie would do as long as he made you look good."

She'd slapped him hard enough to jar his teeth. But he'd deserved it. He'd managed to end the marriage and the years she'd pretended he mattered to her. It had hurt like hell when she'd walked out because he'd seen the relief on her face. That was the heartbreaker. She'd been wanting to go for a long time. She'd never needed him. If anything, he'd held her back.

MADDIE LOOKED TOWARD the dark, empty ridge, willing Jamison to appear. She and Lucy had moved the flock to a nearby wide meadow and bedded the sheep down for the night.

Then she'd grown anxious as she'd watched the ridge, expecting the deputy to come riding in at any moment. But he hadn't.

"I'm going to have to go find him," she told the dog, adding a curse that made Lucy's ears prick up.

She'd thought Jamison could find his way back— at least in daylight. She'd told herself that even being a greenhorn, he could take care of himself. But if that was true, then he should have known to return before it got any darker.

Her greatest fear wasn't even that he'd gotten lost.

It was what he'd found out there.

"Stay here," she said to the dog and swung up into her saddle just as Jamison appeared on the ridge. A huge well of relief washed over her. She sat on her horse, wanting to ride out and meet him and yet putting off what she now feared was the inevitable.

He worked his way down the ridge as the sky turned a deep dark cobalt-blue behind him.

"I was beginning to think you'd gotten lost," she said as the deputy rode up. It surprised her how happy she was to see him even fearing he was bringing bad news. She could admit it now. She'd been more than a little worried about him. The man had grown on her.

"I told you I could find my way back," he said, shoving his Stetson from his forehead to look out across the band. The sheep had quieted. Only the occasional clang of the bell and bleats drifted on the growing night.

Until that moment, Maddie hadn't realized that the air had cooled. She shivered as she waited to hear what Jamison had found.

"You're cold," he said. "Looks like you've got things taken care of here. Why don't we go to camp? I'll cook."

Her stomach growled in response, and she realized she hadn't eaten since breakfast.

He didn't give her a chance to turn down his offer as he reined his horse around and headed for the tent.

"Stay," she said to Lucy then rode after him.

When they reached the tent she couldn't wait any longer. He wouldn't have been gone so long unless he'd found something. She was sure of it. He just didn't want to break the news to her. It made her angry with him. She didn't need him protecting her.

"What did you find?" she demanded as she dismounted and stalked toward him. "Tell me."

"I didn't find Branch."

Her heart squeezed, and she had to swallow. "That's good, I guess," she managed to say. But his face said something else. "What's wrong, then?"

"I found his horse's tracks much farther away than you and I went earlier today."

She was already shaking her head. "Branch didn't leave."

"Maybe not, but his horse went southwest back into the mountains. Where would that come out if a man kept going in that direction?"

Maddie looked away. Her mouth felt dry as cotton. "You already know. If you keep going in that direction, you'd end up in Gardiner."

"The northern Yellowstone Park border town."

She met his gaze in the dying light. "Branch didn't just ride off into the sunset. He wouldn't do that to me."

The words sounded hollow even to her ears. Something had happened up here. Jamison had said that from the start. She was the only one who kept hoping he was wrong. He must think her a complete fool.

She headed for her horse.

"Wait. I'm going to cook—"

"I'm not hungry." She swung up into the saddle and reined her horse around. "I need to check the sheep."

"Maddie—"

"Not now," she said and rode off into the growing darkness, needing to be alone with her foolish hopes.

CHAPTER TWELVE

CLETE MADE CAMP out of the wind in a stand of pines. He had the other three set up the pup tents. He couldn't believe college graduates, some of them with master's degrees, couldn't put up a pup tent. There was a lot of bickering as if they were kids.

By the time they'd finished, he had the fire going and dinner almost done. They'd erected the tents, three in a row, and put his off a ways from theirs. He tried not to take offense at that since there was no way he had forgotten his role in this trip.

"So I'm thinking we must be here," Alex said after dinner as he brought out his map again. Geoff had gone to his tent the moment he finished eating. Tony had poured himself a drink and sat on a log, scowling into the fire.

Clete glanced at the map. "More like here," he said, pointing at a spot along the trail.

Alex grunted. "We didn't get far today."

Again Clete was struck by this need of Alex's to make good time. "What's the hurry?"

"I told you," Alex said as he folded up the map. "I can't wait to get to the high country."

He'd noticed that none of the three had apparently

brought a camera. That seemed more odd than their behavior. This was beautiful pristine country that few people got to see.

"I'm surprised you wouldn't have a camera to photograph this," he said, voicing his thoughts.

Alex looked taken aback. "Buddy, why bring a camera when we have modern technology right at our fingertips." He pulled out his cell phone.

"Modern technology, huh? You'll be damned lucky to get any kind of service up here with that."

"But it has a camera." He grinned as if he'd bested Clete yet again.

"I guess it does," he admitted as Alex put the phone back into his pocket. But he hadn't seen any of them take a photo with their phones. Nor had they commented on the scenery, the weather or the smell of spring and pines that permeated the air.

"I think I'll climb up the side of that mountain to see the view before it gets any darker," Alex said.

"I'd be careful. It's pretty dark already." Clete watched him work his way up to the high ridge. He figured Alex was hoping to get cell-phone service. Sure enough, when he reached the ridge, Alex tried a number. Clete saw the dial on the phone light up like a firefly moving along the ridge.

A moment later Alex was talking to someone, his back to the camp below him. Clete couldn't hear what was being said—no doubt Alex's intent.

As he watched him up on the dark ridge, the same question kept coming back. What was this trip really about? Knowing Alex, it could be just a case of being able to say he'd done it. Or something else entirely.

ALEX GLANCED BACK at the camp. He was tired and more irritable than he'd let on to the others. Tony and Geoff had complained enough for all of them. He was relieved when the number he'd called answered.

"How did it go?"

"Fine," Alex said into the phone. "We got the horses and should make the cabin by early afternoon tomorrow."

"Your guide doing all right?"

Alex glanced back down the mountainside at the camp. Clete was watching him and had been most of the trip. "So far, so good," he said, turning his back again.

He didn't doubt that Clete was suspicious. But with the money dangling like a carrot out in front of him, he wouldn't balk. Once they reached the cabin...well, then Alex wouldn't have to worry about him anymore.

"You said you might be able to bring him in on things."

"That's not an option." When Alex had suggested Clete, he'd hoped the cowboy had changed since their college days. "He's a bigger Goody Two-shoes than he was in college."

"You're sure he doesn't have any idea what you're up to?"

"Not a clue."

"Are you sure about the way you plan to handle this?"

He could handle Clete. The man had a pregnant wife

and a son on the way. That alone would keep him in line. "Trust me. Clete isn't going to be a problem."

"If you say so. How's Geoff?"

"Cranky. He's limping pretty badly and complaining a lot."

"And Tony?"

"Hungry and whiny, but if I can keep him in food and drink, he'll be fine. I need them both." At least for the time being.

"You're making me nervous, Alex. You're making some other people nervous, as well."

It was those other people that had Alex sweating even though it was cold up here on this mountain.

"No reason to worry. I have everything under control." At least he thought he had had—before everything had gone to hell, but he wasn't about to admit that. He excelled at solving problems on the fly as they came up. He'd solve this one, as well.

"That's good because I heard some news that you aren't going to like. That kid who was with the sheepherder up there? He came out of the mountains all messed up, talking crazy, apparently. Had blood all over him. Some former New York City homicide detective who is now working as a sheriff's deputy has gone up there with the rancher looking for the sheepherder. The rancher is a woman, but if you cross paths with her, from what I've heard, I wouldn't underestimate her."

Alex swore under his breath. Just when he thought things couldn't get any worse. For just a moment, he considered cutting his losses and getting the hell out of

Dodge. But he was too smart to think there was anywhere in the world he could hide. He had no choice. He was in this up to his neck.

IT WAS LATE by the time Jamison heard Maddie return to the tent. He'd made them both something to eat since that was something he could do to help her. She was right—he didn't know anything about sheepherding. But he could keep the two of them fed.

He tried to call the sheriff's department but couldn't get cell-phone service. He told himself he would try again tomorrow from up on one of the higher ridges.

He'd hoped to wait and call when he knew something. But unfortunately, he hadn't considered that he'd be up here this long. His phone would need recharging soon.

By tomorrow, I should know something. He'd found an old map in the tent and was pretty sure he knew where they were. He'd been right about which direction the tracks had headed. The closest way to civilization other than the way Dewey had gone was to the southwest— the way Branch's horse had gone. On the map, just as Maddie had said, the trail ended in Gardiner, the north entrance to Yellowstone Park.

But there were no close trails near where they were right now, which made him wonder again about who'd been in this camp besides Dewey and Branch.

As he heard Maddie dismount, he put the map away. He didn't want to upset her any more than he had. It was looking more and more like Branch Murdock had ridden out of here.

She came into the tent, stopping just inside the entrance. "Something smells good," she said, seeing that he'd left hers on the stove. "Thank you." Her gaze met his and held for a long moment. "Thank you for earlier, too." She looked away.

"Sit down. Let me get that for you," he said, but she waved him off.

"You've done enough."

He wasn't sure that was a compliment.

"Anyway, I've been doing for myself for quite a while now," she added.

As he sat down on the far cot, she helped herself to the pan on the stove, standing as she ate. He got the feeling that she wasn't staying long. Either that or she just didn't want to sit in the confined space with him. He was a little surprised she'd come back at all.

"I'm going with you in the morning." She said it as if she'd expected him to argue the point. He didn't. She took another bite of the food he'd prepared. "It's good."

He simply nodded his thanks, and she finally sat down on the far end of the opposite cot but didn't look at him. He let her eat in peace. He'd already shared too many of his suspicions with her. She was angry with him, desperate to believe that the sheepherder she had known all of her life wouldn't have just ridden off and left her and her sheep.

Maddie was strong, but she'd already had some tremendous loss in her life. He hated to see her hurt again. Unfortunately, he feared heartbreak was on its way and there was nothing he could do about it.

MADDIE ATE BECAUSE she knew she needed to if she hoped to keep it together. Also, she couldn't help but be touched that Jamison kept cooking for her. Had she been up here alone, she hated to think of how she would have managed. She felt as if she'd been battered, not just by the wind and this life, but by whatever had happened up on this mountain. She could feel it. As much as she tried to convince the deputy otherwise, she'd known when they didn't find Branch right away that this would end badly.

Now it was just a case of how bad it would get before it was over.

She glanced at him as the wind billowed the tent sides in and out, shaking it wildly with each new gust. A chill moved through the tent in spite of the fire crackling in the woodstove. She felt chilled to the bone, furious to find herself here, especially with Deputy Sheriff Jamison.

He was so damned determined that something bad had happened up here. But what if Branch had just ridden his horse out of here, gone to Gardiner and then taken off to parts unknown? Wasn't that better than the alternative?

She stared at the deputy, wishing Branch really had just ridden into the sunset. Unfortunately, she knew the man, and the deputy didn't. That was why she was terrified of what had really happened to him.

What would she do? Her secret fear was that she would fall apart and Deputy Jamison would be there to witness it. The thought infuriated her.

"When was your breakup?"

Jamison looked up in surprise.

She hated that she'd struck out at him in the only way she could. But did she really want to hurt him? To make him tell his sad story so she could take some comfort in it? "I'm sorry. Never mind. It's none of my—"

"It's been a year since we turned it over to the lawyers to hash out, so I consider that the real divorce. Legally? I got the final papers a month ago."

She glanced at his left hand and the empty space he was rubbing with the pad of his thumb. The indentation had left the skin white where the ring had been *recently*. "A month?"

"I only took my wedding band off a week ago." He met her gaze. "But I guess you could tell that. I'm not used to it being gone. It defined me for too many years. I didn't want to take it off because it was a sign of my failure." He shrugged. "I actually liked being married even if I no longer recognized the woman I'd married."

All the tension she'd felt only moments ago evaporated at his honesty. "I liked marriage, too," she said and had to swallow around the lump that suddenly formed in her throat.

"Thank you for not thinking I was foolish for hanging on for so long. I think a part of me believed that if I didn't take the ring off..." He shook his head.

"None of the bad part would have happened," Maddie finished for him. "I still sometimes think Hank will walk in the door, that none of the other was real."

"You were married a long time?"

She got up to put the pan into the hot soapy creek water he had going on the stove. "Twenty-two years. We married right after college, but we'd been dating since high school." She plunged her hands into the water. It was too hot and yet she kept washing the pan.

"High-school sweethearts," Jamison said. "Lana and I met at college. We both swore we weren't going to turn into our parents. Maybe she meant it. Maybe she was destined to and couldn't have changed course even if she'd tried. I just know how relieved she was when our marriage was over. It only took her a few months before she found someone more socially her equal."

Maddie pulled the clean pan from the water and dried her hands on a hand towel hanging from a hook on the side of the tent. "I'm sorry."

"Please don't be. It was the best for both of us. I feel guilty because my inability to admit the marriage failed had little to do with my feelings about the woman I'd found myself married to."

When she turned she saw that he had a self-deprecating smile on his handsome face. "We lie to ourselves about our lives sometimes."

"Lana thought the man she married was on his way

to somewhere extraordinary. At the very least a partnership in some prestigious law firm or maybe even a role in politics."

"Is that what you wanted?"

He shook his head. "But she never asked me what I wanted, and I was never honest with her until the end."

"She didn't want to be married to a homicide detective?"

He chuckled. "Who would?"

Maddie sat down again, easing herself back onto the cot.

"Lana liked the social circles she'd always traveled in. The up-and-comers. It was a contest with her and her friends. Whose husband was doing better. I felt sorry for her. I'm sure I was an embarrassment." Jamison got up to stoke the woodstove.

"You don't like talking about her. You still feel a sense of loyalty."

He nodded solemnly.

"I feel the same way. I know all Hank's flaws better than anyone, but I can't even remind myself of them now without feeling guilty." Her voice broke. "I'm still angry with him for dying and leaving me." She turned her face away, fighting tears, and mentally kicked herself for starting this conversation. She'd wanted to strike out at Jamison and had only managed to make herself hurt worse. She was grateful, though, that he pretended not to notice.

"It's hard to break those old bonds, let alone even think about—" He cleared his throat and reached for his coat. "I'm going to watch the sheep tonight. Get some sleep."

"Jamison—"

"Don't worry. I won't let anything get your lambs. I also won't leave in the morning without you."

AFTER DINNER AT the trail camp, Clete got everything cleaned up, stored the food in a tree and made sure the campfire was out before he climbed into his tent.

As night settled over them, Alex went to his tent as well, saying he was tired. Geoff had retired earlier. Only Tony had stayed up drinking by the fire until the chill in the air finally drove him to bed.

Clete heard the three talking softly, but with his tent away from theirs, he couldn't make out their words over the sound of the wind high in the pines.

He told himself it was just as well. He didn't want to know what they were talking about. They annoyed him enough as it was. He concentrated on thinking about his wife and their son—the reason he had taken this job. He concentrated on the money and the fact that the job would be over soon.

It just wouldn't be over soon enough, he thought as he fell into a restless sleep.

He woke to heated voices what seemed like only minutes later. But when he checked his watch several hours had passed.

Looking out the end of his tent, he could see two men silhouetted against the night sky. One was smaller than the other.

Alex and Geoff? They were standing over by the horses where Clete had secured them for the night.

"I'm warning you," he heard Alex say. "You aren't going to screw this up for the rest of us, you hear me?"

"Me? You have a lot of gall. I was almost killed because of you. I'm lucky only my leg was injured, but let me tell you, it hurts like hell. I should have gone to a doctor." His voice broke. "If you had any idea what I've been through—"

"I appreciate the sacrifices you've made," Alex said, lowering his voice. "When this is over, I'll make it up to you. But in the meantime—"

"Shut up and do whatever you say, right?"

"You know I can't do this without you," Alex said.

Geoff cursed. "So I keep hearing."

"Is everything all right?" Clete called.

Both men fell silent.

"Fine," Alex finally called back. "Geoff's leg was bothering him, so he tried to walk it off. We're going back to bed now. Got a lot of country to cover tomorrow, huh, buddy?"

Clete said nothing as he watched the two of them exchange a few whispered words before going back to their tents.

What the hell? he thought. He told himself he didn't want to know what that was about. What had almost gotten Geoff killed? Whatever it was, it explained his limp. The fool hadn't gone to a doctor?

Clete lay back down. Just a couple more days and

he would be shed of them. He repeated that thought like a mantra.

That was if they didn't implode before then. Either way, he just wanted his money and to be done with this.

CHAPTER THIRTEEN

"I HEARD NETTIE BENTON was here last night," Undersheriff Dillon Lawson said that evening in Frank's hospital room.

Frank sighed. "I told her to stay away from me."

Dillon shook his head. "Why didn't you just tell her about Pam?"

"Because you don't know Lynette. I'm afraid she'd go after Pam with a baseball bat," he said and couldn't help but smile at the truth in those words. "Nothing could keep her away if she thought it was what Pam wanted."

"How did she take it?"

Frank had replayed the scene over every waking moment since last night. He couldn't bear to think about the hurt he'd seen in Lynette's eyes. Until that moment, he hadn't realized just how much he loved her. Worse, he didn't want to live without her.

But the worst possible thing he could have done was admit that to her. He needed her to keep her distance. "As long as Pam is out there..." Frank looked to his undersheriff.

"You've probably done the best thing for Nettie right

now. But I'm worried about *you*. Pam has managed to get away with attacking you. She isn't going to back off. My hope is that we can catch her in the act next time."

"Next time?" Frank echoed.

"I figured you were probably safe here in the hospital, but once you get out…" The undersheriff's cell phone rang. He checked it and said, "I have to take this."

Frank watched him. Listening to the one-sided conversation, he could tell it was sheriff's-department business.

"What's going on?" he asked when Dillon disconnected.

"Our new deputy, Bentley Jamison, took a call on a possible homicide up in the Beartooths." He filled him in. "We've been holding Dewey Putman until we heard from Jamison or got the lab results on his bloody clothing. Maddie is his guardian, but I've sent word up north to his father."

"This is the first I'm hearing about this? I *know* Dewey Putman. Jamison thinks the boy killed Branch Murdock?"

"Dewey had been in a fight and lied about it. Jamison went up into the Beartooths with Maddie Conner two days ago. You were out of town, so I've been handling it. Our feeling was that it might come to nothing."

"And?" Frank could tell that Dillon had gotten some news.

"We haven't heard anything from Jamison. According to Dewey, the sheepherder was missing, but I just got a call that Branch Murdock's horse turned up in a barn near Gardiner. It appears that Dewey might not be the only one who rode out of the mountains after some kind of altercation."

"Did I hear you say on the phone that the lab got back to you on the blood on the boy's clothing?" Frank asked.

"Lamb's blood, just like he said. I'll let Jamison know as soon as he calls in. We'll let the boy go once I hear that Branch Murdock is all right."

"So Jamison is up in the mountains with Maddie Conner," Frank said, chuckling. "That should definitely break him into being a deputy out here in the Wild West."

He sobered, though, as he realized what this could mean for Maddie. "If Branch's horse was found, then where is the sheepherder?"

Dillon shrugged. "He apparently hasn't turned up yet. But it's suspicious, his horse turning up in a barn. The old guy could have split."

Frank hated to think that might be the case. "Maddie will have to bring her sheep down or stay up there by herself. As it is, she's going to have to find herself another tender. I doubt Dewey will be going back up. Imagine Bentley Jamison herding sheep."

He felt the undersheriff studying him.

"What about you?" Dillon said after a moment. "What are you going to do when you get out of here?"

Frank had thought about that. "Did you know that J. D. West is back in town? He's renting that apartment over Lynette's store. I thought I'd check and see if there are any outstanding warrants on him."

The undersheriff lifted a brow. "I can do that for you. But are you worried about him or Nettie?"

"There's one other person Pam hates even more than me. I'm scared she'll go after Nettie next."

"So maybe having J.D. around could turn out to be a godsend," Dillon said. "Unless you're worried he'll sweep her off her feet."

Frank scowled at him, and Dillon suddenly remembered there was someplace he needed to be.

Lying back in the bed, Frank couldn't help but worry. He had to protect Lynette until this was resolved. Unfortunately, the only way he could see to resolve it was for Pam Chandler to die.

But he knew one thing for sure. He couldn't stand another minute in this hospital bed. He suspected that Dillon had asked the doctor to keep him an extra day, thinking to keep Frank safe here.

"He doesn't know Pam," Frank said to himself as he swung his legs over the side of the bed. He was still weak, head aching and a little dizzy, but he felt well enough to get out of here no matter what the doctor— or Dillon—said.

He found clean clothes in the closet that Dillon had brought for him from his house and got dressed. The clothes he'd been wearing the night he'd discovered Pam in his house had been taken as evidence. Both he and Dillon were hoping that she'd left some of her DNA on them.

The hospital was quiet this time of the night, which made it easy for him to slip out. He walked the couple of blocks to the sheriff's office.

The spring night was chilly, but the cold air felt good. He breathed it deeply into his lungs. He'd never liked being inside all that much. Montana born and raised, he loved the outdoors. This was his home, he thought as he looked toward the Crazy Mountains. The snow-capped peaks glowed in the starlight. A couple more days and there would be a full moon, he thought as he stepped into the office.

"Sheriff," the dispatcher said, sounding surprised to see him. "I didn't think you were getting out of the hospital until tomorrow."

"I got out on good behavior," he told her as he headed for his office for a key to one of the county rigs parked out back.

Key in hand, he continued on out the back door to a waiting vehicle with Sweetgrass County Sheriff's Department printed on the side.

He suddenly realized as he started the motor that he didn't know where he was going. So he sat for a moment, just letting the engine idle. He wanted to go to Lynette, tell her he hadn't meant what he'd said and explain everything.

But he couldn't do that. In fact, he couldn't go anywhere in this patrol SUV—if he hoped not to be noticed. He headed home to trade the sheriff's-department SUV for his old truck. Fortunately, he always left the key in it. He wasn't up to facing his ransacked house. Not tonight.

Maybe he couldn't go to Lynette. But he could make sure Pam didn't, either.

NETTIE BENTON HADN'T danced in years. She felt breathless and light as air as she started down the deserted street toward home with J.D. at her side. They'd begun the day with J.D.'s breakfast burritos. He'd been right about the salsa. It had been hot and spicy and fantastic. She'd asked for his recipe.

Then tonight they'd had dinner, dancing their way through Big Timber only to return to Beartooth to dance a little longer down at the Range Rider.

She'd felt J.D.'s approving gaze on her all night. He made her feel young and beautiful and…desirable. Frank had once made her feel that way. She pushed that thought away. Just as Frank had done her.

"Tired of living in the past?" J.D. had asked at the bar as he'd held her in his arms during a slow dance.

"Is that what we've been doing?"

He had given her a sympathetic smile. "I will always be the bad guy. But you don't always have to be the woman waiting around for Frank Curry. Life is too short. Too short for regrets, either. We are who we are, and tonight we're the best-looking couple on the dance floor."

She'd laughed because at that moment they'd been the only couple left on the dance floor. The bartender— some guy Clete had gotten to fill in for him, they'd been told—had finally thrown them out way past closing time.

Outside, the spring night was alive with stars and a partial silver moon that peeked in and out of the high pine boughs. Beartooth was a ghost town this time of the night. Not that it wasn't close to one in the daytime.

Nettie couldn't remember the last time she'd had this much fun. Heck, she couldn't remember the last time she'd had fun.

"Nettie," J.D. said when they reached her house on the mountain behind the store.

She turned to find him standing mere inches from her. She felt her breath catch and her heart beat a little faster at the look in his eyes.

"I think you should invite me in," he said. Before she could run through all the reasons that was a bad idea, he said, "Nettie, we need each other tonight."

She'd had just enough to drink that she thought he might be right. He reached for her, pulling her into his arms and kissing her. She closed her eyes, lost in the warmth of human contact after going so long without it.

Nettie couldn't even remember the last time a man had taken her in his arms, let alone when one had wanted her.

Reaching behind her, she opened the door to her house, and the two of them stumbled in. Wrapped up in each other and the moment, neither of them noticed the pickup parked up the street—or the person sitting behind the wheel.

CLETE WOKE WITH A START. For a moment he forgot where he was. He'd expected to see Bethany lying next to him when he'd opened his eyes.

He sat up a little and blinked, trying to focus his eyes as well as his mind. Opening the flap on the tent, he looked out.

Tony was snoring loudly in the far pup tent. The flap on Alex's tent was open, the tent empty.

As Clete climbed out and stretched, he spotted Alex up on the ridge again. He had his cell phone in his hand. But he wasn't making a call. He was looking at the screen. Was he actually taking a photo? Or reading a text?

As Alex turned and saw him, he gave a little wave, pocketed the phone and loped down the mountainside and into camp.

"Amazing sunrise," he said. His cheeks were flushed, and if Clete hadn't known better, he would have said Alex was high on something. His eyes seemed a little too bright. Clete realized he'd never seen the man this excited. It did his heart good to think that Alex might actually be enjoying this.

"It is amazing up here," Clete agreed and turned as Geoff crawled out of the tent. He was still limping badly. "How's the leg?"

Geoff shot a look at Alex. "I'll live."

"You know those football injuries," Alex said. "We don't have to tell you about those, do we."

"No." Clete knew he was fortunate that his injury had only ended his football career—not left him crippled. But Geoff's injury had nothing to do with football. So what was the big secret? Something that was Alex's fault and had almost gotten the man killed.

"Tony! Come on. Let's get movin'," Alex called. "The day's a-wastin'."

"I'll fix us some breakfast, while you guys break camp," Clete said.

Geoff shot Alex a look as if to say, "I thought we were paying him to do everything."

Clete could tell by the set of Alex's jaw that he knew he had a rebellion on his hands—and he planned to squash it.

"Sure," Alex said. "We put the tents up. I'm sure we can figure out how to take them down. Anyway, we can't expect Clete to do everything. Not unless we want to be here all morning."

Geoff didn't look happy about it. He walked over to kick the tent on the side Tony was curled against it. A loud curse came from inside, instantly improving Geoff's mood.

On impulse, Clete said, "I'll make breakfast right after I make a quick call." He hurriedly climbed the mountainside, suddenly feeling the need to hear his wife's voice. When he got through, the connection wasn't good, and Bethany was half-asleep. He told her he loved her and got off the phone.

Back in camp, he set about making breakfast, noticing that the three were doing a poor job of breaking camp. He'd have to do most of their packing over, but at least they'd taken down the tents and rolled up the sleeping bags.

He knew he shouldn't be surprised that he felt like

a third wheel. He'd never been one of them, even when they'd been on the same team together.

After breakfast, he noticed that Alex and Geoff had their heads together. He'd written off the tension between them as Geoff merely being in pain and blaming Alex for it. But there was definitely something going on between the three.

From the start Geoff hadn't seemed into this trip. Alex was the one pushing it. Hadn't he said something about not being able to do this without Geoff? He was also the one who'd insisted on Clete being part of it.

Geoff, Clete realized, had never liked him. Because he wasn't one of them? Or because Geoff didn't feel he could trust him?

Clete was Montana born. The others had come from other parts of the country to Montana to play college football. They had the support of their wealthy families and probably still did. Alex had hinted that they all owned massive summer homes in one of the "in" places like Flathead Lake or the Bitterroot or Paradise valleys.

The three had never worked until after college, and even now Clete doubted they started on the bottom of anything and worked their way up. Their fathers probably set them up.

He knew he was being as hard on them as they had been on him. But he couldn't help resenting them. No one had ever given him anything. He'd earned everything he had. And while they played at life, he had a wife at home and a baby on the way to support.

Alex, he noticed, was in Geoff's face. Clete expected

fists to start flying any moment. He wondered what they were fighting about now. The three had always kept secrets and shared inside jokes, no doubt to keep people like him on the outside. He told himself he didn't care what their problem was, but it brought back those old bad feelings from when they'd played football together.

"Breakfast is ready," he called.

The two stepped apart. Tony had wandered off into the woods but returned saying he was starved. Nothing new there.

As Alex and Geoff returned to the fire, Alex said, "Geoff's leg is really bothering him." He made a face as if to say he thought Geoff was a big baby. "He wants to go back."

"I really don't think you should go back by yourself."

"You really don't have any say in it," Geoff snapped.

"Sorry, but you're riding my uncle's horse. Unless you want to *walk* out of here—"

"Easy, you two," Alex said, putting a hand on Geoff's arm. "Clete's right. We all go on together or we all go back. What's it going to be, Geoff?"

The larger of the men had his hands balled into fists at his sides. Geoff could take Alex in a fight, hands down. But Alex had always been the leader on and off the football field. No one, especially Tony and Geoff, questioned his authority.

"Either way, you have to pay up," Alex said. "Why don't you start right now by giving Clete what we owe him?"

Geoff jerked his arm free of Alex's hold and wiped

the back of his hand across his mouth. "I didn't bring any cash with me."

Alex chuckled. "Is that right?"

"You know damned well that's right or you wouldn't have called me on it," Geoff snapped.

Clete was beginning to think turning back was the best plan and said as much.

"No," Geoff said. "I'll be fine." He shot Alex a look as if he wished him dead.

"So we're all good," Alex said and smiled.

As Geoff limped off saying he was going to take a leak, Alex said, "He just got up on the wrong side of the bed."

"I don't think so. I think that leg is really bothering him." He thought of Bethany and his son. Any misgivings he'd had before this were now amplified.

"He'll be fine." Alex seemed to relax. "So, let's eat and hit the trail."

"Yeah, the trail." Clete ate quickly then set to work repacking everything and saddling up the horses. To his surprise, Alex fell in next to him, insisting on learning how to saddle the horses.

"Geoff is having some money problems," Alex said, keeping his voice down as he worked. "His fitness business isn't doing so well. Creditors are putting pressure on him…. That's why he's been in such a bad mood. He hit Tony and me up for money. We both had to turn him down. Geoff doesn't know crap about running a business. I thought this trip through the mountains would cheer him up, but the adventure I suggested before this trip got him hurt." He shrugged.

Clete was taken aback by Alex confiding in him—especially with such intimate information. "I'm sorry to hear that."

"Yeah," Alex said. "I just thought you should know. Sorry to have involved you in it."

"His leg really does seem to be bothering him," Clete said again. "You said the adventure before this got him hurt?"

"I had suggested this motorcycle course…" Alex shook his head. "Geoff crashed his bike and got banged up. I offered to postpone this trip, but he was determined he'd be fine. He didn't want anyone to know that he'd hurt his leg. I told him I would help him out financially when this was over."

Tony and Geoff had disappeared into the woods. As they now reappeared, their conversation sounded heated. Alex fiddled with his saddlebag, apparently pretending he couldn't hear them.

"Tony is still refusing to invest," Alex said as if to explain the latest disagreement.

Clete finished saddling the last horse. He was relieved now that he knew what was going on. Even this hike back into the mountains made more sense now—and he'd only have to put up with them for another day and a half. Alex had said they would be meeting a friend in Yellowstone Park and not making the trip back, which was fine with Clete. He could make better time without them.

He began to relax a little, determined to enjoy the mountains and ignore their squabbling since all it involved was money.

CHAPTER FOURTEEN

NETTIE AWAKENED TO an empty bed, but J.D. had left a note that he was expected at the ranch early this morning.

For a long time, she lay staring up at the ceiling, waiting on the inevitable guilt to assault her. To her surprise, she felt none. She was headed for sixty, legally divorced and on her own. If she wanted to go dancing with a charming man and bring him home to her bed, she darned sure could.

But J.D. wasn't Frank.

That thought irritated her. She threw the covers off and went in to turn on the shower. Stepping under the hot spray, she realized how good she felt. Alive. J.D. had made her feel desirable again. She'd kept her figure and aged well, even if she said so herself.

This morning, feeling good about herself, she fixed her hair after her shower and took a little more time picking out what to wear. Her step was even lighter as she walked down to open the store. The sun was shining, and the spring air smelled better than she remembered it.

"You're in a good mood this morning."

Nettie spun around to find Sheriff Frank Curry

standing in the trees next to the back door of the store. She realized he'd been waiting on her. She wondered how long.

"It's a beautiful morning. Why wouldn't I feel good?" she said even though she couldn't help feeling a little rattled to see him.

He made a grumpy sound as she unlocked the store and stepped in after her.

"It's too early in the morning for your usual, isn't it?" she asked as she turned on the lights.

"I thought you'd have coffee going." He glanced at his watch. "Opening the store a little late this morning, aren't you?"

She felt her spine stiffen. "I slept in. I can do that if I want to, you know."

"You can do whatever you want."

She realized he was angry with her and knew he must have seen J.D. leaving her house this morning. Well, so what? He had no right to be angry. She was the one who had reason to be mad at him, not the other way around.

"Yes, you made it perfectly clear that you weren't interested in whatever I did." They stood glaring at each other until she broke the tense silence. "What are you really doing here, Frank Curry?"

He swallowed, pulled off his Stetson and stared at his boots for a moment. "I had to see you. I…" He raised his gaze and seemed to take her in. "You look so pretty this morning."

She didn't want to be touched by his words. "Thank you. But I'm sure that isn't why you were waiting for me."

"I just wanted to apologize for being so rude at the hospital. I have my reasons why I can't…"

"Can't what, Frank?"

"Why I shouldn't be here." He put his hat back on and started to turn toward the door.

"Frank?" She hadn't known what she wanted to say, just that she didn't want him to leave.

"I have to go, Lynette." His gaze softened, and she saw a sadness in his eyes that threatened to break her heart all over again. "Take care of yourself." With that, he was gone.

As THE MORNING sun rose up over the mountains, Jamison reined in his horse on the high ridge overlooking the grazing sheep and put in a call to the sheriff's office.

The dispatcher put him right through, saying the undersheriff had been waiting for his call.

"I'm glad you called," Dillon said when he came on the line. "We have the preliminary results on the blood found on Dewey Putman's clothing. It wasn't human."

Jamison glanced over at Maddie on the horse next to him, knowing how relieved she would be to hear that. "Has he been able to tell you any more about what might have happened up here?"

"No, he's pretty much stuck to the story he told you."

"We still haven't found the sheepherder. There are a few things missing from the sheep camp, food and an ax. Also, someone took the batteries out of the two-way radio."

The line began breaking up. "I think I'm going to lose you," Dillon said. "You need to know that we got a call late last night. A rancher down by Gardiner found a horse in his barn. The horse has the Diamond C brand on it. Do you know what the sheepherder was riding?"

"Let me ask." He covered the phone and looked again at Maddie. She'd been watching him intently the whole time he'd been on the phone. "Describe the horse Branch was riding."

She did and he repeated the information to the undersheriff.

"That's it, then," Dillon said. "Apparently Dewey wasn't the only one to abandon camp. I suppose you can wind it up and come on back down."

"Yeah, thanks." As he disconnected, he felt Maddie staring at him as if she'd been holding her breath. "Dewey's coat had only lamb's blood on it."

She nodded as if that didn't surprise her. "So where did they find Branch's horse?" she asked, having no doubt connected the dots.

"Down by Gardiner."

She was already shaking her head. "I don't know what his horse is doing near Gardiner, but Branch Murdock did not ride it down there. He wouldn't have just left without a word."

"Maddie…"

She said something under her breath he didn't catch. "Why didn't you tell the undersheriff that someone else has been through camp? From the size of the footprints, you said the person wearing the hiking boots was probably male and was limping. He must have been looking for a way out of the mountains. Perhaps on a *horse?* That would explain how the horse ended up near Gardiner. It would also explain the missing food. The person could have taken the radio batteries so no one could get word out about the stolen horse."

"That's one theory," he agreed. "But where was Branch all this time?"

She raised a brow. "Let's not forget, the ax is missing. Because if someone tried to take Branch's horse… he would have done his best to stop them."

He didn't want to point out that they still hadn't found his body or a fresh grave in the area around camp. But Jamison had plenty of unanswered questions himself. "Okay. What do you want to do?"

"You said you found his horse's tracks…. I want to see where they go."

"We already know where they go. Gardiner."

She shook her head. "I want to see for myself."

"Fine."

"But we'll have to hurry," she added. "There's a storm coming in."

Jamison looked at the clear, blue sky overhead and the few puffy clouds on the horizon to the west, wondering where she had gotten that idea.

FRANK MENTALLY KICKED himself all the way back to his office. He shouldn't have gone to see Lynette. But his need to see her had outweighed his fear of his ex and what she might do.

Foolish, very foolish. If Pam had any idea how he still felt about Lynette…

"I thought you were still on vacation," Undersheriff Dillon Lawson said when he saw Frank. "By the way, you look like hell. Couldn't you sleep at the hospital?"

"I checked myself out after you left."

"I thought you were supposed to stay in the hospital another day?"

Frank made a face as he sat down behind his desk, determined to go to work to take his mind off everything. "So have you heard any more from Deputy Jamison?"

"Just talked to him. I told him about the blood tests on Dewey Putman's clothing and Branch Murdock's horse being found down by Gardiner. He didn't say when he'd be coming out of the Beartooths, but he sounded relieved. He's probably anxious to get away from Maddie."

Frank chuckled. He remembered being called down to the Grand Hotel one night. There'd been an altercation in the bar. Some rancher had gotten into a heated argument with Maddie, suggesting she had no idea how to run a sheep ranch by herself.

Maddie had thrown her beer in the man's face. The rancher's wife had jumped in, and when Frank arrived, Maddie had the woman down on the floor.

"Maddie can definitely hold her own," he said. "Still, I'm sorry about Branch running out on her. I sure didn't see that coming. I wonder if she can keep the ranch going after this." He shook his head and saw something in his undersheriff's expression. "What's wrong? It's Pam, isn't it?"

"Remind me never to play poker with you," Dillon said. "She was spotted in Beartooth last night. I had all area law enforcement keeping an eye out for her. A game warden saw her drive through town. She was in one of the judge's old ranch pickups. I think it's time to warn Nettie."

As JAMISON AND MADDIE dropped over another ridge, he lost the sound of the sheep. She had gotten the dog to stay behind. When they'd left, Lucy was lying in the sun, watching the sheep.

He reined in for a moment to scan the landscape. From this high point, all he could see were miles and miles of snowcapped peaks, new green meadows and pine-choked ravines. It felt like flying to be this high in such a place.

The air felt intoxicating. Or maybe it was being here, seeing this with Maddie. Like him, she had stopped, and he could see her breathing it all in as if needing it for her soul.

Out of the wind and away from the flock, he was able to hear the songs of meadowlarks and the babble of the many small creeks fed by the melting snow. Pockets of snow still melted slowly on the north sides of the mountains and in the heavy timber on the slopes.

He rode on. But this morning he wasn't anxious to find the horseshoe tracks again. He could understand why Maddie needed proof. He just hated to think how she would take it if, given all the evidence, Branch Murdock had apparently abandoned not only his flock—but her, as well.

He found the horseshoe tracks that matched the ones he'd seen at the camp. The tracks followed a game trail along the bottom of a rock cliff but soon petered out in the rocks. Jamison brought his binoculars up and scanned the country ahead. It was miles of wilderness to where Branch's horse had been left.

"Down there," Maddie said, spotting the tracks again.

They rode off the ridge, across another wide bowl and up another slope to a breathtaking ridge. Each time, they lost the tracks but found them again.

As he reined in on yet another ridge, he wondered how far they would have to go before Maddie accepted that Branch had ridden out of here. Why he'd left his dog, Jamison had no idea. But he had. His coat and the rope around Lucy's neck attested to that.

As for whoever had visited the camp, the man's tracks had been on top of Branch's and Dewey's, suggesting he'd come by *after* they'd both left.

"If you kept going in this direction, where would you come out?" he asked.

She shot him a look to see if he was seriously asking this. "We both know the answer to that. Gardiner, the north entrance into Yellowstone Park. But we are still miles from there."

"Where is the closest hiking trail?" he asked as he scanned the land ahead with his binoculars.

"None are close," she said, sounding distracted.

"The assumed hiker who came into camp must have been lost and stumbled onto the sheep camp, then."

"That's one theory," she said, echoing his earlier words.

When he lowered the binoculars, he saw that she was squinting into the distance. The mountain ranges seemed to go on forever—just as the horseshoe tracks did. The wind had come up again and now flattened the grasses and wore at the rock ridges—as well as at his nerves.

"May I see your binoculars?" Maddie asked.

He handed them over and watched her frown. "What is it?"

"That stone Johnny on that rise is new."

"I beg your pardon?" he asked.

But she didn't answer before she rode toward the rise.

Catching up, he watched her dismount and lead her horse toward a pile of rocks on a high point at the edge of the rise. The rocks had been stacked up to make a pillar a couple feet wide and about four feet high.

"Are you seeing this?" she asked.

"It's a stack of rocks, though I can't imagine how they got like that." Nature worked in unusual ways, but these were stacked too neatly, he thought, to be natural phenomena.

"They go by a lot of names. Cairns, rock Johnnies, sheepherder monuments," she said over her shoulder.

"You're saying someone purposely built this?" he asked, joining her. "Why?"

"Most are old trail markers, grazing pasture boundaries, landmarks. The Native Americans used them to let those who followed know where to find water. Sheepherders often built them to pass the time or make a windbreak for warmth. They come in handy on a foggy day. No two are alike so you can tell where you are."

"You can't think Branch made this? Not this far from camp."

She didn't answer as she studied the stack of rocks for a moment, leaning down to eye the flat rock balancing at the peak. "The top rock points the way."

"To what? Water?"

She shook her head. "There are too many small creeks all along these mountain ranges for that to be why it was built here. This formation is new. Someone left it for a reason." She swung up into the saddle again. "Let's see where it leads."

They rode another couple hundred yards before they found a second cairn.

"This one is new, too," she said as they both dismounted and walked over to it.

"How can you tell that?"

"See where the lichen was recently knocked off the rock?"

He could see what she meant. The lichen had been

dislodged, leaving a spot like a fresh wound on the rock—unlike all the rocks around it.

Jamison knelt by the cairn. This one was smaller, but after seeing the other one, he could tell that it had been made by the same person and recently. The structure was identical. At the base, he spied something that had blown up against the bottom rock.

"What did you find?" Maddie asked.

"Part of a hand-rolled cigarette." Cupping his hand to protect it from the wind, he held it to his nose. "Same tobacco as what I found in Branch's coat pocket. The boot prints are the same, too," he said, pointing at a spot in the soft earth.

He turned to look at her. "You said Branch wouldn't have gone this far from camp. Isn't it possible he was leaving these to let you know he left and went this way?"

Maddie studied the stack of stones. Like the other one, this had a flat pointed stone on top. It was aimed back into the mountains where the snow looked both lower on the peaks—and deeper.

It made no sense for Branch to wander this far from the sheep unless he was headed to Gardiner, leaving the sheep and his responsibilities behind. His boot prints were in the dirt around the cairn, even part of one of his homemade cigarettes. Jamison could tell that, like him, she couldn't deny what she was seeing. But unlike him, she wasn't ready to accept it.

"There's something back here he wants us to see,"

she said as she turned, walked back to her horse and swung up into the saddle again.

While he couldn't imagine what, he knew they had to follow the trail Branch had apparently left—no matter where it led them.

NETTIE TOOK OUT the garbage after opening the store. As she walked along the side of the building by the stairs to her upstairs apartment, she thought about J.D. He hadn't returned. It made her curious how things were going with his family. He never seemed to want to talk about it.

She opened the lid of the large trash container. As she did, she remembered seeing him stuff the pile of rags down as if wanting to hide them. It had seemed odd at the time but she'd forgotten about it—until this moment.

Standing on her tiptoes, she peered into the trash. No rags. She dumped her trash to one side, then using another plastic trash container lid, she moved aside the trash from the corner where she'd seen J.D. throw the rags.

The trash shifted to the side, and she pulled back in surprise.

It wasn't dirty rags.

It was a pile of white bandages, and they weren't dirty.

They were stained with blood.

JAMISON AND MADDIE followed the tracks Branch's horse had left behind—and the cairns. Maddie knew Branch had built them, although she couldn't imagine why.

What if she was wrong about him? Maybe he *had* gone "sagebrushed" and half-mad, his tender gone, and he'd stumbled back into the mountains building one stone Johnny after another for no good reason. Wasn't it possible he just couldn't take it anymore and after Dewey had abandoned him, he'd been mad at Maddie for hiring the boy, had headed for Gardiner?

But while her mind argued against it, she thought of Dewey and the terror in his eyes. What if he'd seen Branch going mad? Maybe hallucinating... How else could she explain the "crying" Dewey swore the two of them had heard? It could have just been coyotes, but if Branch told him it was human and crying—

Even old Branch was spooked.

"We need to backtrack," the deputy said as he scanned the country ahead. "I've lost the tracks, and I don't see any more rock piles."

She brought her horse up next to him. They hadn't seen another cairn for a while. The last one had looked as if it had been hurriedly stacked together. The top part had either fallen down or been knocked down.

She hadn't realized how long they'd been at this. The wind had blown in dark cumulus clouds that accumulated on the mountain peaks, growing darker and larger as they moved toward them. This morning she'd smelled a storm coming in. She'd hoped it might go south of them. Or at least not blow in until they were finished.

Finished what? she asked herself. They'd lost most of their daylight because of the clouds, and she could feel the temperature dropping. Jamison was right. Branch had ridden out this way. She couldn't argue it any longer. He wouldn't have ventured this far from sheep camp unless—

Her gaze lit on what appeared to be an incomplete cairn on a rise below them. It was as if Branch had started it but quit for some reason. She rode down off the ridge even though it was very steep. When she reached the rise, she dismounted and walked to the scattered stack of rocks.

On closer inspection, it looked as if someone had knocked the cairn over rather than Branch just having quit building it. She glanced around then down.

A gasp escaped her lips as she looked down the steep rocky slope from the demolished stone Johnny. "There!" she cried, pointing to the spot as Jamison joined her.

"Stay here," he ordered as he dismounted and started down the steep slope. The rocks were loose shale that gave way under his weight. He began to slide, the top layer of rocks sliding with him.

Maddie watched, heart in her throat. She couldn't see more than a boot sticking out of the brush and rocks below her on the mountain. She already knew in her heart, and yet she watched Jamison's face for confirmation as he reached what she knew was a body. Branch Murdock's.

CHAPTER FIFTEEN

NETTIE HADN'T BEEN able to get the bloody bandages out of her mind all morning. She knew the bandages couldn't have been from any injury J.D. might have incurred. She thought about last night in his arms on the dance floor and later in her bed. He'd been fine.

Anyway, the pile of what she'd thought was dirty rags had been on the passenger side of his truck. She remembered the way he had wiped down that side of his pickup after he'd disposed of the bandages. Who or whatever had been hurt and riding on the passenger side of J.D.'s pickup?

Her heart began to pound as she busied herself restacking canned goods on the shelves in the store.

What was J.D. involved in?

Then she chastised herself. She was letting Frank Curry poison her mind against the man.

"Hey, beautiful." She jumped at the sound of J.D.'s voice directly behind her. "Sorry, didn't mean to startle you." He grinned. "You look like you've seen a ghost. Are you all right?"

She stared into his handsome face. He looked so young, so concerned, she couldn't help but weaken.

This was J.D. She knew him. What did she think he'd done? Killed someone?

That was crazy. He certainly would have gotten rid of the evidence if he'd had anything to hide.

But he *did* try to hide the bandages in the Dumpster, she reminded herself.

"What are you doing back?" she asked too sharply.

He frowned. "I thought we could go across the street for lunch. What's wrong?"

"Sorry, it's just…" He'd come back to take her to lunch. That was so sweet and thoughtful after last night… Did she really want to get into this now? Would there be a better time? Anyway, she needed to put her mind to rest.

"J.D., I found something in the trash…."

He frowned. "Yes?"

"The trash out by the side of the store."

"What was it?" he asked. He looked so innocent, so trusting. He was going to make her ask.

She told herself she was going to look like a fool. Worse, he would realize she didn't trust him. She swallowed. "I found some bloody bandages. I was afraid someone had gotten hurt."

"Bloody bandages? Nettie, I put those in there."

She felt an instant relief. He hadn't lied. This was good, right? "Did you hurt yourself?"

"Naw. Oh, hell, I didn't want you to see those." He looked away and she held her breath, now afraid of what he was going to tell her. Or if maybe he was trying to come up with a lie.

"You don't have to—"

"I hit a dog." He met her gaze again. His eyes filled with pain. "I had a first-aid kit in the truck. I wrapped the poor thing up and got him to the vet."

A lump had formed in her throat. "Did the dog make it?"

He looked away again. "I haven't called to find out," he said with a sigh. "You must think I am such a coward, but I feel guilty enough without finding out that the dog died." He looked at her and there were tears in his eyes.

Nettie moved to him quickly and put her arms around him. "I'm so sorry I asked."

"It's okay," he said, hugging her back. "I didn't want you to see the bandages. I felt so bad about the dog. I tried to push them down in the trash...."

"I wouldn't have seen them, but I dropped something and was moving the garbage around..." The lie caught in her throat.

"Did you find it?" He'd gone stiff in her arms.

"What?"

"What you lost. Did you find it?"

"It was just a pen I hadn't meant to throw away," she said, letting go of him. "I forgot all about it when I found the bandages."

He released her and stepped back to smile down at her, but his smile never reached his eyes. "I'm sorry I caused you concern. I could go look for your pen."

She shook her head, relieved that what she was about

to say was actually the truth. "The garbage was picked up this afternoon."

He nodded and she feared he didn't believe her—just as she hadn't him. "I guess it's all good, then. So, are you still up for lunch?"

JAMISON SLID DOWN to where the body had landed. One look at the man crumpled in the boulders partway down the ravine and Jamison knew he was looking at Branch Murdock.

The elderly man had been dead for several days. Some critters had gotten to him, but they'd been small, so not much damage had been done. The body was partially covered with rocks as if someone had purposely tried to hide it.

If it hadn't been for the unfinished cairn, they would have never found Branch's remains, Jamison realized. This was far enough from camp and not near any hiking trails, and this was big country. Few people would ever see it. That was one reason a lot of residents argued against wilderness areas that made it illegal to access it by anything but foot or horse. They wanted four-wheeler access for those unable to walk or ride a horse.

Jamison crouched near the body to inspect it closer. The side of the old man's head had been bashed in with a rock. As a detective in New York, he'd seen his share of gunshot wounds, so he knew what he was looking at. The sheepherder had been shot twice. The first shot had merely grazed his skull. The second had caught him in the chest.

Apparently neither wound had killed him, though. The murderer had been forced to climb down here and use a rock to finish the job. It had been an ugly ending.

Above him on the rocky slope came the sound of the loose rocks moving. It made a tinkling sound like bells. He waved Maddie back, turning to block her view of the body, but that didn't stop her. She slid down the slope, stopping just a few feet from him.

"It's Branch, isn't it?" she asked but didn't come any closer. "Did he fall?"

Jamison heard the hope in her voice and wished he could tell her it had been an accident. But the murder weapon—the bloody rock with strands of the man's hair on it—was lying next to his body.

He wanted to spare Maddie the gory details, but he knew better than to lie to her. There was no keeping this from her.

"Branch didn't fall," he said. "He was shot twice, but that wasn't what killed him. Someone took a rock to his head then tried to cover up the body with stones."

She let out a whimper and then her eyes flared with anger. "Dewey didn't do this. He wouldn't." Her voice broke. "He *couldn't.* He's just a *boy.*"

Jamison said nothing. He'd learned a long time ago that anyone could kill under the right circumstances. Or was it the wrong ones? He'd arrested little old ladies; nice, apparently respectable men; and young boys who'd never even kissed a girl or had their first beer.

Maddie stood hugging herself, her face a mask of pain.

He watched her struggling not to cry for a moment

then stepped to her and put his arms around her. She tried to push him away, saying, "I'm not going to cry. I never cry," before she burst into tears. After a moment, her body became less rigid, and she leaned into him.

The wind blew around them in an insistent wail as the temperature dropped so rapidly he knew she'd been right about a storm coming in. He held her like that until she choked out a couple more sobs and pulled free to wipe her eyes. He could tell she was angry with herself for showing weakness. Doing it in front of him made it all the worse for her, he knew.

He'd wanted to tell her that she'd been tough for long enough, but he knew where that would get him with her. Instead, he stepped back and looked toward the dark clouds on the horizon. The storm was close. Ice crystals glittered in the air around them. Any moment it was going to start snowing.

He pulled out his phone but saw that not only did he not have service, his battery was also running low. "I need to climb up on the ridge and see if I can reach the sheriff's office."

"Go. I have to stay here for a moment."

Jamison didn't like leaving her, but he had little choice. That stubborn, determined look was in her blue eyes again, and he didn't have time to argue, not with the storm almost upon them.

On the ridge, he got the sheriff's-department number to go through, but he had a hard time hearing. The wind had picked up, blowing up dirt that whirled around him like a dervish. He gave his name and asked for the undersheriff the moment the dispatcher answered.

"Dillon, it's Deputy Jamison," he said when the undersheriff came on the line. "I found Branch Murdock. He's been murdered. We're going to need… Dillon?" Nothing but static. He tried the number again, but this time he got a message on his phone telling him his call hadn't gone through.

How much had Dillon heard? He had no way of knowing. All he could hope was that the undersheriff had heard enough and would be sending a chopper.

MADDIE STOOD OVER Branch's body. She couldn't bear to think of him dying alone in this ravine. She was determined to say a few words over him. But as she stood there, she knew there was nothing she could do or say. No prayer came to her lips. He was gone. No matter what she believed about a life after death, Branch Murdock was gone.

Still, it didn't feel right leaving him here, but she could feel the storm building around them. There had been a hint of snow in the air that she'd awakened with this morning. She knew the smell even when the sun was shining and there wasn't a cloud on the horizon. Snow at this altitude and in early June could make it difficult for them to return to camp—let alone get Branch's body out of the mountains for days.

The thought broke her heart. "I'm sorry, Branch," she said and fought the tears that threatened to overwhelm her again. She'd failed him. Whatever had happened up here, it was her fault. Hadn't she had a feeling that sending Dewey was a bad idea? "I'm so sorry."

Jamison called to her from up on the ridge. As she made her way back up to him, snowflakes began to whirl around her.

"Did you reach the sheriff's office?" she asked, feeling the cold biting at her cheeks. She pulled her slicker from behind her saddle and put it on as she waited for Jamison to answer. She could tell the news wasn't good just by looking at him.

"We were cut off. I'm hoping the undersheriff got at least some of it."

She shivered, already chilled as more snowflakes fell. Visibility was already getting bad. They needed to get back to camp or they could get turned around in the storm and be trapped out here.

But she couldn't bear the thought of leaving Branch down there in the rocks. "We can't just leave him," she said, motioning to his body.

"It's now a murder investigation, and there's nothing we can do for him. Isn't it possible Dewey made the stone Johnnies, as you call them, to lead us to Branch's body?" Jamison asked as he drew on his own slicker for the ride back to camp.

"Branch made them. You found one of his cigarettes and his boot prints."

"But it makes no sense. If he was leaving, why leave a trail of rocks?" Jamison asked as he climbed into the saddle.

She'd been asking herself the same thing. The country ahead was much like what they'd been traveling through. Rocky ridges, granite cliffs and green meadows filled with grass and early wildflowers.

"Maybe he *was* sagebrushed," she said, trying to remember if she'd missed something in Branch's behavior before he'd left the ranch for the high country. She couldn't remember anything out of the ordinary, but she'd been distracted, worrying more about Dewey than Branch.

Why hadn't she listened to her intuition? Because she'd needed her sheep grazed up in the high country. Even then, she'd known they wouldn't be able to do this much longer. Without the grazing rights, she would have to provide feed. Stretched to the max already, she'd known it would break the ranch. She would lose the place. After all the years of fighting to survive, she would have lost the last thing she had left.

As she mounted her horse, she glanced down again at Branch's body lying in the rocks. It was over. How could she ever have the strength to keep the ranch going after this?

"*Someone* followed him out here and killed him," the deputy said.

"Not Dewey." She desperately needed Jamison to agree. But he didn't know Dewey and she did. Dewey was young, yes. But he could never bash a man's skull in to finish him off. Even the thought was repugnant.

"Dewey isn't capable of such a thing," she said adamantly when in truth, she needed to hear the words, needed to believe them in her heart. Because if Dewey had killed Branch, then she had destroyed both men's lives.

"He said Branch was mean when he drank." Jamison sounded distracted. What was he looking at?

It was bad enough that Branch was dead. But if Dewey was involved… "We need to get back to camp," she said, realizing the deputy was still looking toward the south and the way to Gardiner. He was still convinced Branch had been leaving when he was killed.

What would Dewey have done if Branch *had* been acting crazy and then had left him alone up here with two thousand head of sheep? Would Dewey have gone after him, as Jamison seemed to think, and tried to stop him?

Jamison was still looking across the ravine.

"So you think Branch made these stone Johnnies when he was drunk?" she demanded, realizing that could have been the case. What did she really know about sheep camp? Or even how Branch Murdock was once he got up here in all this isolation? She knew he desperately missed his wife even after all these years. How could she know what demons haunted him?

"I don't know if he was drunk," the deputy said. "I don't know what to make of the crying sound Dewey said they heard, either."

She didn't hold much store by Dewey's claim. When she looked over at Jamison again, he was still squinting toward the dark clouds to the west. But she realized it wasn't the storm that had his attention. "What is it?"

"I'm not sure." He pulled up the binoculars. "Did Branch have a pistol?"

"And a rifle." She started. "I just assumed that he would have both with him. But if they aren't here… Dewey didn't have either of them."

"No," Jamison said. "But that doesn't mean he couldn't have used either of them, then dumped them before he rode out of here."

She thought of the boy they'd found in hiding in her barn stall. He'd been in a panic. Terrified.

Her heart began to pound as she realized something she'd been fighting hard not to admit.

Dewey had known Branch was dead! Had he followed the tracks just as she and Jamison had done? Had he found the body and seen that the sheepherder had been shot and then panicked?

Or was there an altercation? A fight, as Jamison suspected, and somehow Dewey had gotten Branch's gun and killed him? Even if that was the case, what had the two of them been doing back in here? She reminded herself that Branch had been building rock monuments for only God knew what reason.

Her sorrow over Branch's death and possibly Dewey's part in it made her feel thickheaded. None of this made any sense. But then, this kind of tragedy was often senseless.

"Wait a minute," she said. "How did Branch's horse get to Gardiner?"

Jamison didn't seem to hear her. "There's something over there." He was still staring through the binoculars at something across the ravine.

All she could make out through the whirling snow was a stand of dense pine beneath a rock-cliff wall on the opposite mountain.

"I've been asking myself the same thing about Branch's horse." Jamison put away the binoculars. "I'm going to ride over and see what that is in the trees. I think there's a reason Branch left these stone monuments for us. I want to check out what's over there."

"Then we better hurry." If there was something on the opposite hillside that the old sheepherder was determined they see, she intended to be there when Jamison found it.

CHAPTER SIXTEEN

NETTIE'S GOOD MOOD had disintegrated from this morning. It had all begun with the sheriff's odd visit. He'd said he was sorry for what he'd said. But what was that about him saying he shouldn't be here at the store?

She would never understand him, she thought. Whatever the purpose of Frank's visit, he'd left her feeling off balance. Before that, she'd been feeling good about herself, more confident, although she hated the reason. It was hard to admit that it had taken a man to make her feel better about her life. But that was what J.D. had done.

Until she'd found the bloody bandages. She wished she hadn't confronted J.D. about them. Their lunch had been awkward. J.D. seemed glad when it was over and he could leave again.

She thought of the note he'd left only that morning about needing to go out to the ranch. *Last night was wonderful. I'll be thinking of you all day.*

Nettie felt like crying. She'd allowed two men into her life and she wasn't sure about either of them. J.D.'s explanation of the bloody bandages had been believable enough. It was the way he'd acted after she'd questioned him. She knew it could have just been disappointment when he realized she didn't trust him.

She had thought about calling the local veterinarians to see if any of them remembered a man matching J.D. bringing in a dog that had been hit by a car. The fact that she had even considered doing that showed how little she trusted him.

Then there was Frank. It wasn't her imagination that he pulled her in then pushed her away and had been doing it for some time. She felt like a yo-yo around him.

"Frank needs to make up his mind what he wants and then take it," J.D. had said last night at the bar. "He'd better, before someone else takes it from him." He'd grinned and pulled her out on the dance floor.

Nettie felt sad, remembering how much fun she'd had with J.D. She was pretty sure that was long over. In her dark mood, she'd barely looked up when the bell over the front door jangled and in came what she decided was going to be her last customer of the day.

Bethany Reynolds looked as if she'd just climbed out of bed. She was wearing bunny slippers and pajamas under a ratty chenille robe that was too small to cover her protruding stomach. She looked as if she'd been crying.

Nettie had never said more than two words to Bethany. She still thought of her as a girl, a troubled girl, at least according to local gossip.

Bethany had thrown herself at Clete Reynolds, got him to marry her and then had an affair with an older man. Nettie shuddered at the memory of that scandal since everyone knew the older married man, not that he was innocent in any way.

And now Bethany had gone and gotten herself pregnant—with her husband at least. According to the grapevine, the girl and her husband had gone to marriage counseling and now everything was fine between them.

Nettie wouldn't lay odds on that. She watched Bethany shuffle around the store until she couldn't stand it any longer. "Can I help you?"

Bethany shook her head, looking as if she was going to start bawling again. Running a general store this far from anything, Nettie heard a lot of sad stories from the people who came and went every day. She had a couple of her own sad stories, so she was in no mood for anyone else's today.

She wished Bethany would just buy something and leave. But when the pregnant girl continued to wander around the store as if lost, Nettie finally couldn't take it anymore.

"Okay, what's wrong?" she asked with a groan. "Spit it out. I don't have all day."

Bethany burst into tears. "It's Clete," she said between sobs. "I haven't been able to stop worrying about him ever since he left."

"He left you already?"

Bethany shook her head. "He took some men up into the Beartooths. They're hiking to Yellowstone."

"This time of year?" Nettie instantly regretted her words.

"That's exactly what I said!"

"I'm sure it's fine." She wasn't at all sure since when she'd glanced in that direction just moments ago, she'd seen that the peaks were shrouded in dark clouds. Everyone knew what that meant this time of year. Snow. It could easily dump a couple feet overnight.

What had Clete been thinking taking anyone up there for a hike? Worse, what had he been thinking leaving such a pregnant young wife?

Bethany was crying harder.

"Look, Clete is born and raised here," Nettie said, trying to console her. "He knows how to handle himself in all kinds of outdoor situations. He'll be just fine. But he wouldn't like you carrying on like this. Think about your baby and stop that *bawlin'*."

The girl choked out a few more sobs and finally pulled herself together.

"There, that's much better," Nettie said with relief. "It's just all those hormones from being pregnant. There is nothing to worry about."

Bethany shook her head. "Clete called me this morning. He…he said…" Her voice broke and a sob escaped.

"Did he say he was in trouble?" Now Nettie was worried.

"He said he loved me and the baby and to take care of ourselves." With that she burst into tears again.

"Oh, for cryin' out loud. That's what has you so worked up?"

"You didn't hear his voice. It was like…like he was saying goodbye."

She stared at the girl, trying to remember being Bethany's age. Bethany made her feel old. And yet she couldn't ignore the chill that had run the length of her spine. *It was like he was saying goodbye.*

Nettie glanced toward the Beartooths again and the one jagged peak that had given the town its name. Definitely snowing up there.

"I'll tell you what I'll do," she said as she led Bethany over to the counter where she kept the candy. "I'll get you a nice cold drink and a chocolate bar. That will pick you right up. And then I'll call the sheriff and see what he thinks, okay?"

Bethany sniffled. "Clete had second thoughts right before he left as if he sensed he shouldn't go. I pretended to be asleep when he left because I was angry with him for going, but I was watching him. I saw him. He almost changed his mind. And then he took his gun and extra ammunition."

"A lot of people take guns into the mountains because of the grizzly bears and other varmints," Nettie said.

"Not a *pistol*. Clete always takes pepper spray. He knows better than to use a pistol on a grizzly bear. He took that gun because he didn't trust those men and I don't, either."

"Well, we'll just let the sheriff sort it out."

But when Nettie called, she couldn't reach Frank. Instead she talked to Undersheriff Dillon Lawson.

"How long ago did Clete go back in? How many people are with him? Do you know what route he planned to take?"

Nettie tried to put Bethany on the phone, but she was leaning against the wall, both hands over her swollen belly and shaking her head as if she was trying hard not to cry again.

"Let me ask her," Nettie said to the undersheriff. She asked Bethany then repeated the answers. "Yesterday. Clete and three others. As far as she knows they were on foot and planning to come out at Tower Junction. That's all she knows."

"A storm has blown in up there," Dillon said. "But Clete managed to call out before it hit?"

"Yes. He sounded worried. At least that's what Bethany got out of the short conversation. She said it sounded as if he was saying goodbye."

"We have a deputy up there in the mountains. Tell her not to worry. I'll pass this information along to the sheriff. He just walked in."

"I'll tell her." Nettie hung up and looked over at Bethany. She repeated what the undersheriff had told her.

For just an instant Bethany seemed to relax, but then she let out a cry.

"Now what?" Nettie demanded.

"My water just broke." She looked at Nettie with huge eyes. "The baby is *coming*. I've been having cramps all morning."

"And you only just thought to mention that?" Nettie picked up the phone to call an ambulance but realized she could get Bethany to the hospital faster on her own.

"JAMISON CALLED," DILLON said when Frank walked into the sheriff's department. "We were cut off, but he found Branch Murdock. He said he's been murdered. He wanted us to send a chopper, but with this storm blowing in—"

It took Frank a moment to make sense of what the undersheriff was saying. "Branch was *murdered?*"

"That's what he said. I've been trying to reach him without any luck."

Frank knew Branch. He felt a deep sadness to hear of his passing, let alone that he'd been murdered. For some time now he'd been so involved in his own problems that he felt as if he hadn't been doing more than sleepwalking through his job.

"I'm going to have to pick up Dewey Putman," Dillon said.

"Let me go. I want to talk to him first," he told Dillon.

"I thought you were taking a few more days off." The undersheriff sounded worried about him.

"I'm fine." Frank still had a headache, but he wasn't about to admit that. "I need to keep busy right now." That at least was true. "Let me know if you hear from Jamison again." He didn't have to add, "Or hear anything on Pam." That was a given.

Dewey's father had come down out of the oil fields after getting the calls from Maddie and the undersheriff. Since the divorce, Chester Putman kept a small house in Livingston where Dewey had been living until he'd gotten into trouble. Chester had apparently made Maddie

Dewey's guardian and asked her to help the boy since he couldn't very well take him north to the oil fields.

"I need to speak with your son," Frank told him when he opened the door. Chester Putman was a stocky former railroad worker. Livingston, Montana, had at one time been a huge railroad town, but when the railroad pulled out, it left a lot of workers on pensions. Chester was one of them.

Chester Putman stood blocking the door, and his look said he wasn't going to move.

"Look, I can do it here or I can get a warrant for his arrest," Frank said. "Up to you. Branch Murdock, the sheepherder Dewey went up in the mountains with? He's dead. Murdered."

Chester didn't seem surprised, which led Frank to wonder if Dewey hadn't been more honest with his old man than he'd been with Deputy Jamison.

"I think we'll just call a lawyer."

"Also up to you." Frank saw Dewey come into the room behind his father. He looked scared, but he held Frank's gaze. "But one way or another I'm going to get Dewey's side of this."

"I'll talk to him," Dewey said.

Chester looked reluctant but stepped aside.

Frank moved into the living room. He motioned for the boy to sit. Chester stood near the door, his back against the wall, arms crossed over his barrel chest.

Frank turned on his small recorder. "I need to know if you killed Branch Murdock," he said to Dewey the moment they'd both sat down.

Dewey's face crumbled.

"Just tell me the truth. You knew he was dead, didn't you?"

The boy nodded. "But I didn't kill him. I swear."

"Talk to me," Frank said, leaning toward him.

"He was acting so strange. He was scaring me. So I followed him. He was building these rock formations. He saw me and…"

"It's all right," Frank assured him. "We know you got into a fight."

Dewey was crying now. "He got mad at me for following him. Told me to go back or he was going to whip my ass. I just needed to know what he was doing, why he was piling up those rocks. He took a swing at me. I *had* to fight him back. I thought he was going to kill me, he was so mad."

Frank nodded. "Then what happened?"

"I left. I was going back to camp like he told me when I heard the shots. I didn't know what happened. I thought he might have killed himself or… I don't know."

Frank could tell that he did know or at least had a pretty good guess. "So you went back."

"I found him dead. I swear. He was shot and his head was all caved in and there was this sound on the wind." He shuddered. "We'd been hearing it at night, but right then it was really loud. It had been freaking us both out, but maybe it was getting to Branch worse after what we saw."

"What did you see?" Frank asked, feeling his stomach tense.

Dewey looked away. He swallowed and said, "A flying saucer." He looked at Frank and saw his skepticism. "See? That's why I didn't tell anyone. I knew no one would believe me."

"A flying saucer?"

"Some kind of spaceship. I don't know. It was dark but we both saw it. It flew right over the tent so close it made my hair stand on end."

"So what did Branch say it was?"

"He didn't say. But I'd read about aliens landing in Montana. They pick a place in the middle of nowhere and mutilate animals. I know it's true. I saw it in the newspaper not all that long ago."

It was true about the mutilated animals. The alien part was one of the theories that had been circulating at the time.

"The next morning I found…" Dewey's voice broke again. "Some lambs that had been mutilated."

Frank didn't know what to make of this. "So you followed Branch back into the mountains."

Dewey nodded. "I tried to talk to him about the mutilated lambs…"

"Tell me what you did after you started to leave, went back and found Branch dead."

"I took off. I could tell there was nothing I could do for him. His head…" The boy's voice broke.

"Where was his horse?" Frank asked.

"I don't know. It must have run off or they took it."

"The aliens?"

Dewey looked away toward the window. "You didn't

hear the crying sound on the wind. It was like nothing I've ever heard before." He looked at Frank again. "They were out there. Branch knew it. I think he went looking for them—and found them. Even Branch said he'd never heard anything like it. He pretended he wasn't scared, but he was. He was as spooked as I was. We weren't on that mountain alone." He began to cry. "They killed him. I swear I didn't. I swear."

"It's okay," Frank said as he got to his feet. "I'm having a hard time swallowing the part about the aliens, but I believe you didn't kill him."

JAMISON FEARED HE was probably seeing things in his quest to make sense of the cairns and Branch's death. The simple answer was that Dewey had followed the old sheepherder out here. They'd argued and Dewey had killed him.

The problem was it didn't answer the question of the cairns and why Branch had made them. Or how the sheepherder's horse had ended up down by Gardiner.

The storm had darkened the sky to the west and now rushed toward them on the fierce wind, hurling snowflakes at them. As the temperature dropped, the clouds grew darker, snuffing out the daylight.

Jamison kept his eye on the mountainside ahead. Earlier, he'd caught a flash of light in the trees. He'd also heard something on the wind. It was faint, an almost teasing sound like that of a high-pitched whine. Not a steady one since it seemed to come and go with the wind gusts. He was surprised Maddie hadn't heard it. Or maybe she had and, like him, she'd thought it was just the wind.

Now, though, with the building storm, the whine was louder and more persistent. Jamison didn't know what to make of the sound or the flicker of light he'd thought he'd seen in the trees across the wide ravine. But given that the old sheepherder had left them a trail in this direction—and had gotten himself killed possibly for it—Jamison was determined to find out. He didn't believe the sheepherder had gone loco. Not after hearing the stories Maddie had told about the man.

What Jamison kept coming back to was the dog. Maddie had said they were inseparable. He couldn't help thinking that for some reason Branch hadn't wanted his dog with him. But what out here had he hoped to protect the dog from?

Even if the man had gone over the edge, so to speak, and headed for Gardiner, determined to leave his life behind, he wouldn't leave his dog. Jamison thought of the short length of frayed rope that had been tied around the dog's neck when they'd found her. Branch had apparently tied up the dog at some point. Lucy had gotten loose and taken off possibly in search of him. Then Branch had returned and realized the dog was gone.

That could explain why the sheepherder had left his coat for the dog to find. Because this wasn't the first time Branch had come out here and he didn't want the dog getting in the way while he built the cairns?

Jamison had to make sense of this. It had become a riddle that he was determined to solve. A young boy's future lay at the heart of it. Unfortunately, he could feel the clock running out as the storm blew in with a vengeance. The smart thing to do was hightail it back to camp. He promised himself he would—just as soon as he had a look in the dense stand of pines.

The pines ran from the bottom of the wide ravine to the rock cliff on the mountain above them. Jamison rode along the edge of the stand of trees until he saw a gap. Climbing off his horse, he led his mount through the opening.

It was dark in the pines, the boughs forming thick arches over his head that kept out the light as well as most of the falling snow. The whine he'd heard earlier grew even louder. The eerie sound sent a chill along his spine.

He hadn't gone far when he saw where more than a dozen smaller pines appeared to have been sheared off about six feet above the ground.

He was thinking how odd that was since the destruction had been recent, the exposed wood beneath the bark bright in color. Wind could shear off trees like that. Or ice storms. But in this case, he didn't think that was what had caused this. The destruction was too contained within the stand of pines.

As he moved deep into the trees he caught the flash of light again. Metal. He stopped in his tracks as he saw what had chopped off the trees.

CHAPTER SEVENTEEN

JAMISON STARED IN SHOCK. Lodged in the pines was the wing from a small plane. "Stay back," he called to Maddie when he heard a limb snap behind him.

That earlier whining sound he'd heard was now a shriek. It was coming from deeper in the pines and higher on the mountain. Was this the crying sound Dewey said they'd heard?

It was much darker back in here under the thick boughs of the pines, and colder. The lack of sun, even a weaker spring one, had done little to defrost the cold in the trees or melt the piles of snow that had blown in from winter.

Partway into the pines, Jamison glanced back. To his surprise, Maddie was standing a good distance behind him in the pines as if too shocked to move.

A few more yards into the cold darkness of trees and he caught the smell of death. He stopped for a moment to study the tracks in the soft earth next to a pile of snow. The tracks matched the ones he'd seen outside the sheepherder's camp. Just as in those, the man wearing the hiking books appeared to be limping. Some of the snow next to the tracks was red with blood.

What little sky Jamison could see through the tops

of the pines had turned a slate-gray. But the now-falling snow was getting caught in the branches, little of it making its way to the ground around him. What snow did make it through the pine needles floated in the air around him as he followed the tracks to the downed aircraft.

The two-seater plane had left a trail of broken limbs. Jamison found the plane's left wing lying a few yards from the fuselage. While the trees had probably slowed the plane's speed, the sheer rock cliff had stopped it dead.

He worked his way toward the granite cliff and found the nose of the fuselage half buried in the dirt and rocks. The wind rushed over it like a musical instrument with only one sour note. The sound would have driven anyone crazy and carried for miles. He could see how Dewey and Branch might have thought it crying by the time this loud whine reached the sheep camp.

The scent of death grew stronger as he approached the plane's cockpit, confirming what he knew had to be the case. The pilot was still at the controls. It was hard to say how long the man had been dead. But one thing was clear—he'd been trapped in the wreckage. Someone had tried to bust him out. A long-handled ax leaned against the fuselage next to him.

Whoever had tried to rescue him had failed and given up, leaving the pilot to his own devices. At one point the man had apparently tried to chop off his legs to escape and either died of his injuries or blood loss.

Jamison assumed, given the tracks, it had been the

passenger who'd tried to free the pilot. Leaning in, he saw blood on the passenger side of the plane. The passenger had escaped but had been injured, thus the blood and the limp, he figured.

Having gotten out and though hurt and limping, he'd made his way to the sheep camp where he'd taken food and the ax he'd used to try to get the pilot out. So why hadn't he used the radio to call for help instead of taking the batteries?

The answer was just as obvious as how the man had known about the sheep camp. Branch.

Jamison turned, sensing Maddie behind him. She'd moved within a few yards of the plane and stood staring at it, in obvious shock. "Is the pilot—"

"Dead." He figured she already knew that. Living on a ranch, she would be familiar with the smell of death. She would have learned about life and death early on. But it was one of those lessons that was difficult at any age.

"I was just getting ready to look inside. Please don't touch anything and watch where you step."

"I didn't walk in the tracks."

He smiled at her, more and more amazed by the woman. She wasn't just strong and determined; she was also smart and more capable than any woman he'd ever known.

But what surprised him were those moments when he was acutely aware of her as a woman. She stood there in the too-large clothes, but he'd seen beyond them and her tough exterior. She was all female, and her attempts to hide it made him all the more aware of it the longer he was around her.

Turning from her and those distracting thoughts, he moved to a spot where he could peer into the back of the plane. He wasn't all that surprised to see the duffel bags stacked behind the two seats. One had broken open during the crash, exposing the sealed plastic bags filled with a white powder inside.

He stuck his finger in a broken plastic bag and touched it to his tongue. Cocaine. Each duffel bag appeared to hold close to ten kilos. About two hundred pounds for all the duffel bags.

Jamison did some quick math. At two-point-two pounds a plastic bag...he estimated the street value at more than five million dollars.

"Are there more bodies?" Maddie asked, concerned.

He shook his head as he turned to look at her. "Just drugs. The plane is loaded with cocaine. More than five million dollars' worth."

She let out a surprised sound. "The dead man was a drug runner?"

"At least he was the pilot. The other one survived the crash, but he's injured. Limping."

Maddie hugged herself, her eyes wide. "He's the one that was in the sheep camp?"

Jamison nodded, his stomach roiling. Where was the limping injured passenger now?

CLETE SENSED A CHANGE in the group as they neared the forest service cabin. He, too, was relieved that their day was about to end. Alex had tried to keep up morale during the ride, joking and teasing.

But Tony and Geoff had been sullen. The three were definitely at odds. At least now Clete knew why. If Alex was to be believed. But why would Alex lie about something like that?

He hated such suspicions. Maybe it wasn't all their fault that he'd never been close to these three men even when he was on the team. Clete had to admit he had a chip on his shoulder when it came to their wealth. Maybe he was the one who kept them at a distance instead of the other way around, he thought. He felt bad about judging them the way he had.

Not that he wouldn't be glad when he got them to Yellowstone and washed his hands of them. Depending on the weather, he might call a friend in Beartooth and get him to bring a horse trailer. He wasn't sure he wanted to chance a ride back through the Beartooths alone with four horses.

He'd seen the dark clouds in the distance and could smell the cold in the air. Tomorrow they would be slogging through snow. He just hoped it didn't dump too much, or they might be forced to turn back. Alex wouldn't like that.

He still had time to make that decision about the horses before they reached the Yellowstone Park boundary. Another day with these three sounded like a life sentence given the tension between them. All he needed was a snowstorm to add to the problems.

The moment they reached the cabin, the three

seemed to perk up, though. The cabin had been built for hikers to stay in along the trail. But it provided a dry place out of the weather.

"If you get a fire going in the fireplace," Clete told Alex, "I'll see to the horses."

The truth was, he just wanted the time alone and was glad when they all took their own saddlebags and disappeared inside.

As he worked, Clete thought of Bethany, praying she was doing well and that the baby would wait until he got home. He thought about trying to call her but figured especially with the coming storm, he wouldn't be able to reach her. Also, he didn't want to worry her. He was afraid his call this morning had scared her. All the reassurance in the world wasn't going to alleviate her concerns about this trip. He feared that she'd heard something in his voice this morning.

He and Bethany had been through so much over the past year. But things were better. *He* was better. He was learning how to be a decent husband. It shamed him to think how he had taken his wife for granted.

As he unsaddled the horses, he swore he was going to make it up to her—and his son. The money he made from this trip would help. It didn't seem like enough, though—not with two days to go before he was home again.

He could feel the change in the weather. The air had cooled, and he swore he could see ice crystals dancing in the air. If they were lucky, the storm would go to the north of them. But he wasn't going to worry about it since there was nothing he could do.

When he finished unsaddling the horses and carried his saddlebags into the cabin, he was hit by the strong smell of booze. The three men had their heads together but quickly stepped apart when they saw him.

Alex had gotten a fire going in the fireplace, and the men seemed to have settled in. Tony had a drink in his hand, and Geoff was making another that Clete suspected wasn't his first.

"What are we celebrating?" Clete asked.

"We're going to cook tonight," Alex told him as he closed the door behind him. "Geoff, make our friend a drink so he can relax while we cook."

"I don't need—" He had started to tell them that he didn't drink. He'd quit when he and Bethany had started marriage counseling. He'd drunk enough when he'd found out his wife was having an affair. A man who owned a bar had to be careful about booze, anyway.

But Alex hadn't let him finish. "No arguments. You've been great to bring us up here. We appreciate it. Isn't that right, guys?"

Tony and Geoff muttered their agreement as Geoff made him a drink heavy on the booze and handed it to him.

He didn't want to make a fuss. Nor did he want to sound superior for not having one since all three of them had a drink.

"Put your feet up," Alex said as he took the saddlebags with the food from him and motioned for Tony to help him.

"Should be interesting to see what the two of them cook," Geoff said as the two men disappeared into the kitchen area with Clete's small propane stove.

"It is pretty easy to make freeze-dried meals," Clete said, taking one of the chairs in front of the fire. He did as Alex said and put his feet up. It felt good. He could hear Alex joking around in the kitchen with Tony. Even Geoff seemed more cheerful as he made himself another drink and joined Clete.

Clete took a sip. It was strong and went down almost too easy. "How's your leg?"

"Fine," Geoff said as he pulled down his jean pant leg to hide the bandage, but not before Clete had seen that the bandage was soaked with blood.

He took another drink, biting his tongue to keep from saying anything. He just hoped the leg didn't get infected. But Clete told himself he wasn't going to worry about it.

He took another drink and felt the alcohol warm his blood. The fire crackled and popped, the room warming with him.

Just another day with these fools. He could do this.

The moment his drink glass was empty, Geoff refilled it. The smells from the kitchen assured him that Alex and Tony were doing all right, so he decided to go with the flow. They were in a great cabin in a beautiful place, they had food and a warm fire and the three weren't fighting. He was going to enjoy it while it lasted.

JAMISON FELT HIS heart beat faster as the pieces of the puzzle began to fall into place. The crying Dewey said they'd heard on the wind. Branch would have gone to investigate.

"Branch made the cairns to lead us to the plane..." Maddie said.

Jamison nodded. "He must not have realized the passenger was still around when he was making the last rock marker."

"The man from the plane, realizing Branch had found the plane and seen the drugs, killed him." He heard the relief in her voice. "Dewey must have found Branch dead and panicked."

"That would be my guess. I doubt Dewey knew anything about the plane or the drugs."

She let out a heartbreaking sound. "If Dewey didn't know about the plane...no wonder he was so terrified. He knew we'd think he killed Branch because as far as he knew, there was no one else up here."

That definitely was the way it looked to him. "The passenger was injured. He was bleeding and limping badly. He probably wouldn't have gotten out of here if he hadn't had Branch's horse." He could feel Maddie's intent gaze on him. "You were right about Branch." He saw that gave her little comfort.

"The man left the horse near Gardiner," Maddie said, hugging herself from the cold and the latest tragedy in her life. The wind had the plane wing singing. He could well imagine what it had done to Branch and Dewey when they'd first heard it. The eerie sound sent a shiver up his spine even though he knew what was causing the sound.

"Which means the man made it out," Maddie said, putting it together. "He's coming back, isn't he? He can't leave over five million dollars' worth of drugs in these mountains. Only he won't come back alone. He'll need help getting the drugs out, and we already know what the man is capable of."

She had assessed the situation quickly—just as he had. As he backed away from the plane, he saw his own tracks in the soft dirt. Several days had passed, so the passenger would probably be returning soon. There was too much money in the back of that plane, just as Maddie had surmised. The passenger *would* be armed when he came back with help. All Jamison could hope was that the storm would slow them down and that with any luck, the snow would cover his tracks and Maddie's.

But the passenger already knew about the sheep camp. The man would have to know that someone would come up the mountain eventually to check on the sheepherder. Unless the passenger from the plane already knew that he and Maddie were up here.

Jamison swore under his breath. He had to try to reach the sheriff's office as quickly as possible. For all he knew, the drug runners were on their way here right now.

"Come on," he said as he moved away from the plane. The snow whirled around them in the wind the moment they stepped out of the trees. They reached their horses as more snow began to fall, turning the world around them into a blur of white.

He tried his cell phone. No service.

"You might have better luck on top the mountain," she said, pointing to the next high ridge.

He'd never seen such huge snowflakes as they rode out of the ravine to the ridge. When he was a boy his family used to take winter vacations to Vermont where he learned to ski. But never had he witnessed this kind of snow.

On the high ridge, he tried the phone again, relaxing a little when it showed service. The line rang three times. He heard someone answer, but when he started to speak, he realized he'd lost service. He swore and tried again. This time nothing happened, and it was snowing almost too hard to see the screen.

"Jamison." It was the first time she'd used his name. It felt strangely intimate on this high ridge, snow whirling around them in the wind. "I'm sorry. I don't own a cell phone or you could try mine, but we have to get moving. We have to reach camp before the visibility gets any worse."

He stuck the phone in his pocket and pulled on the leather gloves she'd given him to wear before they'd left her ranch. He'd read stories about ranchers getting lost in the distance between their barn and their houses in Montana snowstorms. Because of that, some ranchers tied a rope from the house to the barn and used it on days like this. He hadn't been able to imagine anything like that. Until this moment.

The clouds and the falling snow seemed to obliterate everything. Suddenly they were surrounded by nothing but white. He had no depth perception and couldn't see more than a few feet in front of him.

"Give me your reins," Maddie called through the wind. "We have to stay together."

He could barely see Maddie and her horse in front of him, but he had faith that Maddie knew what she was doing.

NETTIE WAS SO GLAD to get back to the store after her wild ride to Big Timber with a hysterical Bethany Reynolds. She'd gotten Bethany to the hospital in plenty of time and was glad she hadn't waited for an ambulance.

Nettie hung around until a nurse came out to tell her that Bethany had delivered a healthy ten-pound, four-ounce baby boy and was doing fine. The girl's mother and a sister were on their way from Billings.

The nurse had asked Nettie if she wanted to see the baby, but Nettie declined.

Instead she returned to Beartooth, though she was too antsy to go home. She opened up the back door of the store and busied herself by doing paperwork in the office. She was there when she heard someone knocking.

Her heart did a little patter thinking it was probably J.D. She hadn't seen him since lunch. Maybe he'd forgiven her for not trusting him.

That thought was interrupted as she came out of the office and saw Taylor West standing on the porch just outside the front door of the store. He was frowning but quickly removed his Stetson and the frown when he saw her.

"Hello, Nettie," he said cordially as she opened the door. Taylor was always cordial. Everyone liked him and with good reason. He and J.D. shared the same good looks, but little else. Taylor was the more serious of the two and the more responsible. But J.D. had the better personality, she thought, and realized she could have been biased.

"Taylor." She couldn't have been more surprised to see him since she thought he was out at the ranch with his brother.

"I hate to bother you. I hope I didn't get you from anything important."

"Just paperwork. I love anything that takes me away from that."

He turned his hat nervously in his fingers. "I understand J.D. is staying in your apartment upstairs. I was hoping he might be around, but I don't see a light on up there."

She stared at him, dumbfounded for a full minute. "He isn't out at the ranch?"

Taylor looked confused. "Why would you think he was at the ranch?"

Because that's where he said he was going this morning in the note he left beside my bed.

"I haven't seen him," Taylor said. "I heard he was back and thought he might stop out..."

Now it was Nettie who was confused.

"He hasn't been out to see you." It was more of a statement than a question, but Taylor answered anyway.

"No. Do you have any idea where I could find him?"

"Not a clue." She thought she'd known, but clearly she'd been wrong. "He…he's just renting a room from me, so how could I know?" She hated the bitterness she heard in her voice. J.D. had lied to her. Frank had tried to warn her, but she hadn't listened. She was so determined to believe that J.D. had changed.

"I'm sorry. Of course you wouldn't know. I just thought…" He looked away, clearly embarrassed, and she knew then that he'd heard she'd been at the bar with J.D. last night. Everyone in the county would know by now.

"I thought he was back to patch things up with you," she said. "That's what he led me to believe."

Taylor nodded, sympathy in his gaze. "Well, if you see him…"

"Oh, I'll be sure to mention I saw you."

After Taylor left, Nettie was too angry to go back to her paperwork.

There is no fool like an old fool.

She glanced at the clock as her stomach growled. She'd been waiting for J.D., thinking she might make them dinner, so she hadn't even bothered to grab something while she was in Big Timber.

Now she felt starved. Anger did that to her. Locking up the store, she walked over to the café. The Branding Iron was empty this early in the evening. Kate LaFond had inherited the store from the former owner after he'd died—not that anyone had known about that when she'd arrived in town. Nettie had known the woman was hiding something—and she'd been right.

But it gave her little satisfaction now. She and Kate had formed a kind of truce since all of the details about her past had come out. Or at least Nettie had quit butting into the woman's business.

Kate was now married to Jack French and lived on his family ranch northeast of town. Nettie had expected Kate to put the café up for sale, especially after her only waitress, Bethany Reynolds, had gotten pregnant and quit.

As she pushed open the door, Nettie noticed the waitress-wanted sign in the front window. Kate looked up from behind the counter as the bell over the door tinkled.

"You've probably already heard," she said to Kate as she took a stool at the counter. "Bethany had her baby. Ten pounds, four ounces. A boy."

"I hadn't," Kate said. She was a dark-haired, pretty thirtysomething. Jack French had fallen like a rock off a cliff for her. "Good for Bethany. Clete must be excited."

Nettie didn't bother to tell her that Clete was up in the Beartooths. She'd told the undersheriff. Once the storm up there quit, he'd check on Clete and the three men he'd gone up there with. By then, Dillon would be able to take news of the baby. What would have happened if she hadn't been there for Bethany? It made her angry at Clete for deserting his wife for a hike in the mountains.

"I see you have a help-wanted sign in the window for a new waitress," Nettie said as she idly picked up a menu. The selection hadn't changed much since Claude had owned the place. Nettie had memorized the menu years ago.

"Want the job?" Kate joked.

"What are you going to do with the apartment upstairs?" It was hard enough to rent the one over the store. Nettie was hoping Kate wasn't going into competition with her.

"I'm thinking it might go with the waitress job if I can find the right person."

"Good idea." She put down the menu. "Turkey sandwich to go, please, with mayo and lettuce, no cheese."

"Have you thought about getting help over at the store?" Kate asked as she put the order up and dinged the bell to let Lou, the cook, know they had a customer.

"The store isn't that busy." And what would she do all day if she didn't have the store? The problem was that she wasn't getting any younger, was she? She'd never given any thought to the day when she couldn't work and sure didn't want to now.

Earlier she'd felt young and alive. After hearing about J.D.'s lie, she now felt like a fool—and her age again.

Kate wrapped up her sandwich when it came out, put it in a bag and handed it to her. "I'll put it on your tab. If you hear about anyone looking for a waitressing job…"

She nodded distractedly and left. While the mountains were socked in with the spring storm, it was still nice down here in the valley.

As she stepped off the boardwalk in front of the café and started across the street, Nettie thought about what she would say when she saw J.D. again then realized it was going to be sooner rather than later.

His pickup was parked across the street next to the store. His brother, Taylor, had just missed him. Something told her that hadn't been a coincidence on J.D.'s part.

Nettie was so lost in thought that she didn't hear the vehicle come roaring up the street. It seemed to come out of nowhere, engine revved. All she caught was a glimpse of chrome grille, and then she was flying through the air.

CHAPTER EIGHTEEN

MADDIE FELT COMPLETELY devoid emotionally. Branch was gone. That loss had left a gaping hole in her heart, another one after the two she'd already suffered not that long ago.

Ahead, the snow obliterated everything. She knew these mountains and yet she couldn't be sure she wasn't going in circles. Had she been alone she wouldn't have cared.

Her life, as tenuous as it had been, was now unraveling. That horrible whine they'd heard on the wind had died down with distance. But she could still hear it—feared she would always hear it echoing in her mind. Poor Dewey. He must have been so confused, so frightened.

And Branch, what had he thought of the sound? He'd been curious enough to try to find out what was causing it apparently. How else had he found the plane?

The reminder that Branch was gone hit her again. She would never be able to keep the ranch without him. It was over. On her father's deathbed she'd promised him there would always be a Diamond C.

He'd smiled and taken her hand and told her to get married and have lots of children. He'd told her that the ranch would kill her. It had killed him at an early age. She and her mother and Branch had kept the ranch going after that.

But now everyone was gone but her.

Just the thought of Branch and how he'd died choked her up again. She didn't want to cry. Her tears would freeze on her face along with the snowflakes. She hated to think of the kind of pressure she had put on him. Branch knew how much she depended on him. What had he thought when he found the plane full of drugs?

He had built the cairns so law enforcement would find the plane. Had he seen the bags of cocaine in the back? Had he not thought even for a moment that he could walk away from this lifestyle and never have to worry about money again?

Not Branch. He was as straight-arrow as they came.

She felt sick. He was gone and the drug runners had crashed in country she knew and loved. Now it felt violated, dirtied by their greed and violence.

"Maddie?"

She reined in as Jamison rode up next to her.

"Maybe we should try to get out of the storm," he called through the whirling snow. He thought they were lost.

"The camp is over the next mountain," she said, praying that was true. She'd lost track. Maybe they'd ridden too far. Or maybe, like she'd thought earlier, they were just going in circles. They were caked with snow, and she knew he must be as chilled as she was. They needed to get out of this weather and soon.

She spurred her horse forward, telling herself that if their camp wasn't over the next ridge, they would look for a place to get out of the storm.

As they topped the ridge, she heard the sheep. She'd never been so glad to hear anything in her life.

"YOU DON'T REALLY believe aliens landed in the Beartooths, do you?" the undersheriff asked after Frank filled him in on what he'd learned from Dewey.

"I think Branch and Dewey saw something, and whatever it was, it got Branch Murdock killed. I believe the kid. He didn't kill Branch."

Dillon looked as worried as Frank felt. "Then Jamison and Maddie Conner are up there with a couple thousand head of sheep in a snowstorm with a possible murderer?"

"Let's hope not. Either way, there's no getting them out until the storm lets up, which probably won't be until morning. Jamison is smart, and Maddie knows the area. If they have shelter, they should be all right."

The dispatcher suddenly appeared at Dillon's door. "There's been an attempted hit-and-run in Beartooth." Her gaze shifted to Frank. "Nettie Benton was almost run down. She's…unconscious," she added as Frank shot to his feet. "An ambulance is on its way."

"Pam," Frank said like a curse.

"We don't know it was Pam," Dillon said on his heels.

"Like hell we don't." Frank headed for his own rig.

He could hear Dillon on his radio to any law enforcement in the area.

"Frank, damn it, wait for me."

But Frank was already sliding behind the wheel of his patrol pickup, a prayer on his lips. He didn't know what he would do if he lost Lynette.

He cursed himself for not telling her how he felt. If only he had asked her out. He'd wanted to not long after her husband had left. But he'd figured she might need more time. What a fool he was for dragging his feet.

Now it might be too late.

NETTIE OPENED HER EYES. She could hear voices, but they sounded off in the distance. She blinked, blinded by the daylight's brightness, and closed her eyes again.

"Nettie, can you hear me?"

At first she couldn't put a name to the voice.

"Nettie?"

"The ambulance is on the way."

She recognized *that* voice. Kate LaFond. And opened her eyes again.

"She's coming to," J.D. said as Nettie felt her eyelids flutter.

The relief on his face made her keep her eyes open. To her shock, she found she was lying on the ground at the edge of the highway through town. Several of the locals were standing over her, including Kate LaFond.

"What happened?" Nettie asked as she tried to sit up.

"Stay put," J.D. ordered. "We've called for an ambulance."

"I don't need an ambulance," she snapped. "I'm fine." She pushed her way up into a sitting position, aware of the ache along her one side. She rubbed her shoulder and asked again, "What happened?"

"A truck tried to run you down," J.D. said.

"What?" Nettie couldn't make sense of his words.

"It's true," Kate assured her. "I saw it all from my front window. If J.D. hadn't seen what was happening and thrown you out of the way…"

Nettie's gaze shifted to J.D. "You saved my life?"

"It wasn't that—"

"It was *that* heroic," Kate interrupted him. *"He saved your life."* She glanced at the others who had gathered. "Did anyone get the license-plate number on that truck?"

There was a general shaking of heads.

"All I saw was that it was dark-colored." Kate looked to J.D.

"It happened too fast. You didn't see the driver?"

Kate frowned. "I did kind of. I think it was a *woman*."

The sound of sirens filled the air.

"I really don't need an ambulance," Nettie said and reached for J.D.'s hand so he could pull her to her feet. She would be sore tomorrow. "Thank you." She met his gaze. "I appreciate you saving me, but you and I need to talk."

Right behind the ambulance was a sheriff's-department vehicle. The moment it stopped, Frank rushed toward her.

"Are you all right?" he demanded. "I heard there was a hit-and-run and that you were…" His voice broke.

"I'm fine. Please, send the ambulance away. I don't need it."

"I insist you let the paramedics take a look at you, and if they say you're fine…"

Nettie sighed but realized she didn't have the strength to fight him. As Frank led her over to the waiting paramedics, she noticed that J.D. had disappeared.

"I told you I was fine," Nettie said after the paramedics had assured him that she didn't seem to have any serious injuries and no broken bones. "I was just a little dazed there for a while."

"I need to talk to the eyewitnesses," Frank said. "You're going to your house, right? There's no reason for you to go back to the store this late."

"Frank, don't try to—"

He held up his hands in surrender. "So you'll be at the store when I'm through talking to the eyewitnesses?"

"Yes, but I can't tell you any more than they can. It happened too fast. Kate said all she saw was a dark-colored truck. She thought it was a woman behind the wheel."

He chewed at his cheek. She could see how furious he was. Furious and scared that she'd been hurt. Damn him for doing this to her. For caring and making her care about him.

She turned away from him and started toward the store. She could feel his gaze following her and did her best not to limp even though her side still hurt. As she started up the porch steps, she noticed that J.D.'s pickup was gone. He'd saved her, but when she'd told him they needed to talk, he'd disappeared. "Men," she muttered under her breath.

JAMISON WAS AMAZED Maddie had been able to get them back to camp. The world around them was a madding, whirling, cold white that messed up his equilibrium. He feared he would have still been going in circles if it had been left up to him to lead them back.

"Go ahead inside the tent and get changed out of your wet clothes," he told her. "I'll take care of the horses."

"No, you're as cold and wet as I am. This will go faster if both of us do it." She called Lucy and the dog came running, slipping inside the tent to curl up on the rug between the cots.

Jamison had never been this cold, but then again, he'd never been caught in a blinding blizzard before.

They finished with the horses and hurried into the tent. He started the stove, anxious to get a fire going. Also wanting to give Maddie a chance to change clothes in private.

Once he had the fire going, he asked, "Coast clear?"

"Are you always such a perfect gentleman?" she asked, sounding amused.

He turned to find her grinning at him. She'd changed her clothing and was hanging up her wet things on the frame of the tent. "Not always."

"Change your clothes. If you want I can step outside."

"Don't be silly. I'm not bashful."

She laughed as she wrung melted snow from her long hair. "Aren't you?"

He moved past her and the dog and began to strip off his wet clothing, his back to her. It was freezing inside the tent. Wind and snow buffeted the canvas, which had frozen from the cold. He could see the shadow of snowdrifts around the side of the tent.

"How long do these kind of June storms last?" he asked as he pulled on warm, dry clothing. The tent was starting to heat up a little. He was glad he'd stocked wood. They'd have enough that was dry to last them for a while, anyway.

He realized Maddie hadn't answered his question. He turned to find her staring at him. No, she was staring through him.

"Are you all right?"

She blinked and her gaze rose to his. He saw the pain and sadness.

"Stupid question," he quickly amended. "Is there anything I can do?"

Her expression mirrored the battle he knew had to be going on inside her. She'd changed into jeans and a flannel shirt, one so large he suspected it, too, had belonged to her husband.

As she shook her head and sat down on the edge of the cot, she said, "I was just thinking about Branch. He really was the last of his kind. This is the end of not just his life but an era. I won't be bringing my sheep up here anymore."

"Maybe by next June—"

"No." She shook her head and leaned down to pet Branch's dog. "It's been coming for a long time. Branch and I both knew this might be the last year." Her voice broke. "You know, as crazy as it sounds, this would be the way he'd want to end things. Up here in country he loved. Branch would have been miserable retired. He always said he'd take a bullet to his head over a rest home. I assured him he'd never see a rest home, that I wouldn't let it happen." Her eyes filled with tears.

He moved to join her on the cot and reached for her hand. To his surprise, she let him take it in both of his.

"Tens of thousands of sheep have grazed in these mountains as far back as the late-nineteenth century," Maddie said. "I guess I'm glad the Diamond C will have been the last ranch to do it."

He looked over at her, hearing the break in her voice, feeling her pain. "Maybe you can find another sheep-herder—"

"No," she said, shaking her head. "Sheep ranching has changed. It's a dying way of life. I continued the sheep drive because it was the way my father and my grandfather had done it. But I can't compete anymore with factory farming, and this is just too damned hard."

She brushed at an errant tear and looked over at him. He'd forgotten how blue her eyes were. There was something so tender and so wounded about her and yet still so damned determined to stay strong. He wanted to take her in his arms and hold her. More than hold her.

The wind whipped at the tent, shaking it loudly. A chill moved through in spite of the fire in the woodstove. Outside snow pelted the canvas, the drifts growing higher around the tent. It felt as if they were like the reverse of a snow globe as they huddled out of the blizzard and waited.

"It's going to be a long night," Maddie said and met his gaze.

He reached over to brush that errant lock of hair back from her face. "You are so beautiful." She started to speak, no doubt to tell him that wasn't true, but he pressed a finger to her lips. Her eyes filled and he saw her swallow.

"I have never known such an amazing woman," he said as he cupped her face in his hands. "Maddie, I thought no woman could ever make me feel like this again."

MADDIE TOOK ONE of his hands and pressed it to her lips. He made her feel as if she really was amazing, but inside she'd never felt more like a failure or more vulnerable.

She looked at him. His jaw was shadowed with four days' stubble. They had both washed up each morning in the creek, but she hadn't thought to bring him anything to shave with. With each day, Jamison looked more as if he belonged up here. Or maybe she'd just grown used to his being here.

Looking into his gray eyes, she was reminded of how she'd at first thought of a wolf. A lone wolf, at that. Now, though, the color of his eyes reminded her more of soft misty fall mornings. She had seen such kindness and gentleness in this man—along with strength—that it now seemed reflected in his silvery gaze.

She looked deeply into those eyes and found herself wondering about him. She had never wondered about other people's lives. She'd been too busy with her own troubles to concern herself with anything else.

But the longer she'd spent with this man, the more she wondered what he was doing here. Not up on this mountain. But working as a deputy in Sweetgrass County, Montana. His recent breakup with his wife was part of it, but not all of it. She wondered what he'd come to Montana searching for and if he would find it.

She'd underestimated him when she'd first met him. It had been his hands. Pale. Not a callus on them or a scar or any sign that he'd ever used them to do any kind of manual labor. Add to that his accent and how he was dressed and she'd thought him soft. Weak. A city green-horn who couldn't rough it.

"I was wrong about you," she said. She'd never thought of herself as being judgmental, but she had been. "You are much more capable than I'd thought you were."

He looked at her, his eyes lighting up as he laughed. "Your expectations must have been very low for you to give me that much credit."

"I'm sorry I called you a greenhorn."

"Don't be. You're right. I know nothing about your lifestyle. Who knew that sheep didn't have upper teeth or that if knocked onto their backs, they can't get up by themselves? And I definitely didn't know that anyone would herd sheep a hundred and fifty miles back into these mountains to summer pasture."

"You must think I'm crazy."

He shook his head. "It surprises me that for all the lamb chops I've had in my life, I never gave a thought to where they came from." He added with a chuckle, "After looking into those big brown eyes out there that might be the last lamp chop I ever eat."

"I wouldn't count on that. We might be eating one before we get out of these mountains. It's that or mutton. That is *if* we get out of these mountains." Her voice broke.

"We will get out." Jamison stood and pulled her up into his arms.

"Don't worry. I won't fall apart on you," she said against his chest.

He chuckled. "I never thought you would. You got us back here to the camp. I don't think I could have, not in that storm. But you don't always have to be so strong."

She laughed. "Shows how much you know." She didn't feel strong at all right now. She felt her nipples harden and goose bumps ripple across her skin.

Her breath caught in her throat as he bent to press his lips to her throat. His warm breath made her shiver. The soft brush of his rough jaw against her tender skin sent a wave of desire crashing through her. She desperately wanted to pull away, afraid of what she would let happen if she didn't.

But instead she clung to him, as desperate to stay in

his arms as she was to run. "Jamison." She'd breathed his name, a plea, a prayer.

He drew back to meet her gaze, and then he slowly leaned forward until his mouth was only a breath away from her own. She closed her eyes as his lips brushed over hers. A moan escaped her parted lips.

He put his hands on her waist and pulled her closer, deepening the kiss and spreading waves of desire through her.

Maddie told herself she didn't need this, didn't want this. She turned her head away, breaking off the kiss to catch her breath. She felt his warm breath glance across her cheek. His lips brushed from her earlobe down the long arch of her neck to the hollow above her collarbone.

Her traitorous body trembled with a need so strong she didn't think her legs would hold her. His hands slipped under her flannel shirt to touch her bare flesh, stealing her breath. Her body ached and she thought she might scream if he stopped.

She opened her eyes and met his steely gaze, surprised by what she saw there.

Need and desire and absolute terror. He was as afraid as she was of this intimacy that made her heart race, her skin suddenly too sensitive to his touch and her pulse a thunder in her breast. His warm palms moved slowly over her flesh from her waist up her rib cage, stopping just below her breasts. Sensation skittered along her nerve endings, making her flesh dimple under his touch.

She wanted to touch *him,* needed to with a desperation born of grief and desire. With trembling fingers she unsnapped his shirt, a shirt her husband had once worn. But she didn't feel that thump of pain in her heart at the thought of Hank. He was gone. She was still alive.

Maddie pressed her palms to Jamison's muscled chest, her eyes closing against the well of emotions that whirled through her like the snow was doing outside the tent. A sound rose in her throat, a moan that captured in one sound a need that she would never have been able to put into words.

Jamison reacted by dragging her closer. His hands pushed up under her bra to cup her full breasts. She felt her nipples turn rock hard against the warmth of his palms. As his thumb pad skimmed over her breast, desire rushed to her core. She moaned again and leaned into him.

His gaze locked with hers as he pulled her down on the cot and began to unsnap her shirt, one agonizing snap at a time. Cold air rushed over her bare skin as her shirt fell open. He freed her breasts, her nipples hard and dark in his hands, and then he dropped his mouth to hers again. She opened her lips, opening not just her body, but herself to him.

She told herself that this union would be nothing more than sex. But that was before she'd looked into his eyes. This was going to change her. Change them both. The intimacy of what they'd been through and were now about to share reached beyond a simple physical act.

"Maddie," he said against her lips. She could feel his need, as strong and powerful as her own. As his fingers reached for the buttons on her jeans, she stopped him. Her voice sounded strange even to her.

"I've only known one other man, my husband," she said, her voice breaking with emotion. "I don't know… and it's been so long." She lowered her gaze.

He raised her chin with one finger. Their eyes locked. "Trust me."

She swallowed but nodded. "I do trust you."

This time his kiss was gentle. His gaze never left hers as he unbuttoned her jeans and drew them down. Tossing them aside, he pulled the sleeping bag over them.

CHAPTER NINETEEN

ALEX LOOKED DOWN at Clete lying on the floor of the cabin, suddenly alarmed. "How much of the drug did you put in his drink?"

Geoff shrugged. "Hopefully enough to kill him."

"I don't like this," Tony said. "I didn't sign on for *this*."

"Like I signed on for this!" Geoff snapped and pulled up his pant leg to show his bleeding injured leg. "You don't want to get your hands dirty? Well, guess what, I've had to do things I never dreamed I could do. So don't go telling me you didn't sign on for this."

"Knock it off, you two," Alex said as he bent down to check Clete's pulse. It was faint but still there. "Fortunately, you didn't kill him," he said, getting to his feet. He should have handled this part himself, but he couldn't do everything. All he needed was one more complication. "We need to get moving."

"We can't leave him," Tony said.

"He's right. We need to finish him off," Geoff said as Alex started to walk away.

Alex turned back, fighting to keep his temper in check just a little longer. He was sick to death of all the arguing. "We already discussed this. Clete isn't going anywhere for a while. When he does wake up—if he does, thanks to you—he'll be on foot."

"He'll go to the cops."

"Not until we are long gone. And what will he tell them? That he had a few drinks and woke up to find we had taken his horses and left him? It would be our word against his. We'd say he got drunk and violent. We couldn't trust him to get us out of the mountains alive. Believe me, this part I have covered."

"I still think we should kill him." Geoff met his gaze. "I think you should do it, Alex, so you're in this as deep as I am." His look was challenging. "Bury his body out in the woods so no one ever finds him."

"You ever watch any forensic shows, Geoff?" Alex demanded, losing his patience. "They would find him and they would come after us. I'm not getting involved in a murder."

"You're already involved in murder," Geoff shot back. "Or have you forgotten?"

"People know we came up here with him. If he disappeared we would be the obvious suspects," Alex said. "Use your head, Geoff. We're covered. The kid killed the sheepherder. We know nothing about any drugs."

"They'll find our tracks at the plane," Geoff said.

Alex sighed. "Our story is that after we left Clete we got lost, stumbled onto the plane, but it was empty except for the dead pilot. We call in what we found as soon as we reach Gardiner. By then, we will have gotten rid of the coke. They can't prove anything."

"My blood is in that plane," Geoff said.

"We can say the pilot was still alive. You got in and tried to help him. Like I said, they can't prove anything. Our fathers can get us the best lawyers money can buy. As long as we don't spend the money for a while…."

"He's right, Geoff. It's bad enough as it is," Tony said, sounding scared. "But this is *Clete.* He used to be our teammate. So if you decide to kill him, I'm walking away from all of this."

"No one is going anywhere." Alex knew he was losing control of the situation. He couldn't let that happen. He needed them a little longer. "Trust me. We stick to the plan and everything is going to be fine."

But Alex knew not much more could go wrong or they might never get out of these damned mountains.

"This is from Kate," Sheriff Frank Curry said when he found Lynette sitting behind the Beartooth General Store counter a while later. He handed her the paper bag with a turkey sandwich inside. "She said yours got smashed when you were almost run down."

His jaw tightened, making his teeth ache. He was fighting to hide his fear as well as his fury. He'd been in law enforcement long enough to know that being this personally involved and this furious could keep him from thinking clearly. And right now he needed more than anything a clear head—and not to act on what he was feeling.

"Thanks," Lynette said. "But I lost my appetite." She put the sandwich aside and looked at him, waiting. "What's going on, Frank?"

"You were right. Kate said she didn't get a look at the driver, and the few people around didn't—"

"I'm not talking about that."

He swallowed as he looked into her face. A bruise was starting to darken her jaw. He wanted to cradle her face in his hands and tell her how he felt about her. He told himself she was all right. But what about next time?

There wouldn't be a next time. He'd make damn sure of that.

"You can't keep pushing me away and then…" She met his gaze. "Doing whatever it is you are doing right now."

"You're right. I'm sorry." He glanced toward the front window of the store, wondering where Pam was and if she was close by. What would she do when she heard that she'd failed? Try again?

"Frank—"

He cleared his throat. "You and I do need to talk about…us. But I can't right now. I have to find—"

"*Us?*" Her face twisted in anger as she got to her feet and pointed toward the door. "There is no us, Frank. I want you to leave. I mean it. Just get out of here. Leave me alone."

"I can't do that. Lynette, the truck that almost ran you down? It wasn't an accident. I'm sure it was Pam."

"*What?*" Lynette lowered herself gingerly back onto the stool behind the counter. He could tell that she was favoring her side. She was in more pain than she was letting on and it killed him. "Your *ex-wife?*"

He saw that he had to tell her. In retrospect, he should

have told her before. "Pam is the reason I was in the hospital. She and an accomplice tore up my house and—"

"Why isn't she in jail, then?"

"Because she had an alibi. Judge Westfall. She's been staying with him and now she's disappeared again."

Lynette was shaking her head.

"She told me before I passed out that she wasn't through with me. Lynette, she knows an even better way to hurt me is through you." His gaze locked with hers. "She knows how I feel about you. She's always known."

Tears welled in her eyes. "Well, she's the only one who knows."

He had to swallow the lump in his throat. This wasn't the time to get into this. They were both upset. "Lynette, I need you to close up the store for a while. Go on a cruise. Just leave town until—"

"I'm not going anywhere." She made a dash at her tears, clearly her anger buoying her.

Frank sighed. He knew this woman too well. Of course she wasn't going to run. He'd hoped he could talk her into it, especially after what had happened today. But he could see her digging in her heels.

"I thought if I stayed away from you..." he said, trying to explain why she needed to leave. "When we got the call about the hit-and-run, I sent the undersheriff out to Westfall's ranch. I called Dillon after I talked to the eyewitnesses—all but J.D. Do you know where he got off to?"

She shook her head.

"Anyway, Judge Westfall says one of their old dark-colored pickups is missing—and so is Pam. I looked for her last night, but if Westfall is harboring her... Bull swears he doesn't know where she is and that he isn't so sure he saw her the night I was attacked. He's retracting the alibi he gave her, saying she might have deceived him."

"He gave her up?" Lynette knew how close Bull Westfall had been to Pam. The Westfalls were the first family she met when she came to Big Timber. Bull's sister had taken her under her wing.

"Pam made it look as if she was reading by the window so the judge thought she was down at the guest-house," he said. "But there still isn't any proof she was the one who attacked me."

"So where is she now?"

"Maybe on the run but we can't be sure of that. That's why I wish you would leave until we can find her. I don't want to have to worry about you."

Lynette shook her head. "I can handle Pam if she comes back."

"I wouldn't count on that. I thought I could handle her, too. She almost killed us both. Don't underestimate her." He took off his Stetson and raked a hand through his hair. "I can't bear the thought of you being alone out here."

"She's *not* alone," J.D. said. Neither of them had heard him come in the back way. "I understand you're looking for me, Sheriff?" He chuckled. "Just like old times."

LYNETTE WATCHED FRANK and J.D. talk on the store porch. Night bugs fluttered under the porch light. Just from the men's postures, she could see the animosity between them. Her head hurt when she thought about what Frank had told her. Her body hurt from her near-death accident and now Frank had her brain circling like water down a drain.

How he felt about her?

She swore under her breath. J.D. was right. It was high time she quit waiting around for Sheriff Frank Curry. It was bad enough the way he kept pussyfooting around with his intentions toward her. Now his crazy ex-wife wanted to kill her.

She started to move from the window when she saw Frank turn abruptly and head down the porch stairs. It was so like Frank to just take off and not bother to finish their conversation.

Nettie rushed out past J.D. to follow the sheriff to his pickup. If he thought they were finished after what he'd told her, he was sadly mistaken.

"Where do you think you're going?" she demanded as Frank jerked open the driver's-side door to his patrol SUV. She'd seen the look on his face when J. D. West had come into the store. He'd been furious and even if he wouldn't admit it, jealous. Not that he had any right.

She grabbed his arm to stop him from climbing into his rig. "If this is about J.D.—"

"It's about Pam." Frank yanked his arm free and slid behind the wheel. "I need to settle this once and for all. I'm not going to lose you to J. D. West and yet,

I can't chance what Pam will do if she thinks you and I are together."

"Frank, please—"

"I'm sorry, Lynette. I can't let her try to hurt you again." He pulled on the door, forcing her to step back. The door slammed, the engine revved and he pulled out, throwing gravel at the edge of the highway.

Lynette went back into the store and made a quick call to the undersheriff. Frank was going to get himself into trouble, sure as the devil.

As she hung up, she turned to find J.D. grinning at her.

"My plan is working," he said.

"Oh, and which plan is that?" she asked, hands on her hips.

"Frank couldn't be more jealous."

"I told you. He and I—"

"And I told you that Frank just needs a little competition," J.D. said, cutting her off. "If he thinks I'm interested—"

"So you really are just doing this to make Frank jealous."

His brown eyes warmed her as they met hers. "It's an added benefit. Anyway, you're still hung up on Frank, and, sweetheart, he's still hung up on you."

"You don't know what you're talking about."

"Oh, yeah? I saw him sitting in his pickup outside your house last night."

Nettie couldn't hide her surprise. "He just doesn't want me with you."

J.D. laughed. "Can't blame him. But a man doesn't sleep in his truck outside your house unless he cares about you. I saw him early this morning when I left."

She shook her head, afraid to let herself believe anything either man told her. "He's merely worried about me. His ex-wife is the one who put him in the hospital. He thinks she was the person behind the wheel of that truck that tried to run me down."

J.D. let out a low whistle. "Looks like he's gone after her. Once she's in jail—"

"By now she could be in another state."

"Let's hope so." He moved closer. "What do you think about closing up and coming upstairs with me?"

Nettie studied the handsome man in front of her. He'd saved her life today. But even if she hadn't hurt all over, she wasn't going upstairs with him. J.D. was right. She was still in love with Frank. Not to mention, she didn't trust J.D. He'd lied to her about going out to his brother's ranch. She suspected that lie was just the tip of the iceberg.

J.D. had warned her, though. He'd said he was no hero. That he couldn't be trusted. That he wasn't one of the good guys. She just hadn't listened to him.

"Your brother stopped by earlier."

"Ahh," he said and took a step back. "I know what you're thinking."

"Do you? Why did you lie to me?"

"I had every intention of going out to the ranch. I tried, numerous times. But you want to know the truth? I can't face my brother. I'm a coward."

"A coward wouldn't have thrown himself in front of a speeding pickup today to save my life."

He shrugged. "If I'd had time to think about what I was doing…"

"Why do you do that?"

"What?"

"Put yourself down."

"I like to beat other people to it," he said with a laugh, but there was no humor in the sound.

"J.D.," she said, squeezing his shoulder. "It isn't too late to rewrite your life from this point on."

He smiled, his gaze caressing her face. "When I'm with you, I believe that's true."

"Taylor wanted to see you."

He chuckled. "I'll just bet he did. Probably wonders what I'm up to."

"Would it help if I went out there with you?"

"You'd do that?" J.D. sounded touched.

"I would."

"Tomorrow, then," he said. "Tonight, though…"

She smiled as he went to lock the front door and put out the Closed sign. "I'm not sure what you have in mind, but I just survived a hit-and-run accident."

His gaze met hers. He knew that wasn't the only reason she wasn't going to sleep with him again. "All I have on the menu tonight is dinner. I picked us up a couple of steaks earlier, and I'm cooking them for us."

"What are we celebrating?" she asked.

"That we're still both alive, sweetheart. We're still both alive."

JAMISON LAY ON the cot, with Maddie curled in his arms, and listened to the storm raging outside. He could see where the snow had drifted high against the side of the tent, but it was warm under the sleeping bag with her. The fire in the stove crackled softly. Lucy lay curled on the rug on the floor. He couldn't imagine a time he'd felt more content.

"Did you ever imagine yourself trapped in a snow-storm in the wilderness?" she asked.

He laughed. "I could never imagine any of this." He kissed her gently. "There is no one I'd rather be trapped with than you, though."

She smiled, but he saw a change in her eyes. They seemed to dim.

"You didn't come out here planning to stay, did you?"

He met her gaze, surprised by her question. "I just wanted a change. This is definitely a change from New York City." She was right and they both knew it. He had planned to stay for a year, definitely not any longer. He'd just needed to get away. He'd always known he would be going back to New York. His boss had insisted he take a sabbatical instead of quit outright. He was holding his job for him.

He started to tell her that, but before he could admit the truth, she said, "You know the drug runners will come for their cargo."

"They won't be able to travel any better than we did in this storm."

"That's assuming they weren't already on their way

before the storm began." He'd thought of that but hadn't wanted to voice it.

"They will be much more interested in getting the cocaine out of the mountains than anything else." He hoped that was the case, anyway. He'd dealt with criminals for too long not to know that they didn't like leaving loose ends.

They would have to know that someone would come looking for the sheepherder. He suspected that if they had a contact out of these mountains, that person might have already heard about Dewey coming out, acting terrified and covered in blood. Jamison had seen the way news traveled in this county and doubted he was the only person Fuzz Carpenter had told.

So he had to assume the men who would be hiking in to get the drugs would know that a ranch woman and a deputy were in the sheep camp looking for the sheepherder.

"Do you think you can find your way out once the storm stops?" she asked.

"I'm not going without you." He could tell that she'd figured all this out already. Once the storm let up, they would have to get help as quickly as possible.

She met his gaze. "I'm not leaving my sheep. Once the storm stops, they will have to be moved to pasture where the snow isn't so deep. You'll be back before I know it with the cavalry. You can't let those bastards get away with what they did to Branch—and Dewey for that matter, too."

He pushed up on one elbow to look down at her. "Maddie, if you think I'm leaving you here alone—"

She pressed her finger to his lips. "You have no choice. I can take care of myself, and I don't want to spend what time we have left arguing." She put her arms around his neck and pulled him down into a kiss. He didn't struggle long.

MADDIE LOST HERSELF in this gentle, loving man. Jamison had worked his way into her trust, her heart and her bed. She'd given herself to him freely, expecting nothing in return.

She'd never felt so close to anyone, especially someone she'd known for such a short time. She could only assume it was because of what they had been through together.

After finding Branch, she had been ready to give up. Nothing had mattered. But she'd had Jamison to worry about. She'd needed to get him back to the camp.

So she had. That was the way it had been for years. She'd done what had to be done no matter how hard it had been. Or how empty it had felt. She'd been going through the motions for years—even before she lost her husband and son. Saving the ranch had taken so much out of all of them—and it had gotten not just Hank and Matthew killed, but Branch, as well.

She brushed at her tears. "I lost my husband and son four years ago. They got caught in an avalanche up here. It had been a long winter, more snowfall than usual. I tried to talk them out of bringing the sheep up so early..."

"I'm sorry."

"I went on because I had Branch to worry about. Today I realized he probably only kept doing this because of me. He was getting too old for this life. He had to know that and yet, he wouldn't have stopped..." Her voice broke.

He pulled her close. "You were lucky to have each other. Like you said, you kept each other going when probably neither of you had the strength to go on alone."

She nodded against his chest. She'd noticed that he hadn't been toying at his ring finger. The ghost of a line was still there from his wedding ring, but it was fading.

"Tell me what it was like growing up back East," she said, changing the subject. "I want to hear about summer camp."

He laughed.

"Was it as decadent as I suspect it was?"

"You'll be disappointed if I tell you it wasn't, huh."

She listened as he told her about his childhood. She didn't want this night to end and yet, as she looked into his handsome face, she knew it would. She tried not to think about what would happen after that.

But she couldn't help realizing that once she got off this mountain, she couldn't keep telling herself that everything would be all right.

"I think my sheep-ranching days are over," she said later as they lay entwined on the cot. "I'm tired of being part of a dying breed."

"That can't be true."

She pushed up on one elbow to look down into his face. "I sell my lambs for food mostly because wool has been replaced by synthetic fabrics. The number of sheep in this country was once about fifty million back in the early 1940s. Now it's down to about five million."

"What will you do if you don't ranch?"

She laughed and lay back to stare up at the tent's ceiling. In that moment of silence, she could hear snow pelting the top of the tent.

"Do?" she repeated. "Whatever I want. No more frosty mornings spent bottle-feeding baby lambs and cold nights lambing when if I stood in a spot too long, my boots would freeze to the floor."

"You know what I hear in your voice? The hardships, yes. But more the love you have for what you do. You've fought for your ranch. You and an aging sheepherder have kept things together against all odds."

She laughed, but it came out sounding more like a sob. "And now it is just me. I'm sorry, but I no longer have the fight left in me."

Jamison kissed her. "There is plenty of fight left in you. You just have to decide what you want to do with it."

They made love again as the storm raged outside the tent. They must have dozed. She woke later to find Jamison throwing more wood into the stove. He'd made them something to eat. She could smell bacon, the last of it. They would be eating lamb if they weren't able to get out of here tomorrow.

Maddie tried not to think about it. She knew he would launch another argument in the morning about leaving her here alone. She wouldn't be alone, she thought as she listened to Lucy snoring softly on the floor between the cots.

She could no more leave Lucy than she could her sheep. The snow would be too deep for the dog to keep up. No, she would stay here. This was her responsibility. She'd gotten them all into this.

After she and Jamison ate, they huddled together under their sleeping bags and talked about the years they'd spent growing up. Where once she'd thought them so different, their backgrounds as opposite as night and day, she now found the similarities. It was the little things that bonded people, she thought later as the two of them curled up again under the sleeping bags and, listening to the snow piling up outside the tent, fell asleep.

CHAPTER TWENTY

FRANK HAD NEVER been so angry or so scared. He couldn't stand another day of being afraid for Lynette—or being forced to keep his distance from the woman he loved for fear of what Pam would do. He wasn't losing Lynette to J.D., that was for damned sure.

Pam had tried to kill Lynette.

He still couldn't get his mind around it as he drove up the Boulder River Valley. And yet again, there was no proof even though Kate had thought it had been a woman behind the wheel. But there was no doubt in his mind.

He still couldn't believe how far Pam would go to get her vengeance. But why did that surprise him? She'd taken a baseball bat to *him*. He'd hurt her, unintentionally. But Lynette had done nothing to Pam. She'd just had the bad luck of being loved by him.

He had to fix this. Pam had now pushed him too far. That was his only thought as he sped toward the Westfall ranch house. Maybe the judge had rescinded his alibi, but Frank knew that Judge Westfall thought of Pam as a daughter. He'd still help her, no matter what he said. If Pam was there…

Frank didn't let that thought go any further. He'd do

whatever he had to to protect Lynette. He'd failed Tiffany, but he would spend the rest of his life trying to make that right, too.

On the drive up the Boulder, he had found himself caught up in the past as if by rehashing it in his mind he could change it. By the time he pulled up in front of the judge's house, he'd hoped to be calmer. He wasn't.

Storming up the porch steps, he was met at the door by Judge Bull Westfall. Bull had gotten his nickname due to his stature. He was short and compact and looked as strong as a bull.

The man had obviously been expecting him. "She's not here."

"I'd like to see that for myself."

"I already told Dillon—"

"You expect me to believe you? You gave her an alibi the night she almost killed me."

"I'm sorry about that. I never would have said she was here unless I believed it."

"Really? Then you have no problem with me searching the ranch."

Bull stood firmly, blocking the doorway. "I resent you not trusting my word."

"Did I mention that I believe her accomplice the night she visited my house was your grandson Billy?"

"I find that hard to believe."

Frank laughed. "No, you don't. Step aside, Bull. I'm coming in."

"I don't think so. Not without a warrant."

He grabbed a handful of the judge's shirt in his hand

and was about to force his way in one way or the other, when he heard the sound of a siren fill the air.

Frank swore as the sheriff's-department SUV roared up in the yard. Lynette must have called Dillon.

The judge broke free of his hold. "You're damned lucky I'm not going to press charges, *Sheriff*. Although I think a night in jail might do you some good. You are aware there is a restraining order barring you from these premises, aren't you?"

"Pam just tried to kill Lynette Benton," Frank said with a curse. "Tried to run her down in the street."

Bull shook his head, looking more sad than surprised. "I had no idea she was so sick. But Pam isn't here. I won't protect her. You have my word."

Frank heard Dillon get out of his SUV.

"You need to leave, Frank," Bull said. "I'm going to overlook this as long as you leave *now*."

"He's right, Frank," Dillon said as he moved to the bottom of the porch steps. "You don't want to push this any further."

"If you try to force your way into my home without a warrant, I will have the undersheriff here arrest you, and I will press charges," Bull said. "What's it going to be, Frank?"

"Is this because I wouldn't hire your grandson back on the force?" Frank asked.

"This has nothing to do with Billy."

"Like hell. He's up to his eyeballs in whatever Pam has going on."

"Dillon, you're my witness. If Frank doesn't leave now—"

"He's leaving," the undersheriff said as he started up the stairs.

Frank had never been this angry in his life. His blood felt as if it were boiling. He could hardly see straight, and his heart felt as if it were about to burst from his chest.

He wanted to shove Bull aside and search the premises, screw a warrant, but the reasonable side of him made him take a step back.

It was enough. Bull retreated into the house, closing the front door behind him.

"I don't trust him," Frank said and turned to look at the undersheriff.

Dillon had his hat off and was raking a hand through his hair. He looked irritated as hell and disappointed. "Why don't we discuss this back at the office," he suggested. "I'll follow you. You do remember the way to the office, don't you, Frank?"

ALEX HAD NEVER been so glad to see the plane wreckage as he stepped from the falling snow into the thick stand of pines. They'd heard an eerie sound before they'd reached the down site. He realized now that it seemed to be coming from the wrecked aircraft. It raised the hair at his neck and sent a chill through him as he stepped closer.

Geoff had said the pilot was dead, but—

"What is that sound?" he asked, hating that his voice wavered.

"Just the wind whistling off the metal of the plane," Geoff said, sounding amused that it had spooked him.

The crushed metal seemed to gleam in the faint snow-light. Alex had lost faith that they would ever find the damned plane, especially in a snowstorm.

"I told you I knew where I was going," Geoff said belligerently as he limped past him now toward the plane.

"Yeah, but let's not forget the times you got us lost on the way here." Even with the global tracking system Geoff had brought, they'd had a hell of a time finding the plane.

"It wasn't my fault I kept losing the signal," Geoff snapped. "I didn't think I would have to find my way back here in a damned storm."

They were all cold and wet and exhausted from fighting the storm. Alex saw that there was less snow under the dense pines, but it was no warmer. "Well, we're here now and this isn't so bad."

Geoff mumbled something under his breath and headed through the trees away from him. He noticed that his former teammate was limping worse. Geoff had also pulled off his hat and gloves as if he was overheating. Alex shot Tony a glance. But Tony being Tony, he hadn't noticed a thing. He was probably wondering when they were going to eat.

"Tony, take care of the horses," Alex ordered.

"We need to build a fire," Tony argued. "We're going to freeze to death."

"Geoff and I'll get the fire going. You just take care of the horses. We're going to need them to get out of here."

As he followed Geoff to the downed plane, Alex slowed. His gaze took in the tracks, and he felt as if that other shoe he'd been worried about had just dropped.

Along with Geoff's, there were two other tracks in the light snow and dirt under the pines. "Someone's been here." Even with a skim of snow in places, the tracks in the dirt were still visible. One large boot print. One smaller one. Definitely none of theirs.

Geoff glanced at the ground. "So what?" he said as he lowered himself onto a rock next to the plane and out of the weather.

Alex watched him gingerly touch his leg and wince. Was his brain so addled from the pain and the infection in his leg that he didn't realize what this meant?

"It must be someone from that sheep camp you told us about," Alex said, feeling the full weight of his words. That one more thing he worried about was finally staring him in the face.

"The sheepherder is dead, and the kid's scared out of his wits and doesn't know anything. I told you, I took care of it."

"No, someone has been here more recently than that." Alex glanced toward the plane. "Someone knows about our payload."

"So let's get it out of here before they come back,"

Tony said. He stood just a few yards away. He looked cold and miserable.

"I thought I told you to take care of the horses?" Alex barked.

"Let's load them and get out of here. We can be in Gardiner before anyone knows we've been here."

"In this snowstorm?" Geoff scoffed. "I'm not going back out there until it lets up. We were lucky to make it here, but at least this was a fairly short ride. It would be insane to try to reach Gardiner in this storm."

"But you made it out once," Tony argued. "You can get us out again."

"We aren't going anywhere," Alex snapped. "Geoff's right. We wait for the storm to let up."

"But what about these tracks?" Tony asked, sounding scared. "If someone else knows…"

"No one knows." Geoff wiped his sweating forehead and leaned back against the plane in the spot where he'd dropped as if he couldn't take another step.

"You're wrong," Alex said, more annoyed with Geoff than he could ever know. "The sheep rancher and a sheriff's deputy are up here looking for the sheepherder." The other two men stared at him. "I didn't think they would be a problem since they haven't been here long. Apparently I was wrong."

Geoff shook his head. "Nice—you are just now telling us this. But even if they made a call to the feds, no one is flying in here until this storm lets up. Anyway, I doubt anyone got a call out of here. There is limited cell-phone coverage, and I took care of the radio in the sheep camp. Once the storm quits, we hightail it out of these mountains, just like we planned."

Alex wondered when Geoff had decided to take over their little operation. Not that it mattered. Alex could feel the last of this plan turning to dust as it slipped through his fingers. What had he been thinking bringing these two morons in with him?

"You're forgetting that we have a dead sheepherder and possibly an eyewitness, that kid who was with him," Alex said and wondered why he was wasting his breath.

"The kid doesn't know anything. I told you that," Geoff said. "The deputy will think the kid killed the old man. I used the old man's gun to kill him then got rid of it."

"Sounds like you have it all figured out." Alex began to gather wood for a fire. He agreed that no one would be out in this snowstorm since it appeared to be getting worse by the minute. But once it let up that was another story.

It came down to one simple fact: if they couldn't get the drugs out and pay the money he owed for them, he was a dead man. He just hoped his contact hadn't panicked and called someone in the cartel. That was all they needed.

Not that it mattered. Alex doubted any of them would get out of these mountains alive now anyway—even if the cartel didn't show up. Maybe this operation had been doomed from the beginning. As he looked at Tony and Geoff, he knew he only had himself to blame.

That realization struck hard, but once he'd accepted

the truth, it allowed him the luxury of deciding how he wanted it to end. He wasn't through with these mountains. Or the people in them.

"I THINK YOU need more time off," Undersheriff Dillon Lawson said when they were back at the department. Frank had followed him into his office, but while Dillon had taken his seat behind his desk, Frank had remained standing.

"What I need is to find Pam."

"What would you have done if you *had* found her?" Dillon asked.

Frank merely looked at him.

"That's what I was afraid of. This isn't like you. You're coming unraveled, and it's damned hard to watch. Frank, I respect you. You've always been so level-headed and fair. I can't bear to see you throw away your career like this."

Frank knew what Dillon was saying was true. He no longer recognized himself. But then, he'd never been pushed this far. He could take anything Pam dished out. But it wasn't just him she was hurting. What she'd done to Tiffany was criminal. Trying to kill Lynette? He felt a rage in him that burned so hot he could barely stand it. And as she'd said, she wasn't through with him yet. He had to find her and finish this.

"You're playing right into Pam's hands," Dillon said. "She wants to see you break. She wants to ruin you. You can't let her win."

Frank feared it was too late. He knew Pam must be

loving seeing him like this. When they were married she would try to rile him, and when she couldn't, she'd tell him that he had no passion in him. No killer instinct.

He smiled to himself at the thought of how wrong she was on both counts.

"What are we going to do about this?" Dillon asked.

"How about find Pam and put her behind bars?"

They both knew that wasn't going to happen. Even if they could locate Pam, they had no real evidence that she'd done anything. Maybe an assault charge would stick now that she didn't have an alibi, but without any real evidence and her with no prior record, she would probably get off easy.

Not to mention that Pam would be one hell of an actress before a judge. He'd seen that Bull felt sorry for her and blamed him. An allegedly heartbroken woman would play on everyone's sympathy. Pam would be a champion at it.

"We have an APB out on Pam," Dillon said. "That's all we can do right now."

Pam would hide out for the time being. Even if Frank knew where to look, he probably couldn't find her.

"Here's the situation, " the undersheriff said. "Take some time off, get your head on straight. You have vacation coming. Take more of it. We'll forget what happened today."

Frank knew he could be suspended for what he'd done and that Dillon, just like the judge, was trying to help him. "That's the last thing I need right now. I need to work."

Dillon shook his head as his phone rang. "I can't let you do that, Frank. We both know you shouldn't be working right now." He took the call. When he hung up, he said, "It's starting to clear up in the mountains." He disconnected and placed another call. "Get the helicopter ready to lift off as soon as possible. Call me when we're ready to roll." He put down the phone and looked at the sheriff. "Well, Frank?"

He knew Dillon was right. He wasn't capable of doing his job. Not as long as Pam was out there. He began to take off his gun.

"Frank, what are you doing?" Dillon asked.

He laid his silver star on the undersheriff's desk. "I'm quitting."

"Frank, no," the other man said, getting to his feet. "Take some vacation time—"

"It's best this way. Like you said, I'm not acting rationally, and I sure as hell am not acting like the sheriff of this county."

Dillon shook his head. "I'm not accepting your resignation, Frank. As far as I'm concerned you're on extended leave. You're going to cool down, get your head on straight and be back for your star and gun. It will be waiting for you."

Frank started for the door. "Go save Jamison. He's a good man."

"Frank, wait. What are you planning to do? I don't have to tell you what will happen if you take the law into your hands, do I?"

"No, I know how it goes." He stepped through the open doorway.

"We'll talk soon."

Frank didn't answer as he left.

CLETE OPENED HIS eyes to a blinding headache. He attempted to sit up, shocked to find himself on the floor in front of a dead fire. The room had gone cold, but someone had been thoughtful enough to throw his coat over him.

What had happened? He couldn't remember at first. Then he recalled Alex and Tony making dinner. But he couldn't remember eating it. Had he?

His stomach roiled. He lay still, eyes closed, trying to keep whatever he'd last eaten down. The cabin was too quiet. He opened his eyes and glanced around. Where was everyone?

Light came in from the falling white snow outside the windows and illuminated the small space. As his eyes adjusted, he saw that the cabin was empty. Alex, Tony and Geoff were gone—so was their gear.

He lurched into a sitting position to check his watch. It was morning. What the—

As he tried to rise, his head swam. Getting on his hands and knees, he crawled over to look in the only other room, the kitchen. Empty, too. Their sleeping bags were gone as well as their saddlebags. They'd taken off in the middle of the night or first thing this morning?

Clete lay back, closed his eyes again and breathed for a few minutes as he worked to ease the nausea. His stomach rolled like a boat being pitched on a heavy sea. How much had he drunk last night? He recalled only two drinks. Geoff had been making them strong, but normally Clete could hold his liquor. Hell, he owned a bar.

He worked his way up, hanging on the doorframe until he got his feet under him. Stumbling to the front window, he looked out. The horses that had been in the small corral were gone. All of them, including his.

He moved into the kitchen, his mind whirling. All the food and supplies were also gone. As his mind cleared a little, it hit him like a truckload of bricks. He'd been had. Geoff had drugged him. No wonder Alex and Tony had offered to cook. They'd drugged him and left him here without supplies or a horse? Why would they do that? He realized they'd also taken his saddlebag with his gun and ammunition in it. He shouldn't have been surprised, but he was. It was nothing compared to his growing anger.

What he couldn't figure out was *why?* Why hire him to bring them this far just to leave him?

He shuffled into the kitchen. They'd left an almost-empty bottle of booze and part of a cola. He chugged a little of the cola. Then added a little hair of the dog. The vodka made his stomach roil again, but it helped clear his head a little.

In the living room he put on his coat. At least they'd left it, and he was still wearing his boots. They could have left him here naked. Or they could have killed him. The sad thing was that he thought that had been an option. Had he overheard them talking about doing just that?

He took another drink and returned to the living area. He realized that without those three idiots he could make great time on foot. Alone he could reach his uncle's house and his vehicle in no time.

Or, he thought, as he glanced around the cabin, he could go after his horse. *All* of his uncle's horses. Let Alex, Tony and Geoff hike out on foot. The bastards deserved it.

At the thought of Bethany and his soon-to-be-born son, Clete tamped down his anger. Going after them would be stupid. Through the window he could see that the storm had dumped a good foot of snow and it was still coming down. Instead, if he got moving, he could be waiting for them at Tower Junction when they came out.

Also, the sooner he got moving, the sooner he'd be home with Bethany.

As much as he wanted to pay the three men back, he was going home to his wife—then he was going after his uncle's horses—and his money.

A shadow of a memory moved almost within reach. He stood frozen in place, the memory teasing him before coming to him slowly. He had heard their conversation just before he'd passed out. They *had* been talking about killing him!

But that wasn't all.

"Is he out?" Tony's voice.

"Like a light." Geoff this time.

"I wish we didn't have to do this to Clete." Tony talking, sounding more than a little drunk.

"I wasn't the one who ended his football career." Geoff again. "Let's remember who did the damage."

"Because Alex told me he was the one behind that sick prank against me." Tony sounded as if he might cry.

"Who says he wasn't?" Alex this time from the kitchen. "We should eat. We have a long ride ahead of us."

"I still think we should kill him." That damned Geoff.

The bastards. They'd ended his football career and now they'd almost ended his life and for what? Clete began to shake from the cold and the anger. He was amazed they'd left him alive. He realized there was only one reason they had.

They didn't expect him to come after them.

CHAPTER TWENTY-ONE

"YOU CALL THAT a fire?" Tony said with a curse as he leaned over the small blaze.

"We don't want to burn down the entire forest. Nor do we want it to lead anyone to us," Alex said irritably.

"Like someone is going to see smoke through this damned snowstorm," Geoff muttered from his spot away from the fire.

The sky was lightening, the storm appearing to let up. Alex felt antsy. Now that he'd made up his mind, he just wanted to get moving.

"We will be leaving soon, so let's try to relax," he said not for the first time.

Geoff didn't even bother to respond as Tony scooped up more dried pine needles from the base of a nearby tree where the snow hadn't reached. Alex watched him throw them onto the fire. The brown needles sizzled and popped before catching flame.

Over the flames, Alex studied his two former teammates. He'd thought them tougher than they were. He deeply regretted getting into business with them. But how could he have known how quickly they would fall apart when things began to go wrong? Surely they had been tougher in college when they'd been able to take a hit and get back up. Since then, they'd gotten soft apparently.

He considered how to deal with them—just as he had been forced to deal with everything else.

"I should never have let you talk me into this," Tony grumbled, his gaze on the fire. "You said this was going to be a piece of cake. Not to worry. Just think about the money." Tony's gaze lifted to glare across the fire at him.

Alex had no trouble staring him down, though. His bigger concern was Geoff because Geoff was the brighter of the two.

"I still think we should load up and get out of here," Tony said and glanced back at Geoff, obviously hoping he would agree.

But Geoff was in no shape to agree to anything. He had stopped rubbing his leg. Hell, he had stopped moving altogether.

"The storm is letting up," Alex said. "It makes sense to wait. Not to mention, we're all exhausted. Anyway, there is no reason to panic. Like Geoff said, he took care of the radios at the sheep camp, and no cell phone is going to work in this storm."

Tony seemed pacified for the moment.

Alex moved closer to him. "Geoff's leg is infected," he whispered. Geoff had his eyes closed and appeared to have dozed off.

"How do you know that?" Tony demanded.

"Keep your voice down. He's *sick*."

Tony turned to look at Geoff. As cold as it was, even

Tony had to see that Geoff looked sweaty, feverish. "So he sees a doctor as soon as we get out of here. He should have gone before coming up here."

"Well, he didn't. He was afraid the doctor would ask too many questions." Alex glanced again at Geoff, who didn't seem to be paying any attention to them or anything else. "We need to put distance between us and this plane—and as quickly as possible once this storm breaks. Geoff isn't going to make it."

"What are you saying?"

Alex stared at him. "He won't make it."

Tony swore and looked sick to his stomach. "You're the one who talked him into coming. You knew he was hurt."

"We needed him to bring us to the plane. Even with a GPS, we couldn't have found the plane without Geoff."

"You can't just leave him here." Tony sounded close to tears.

Alex wanted to slap him. Instead, he said, "I had no idea his leg was so bad. He kept saying he was fine."

Tony shook his head angrily. "You can't leave him behind. How barbaric is that?"

"We can't get him and the coke out."

"I wish I'd never gotten involved in this."

"So you keep saying, but you did," Alex said. "Now you need to buck up if you hope to get out of here alive."

"You are one coldhearted bastard, you know that?"

"I'm a realist," Alex said. "I say what everyone else is thinking but doesn't have the guts to say."

Tony shook his head again and reached for more pine needles to throw on the fire.

Alex wondered if Tony was finally realizing that if Alex could leave behind Geoff this easily, he could do the same with him.

Tony would be wary now. Alex figured Geoff could be dead by midmorning. But by then, the coke would be loaded on the horses. Then what? Alex had thought about trying to hide the drugs in the mountains and coming back for them later, but he knew that was a pipe dream. As was trying to get the drugs out of the mountains now that the plane had been found by the deputy.

He shook his head, thinking what would happen to him if he didn't pay the cartel the rest of what he owed for the coke. Worse if they heard that the plane had gone down in these mountains and decided to take matters into their own hands.

Would his associate back in the valley double-cross him to save his own neck? In a heartbeat.

Alex swore under his breath, remembering when they'd spoken on the phone. Had he already sold him out then?

He watched Geoff sleep for a moment. Tony was trying to get warm by the fire, looking miserable.

What Tony didn't know, but Geoff no doubt already suspected, was that too much had gone wrong, and it was too late to walk away from this latest adventure. Alex had a new name, a passport and enough money hidden away that he could try to disappear, but it would mean a life on the run, always looking over his shoulder, never knowing when they would find him—but knowing that they would eventually.

Geoff had been so sure the sheepherder and the boy hadn't known about the drugs, hadn't told anyone. But the rancher and deputy had found the plane, found the drugs. That changed everything, and these two fools weren't smart enough to know that.

He watched Tony throw more pine needles on the fire and ask Geoff how he was doing. Geoff mumbled something that made Tony glance in Alex's direction. His worried look made it clear he didn't think Geoff was going to make it, either. Tony turned away, no doubt in tears. Alex was too angry for tears. When he got like this, he wanted to hurt someone.

JUST BEFORE DAYLIGHT, the storm began to let up. Jamison hated leaving Maddie and yet he feared when the storm finally quit, the drug runners would return to the plane.

What would they do if they noticed his and Maddie's tracks? They would know about the sheep camp, anyway. They'd already killed once; he was sure of that. They wouldn't hesitate to kill again.

But he believed he had time on his side. That and the drug runners' need to get their payload out before getting caught. He was counting on the storm slowing them down—or keeping them out of the mountains altogether.

"I'll be fine, Deputy," Maddie said before he'd even told her his plan. "You need to do your job and so do I."

Like him, she had to have noticed the sky lightening as she lay in his arms. "I'll saddle your horse."

She started to swing her legs over the side of the cot, but he pulled her back, turning her to him as he drew her near again.

"I wish I could stay right here," he whispered as he looked into her beautiful face. "Last night..." He shook his head. There weren't words for what he'd felt. Or if there were, he wasn't able to find them. "Ride out of here with me—"

She pressed a finger to his lips and shook her head. "I'll be here when you get back."

He studied her. He knew how stubborn she could be. It was clear she wasn't going with him. "You promise to keep a gun handy?"

She smiled and cupped his jaw. "I *always* have a gun handy. Haven't you noticed that about me?"

He returned her smile, warmed by the look in her blue eyes. "I still don't like leaving you here alone."

"I've been alone for a long time now. Anyway, I have Lucy and my sheep. And you'll be back."

He nodded. "With the cavalry." He kissed her and felt desire spike through him. More than anything, he wanted to make love to her one more time, but he could feel time slipping away too quickly.

The drug runners would be on the move once the storm quit. For Maddie to be safe, he had to get down out of the mountains and back by helicopter as fast as possible. He was counting on the drug runners' first priority being their cargo and the need to escape.

Getting up, he dressed while Maddie put some jerky into a saddlebag for him then pushed him toward the door. "Just be careful."

"I will." He rode out through the waning storm. His horse kicked up the surprisingly light snow. Over a foot had fallen overnight. Maddie had told him to stick to the ridges where the snow would have been blown away by the wind.

He hadn't ridden far when he turned to look back. He could see her silhouetted in the door of the tent. He spurred his horse forward, anxious to get to help. He was too aware that just over the mountains to the south was a planeload of cocaine worth a small fortune. All he could hope was that the storm had slowed down the drug runners from getting to it.

Once the storm finally cleared, a helicopter would be able to get in—but then, so would the drug runners. He was racing against time and praying he had the advantage.

CLETE KNEW HE was getting close as the snow finally stopped falling. The horseshoe tracks had less and less snow in them as he kept going. He'd been moving fast and was thankful he'd stayed in good shape since college. That he was going to be able to catch them came as no surprise. They had been nervous on horseback especially when the trails narrowed and they had to ride along a dozen steep areas.

At several points, it was clear they had gotten turned around and had to backtrack. He'd known that the falling snow would make them even more leery, so they would be forced to move at a snail's pace. His uncle would have a fit if he knew three novices had his horses in blizzard conditions in the mountains. But Clete had a lot more to worry about than what his uncle was going to say.

Ahead, he heard a horse whinny and quickly slowed as he neared a ridge. Voices carried on the wind, but he didn't catch the words. Crouching down, he climbed up the slope through the deep snow until he could see over the ridge.

He spotted the horses tied at the edge of a dense stand of pines—then heard voices. The sound seemed to be coming from the trees. What were they doing down there?

He didn't believe they had merely decided to take the rest of the trip by themselves. Why go to the trouble of drugging him? They were up to something, and it was the real reason they were all back in these mountains instead of on the trail where they should have been.

He had to get closer. It would be chancy since there was no cover until he reached the pines. Keeping low, he moved as fast as he could along the top of the ravine. He dropped down at the edge of a rock cliff, slipping through the snow. If any one of them came out of the trees now, they would have seen him.

As he began to slide too quickly, he grabbed hold of brush sticking up out of the snow but only managed to slow himself down a little. Almost to the trees, he finally was able to dig his heels in and come to a stop at the edge of the pines.

The men had quit talking. Or at least he couldn't hear them. His heart was already pounding from his slide down into the ravine. Now it picked up speed at the thought that they'd heard him.

He hadn't forgotten that they were armed with at least one weapon—his. He suspected they'd brought their own as well since he'd let them load their own saddlebags and he hadn't been watching them the whole time.

He moved into the trees, staying as quiet as he could, and kept to the darkest parts of the forest. The smoke of a campfire hung in the pine boughs. He hadn't gone far when he heard voices again—closer this time. The sound was off to his left. He could almost make out their words. A horse whinnied nearby.

What were they doing? They were nowhere near any trails. Had they gotten lost and just camped here to wait out the storm?

He moved closer. A little deeper in the pines, he saw the broken limbs and sheared-off tree trunks.

What in the—

That was when he spotted one of the plane's wings and heard Alex's voice only yards away.

It had been a cold, wet time. Alex was thankful for the dense trees. Out of the wind and with a fire going, he'd stayed warm enough. He hadn't slept, but Tony and Geoff had. Geoff was much sicker, just as he'd predicted.

He woke them both. "Saddle the horses and load them with fifty pounds each," he ordered once they were both awake.

"Fifty pounds on each horse? That's too heavy." Geoff struggled to his feet but clearly wouldn't be on them for long.

"I know what I'm doing," Alex said as he moved to the edge of the pines to his horse.

"Wait a minute. Where are *you* going?" Geoff demanded as Alex swung into his saddle.

"I need to take care of something, and then we're getting out of here."

"You're going to kill the rancher and the deputy?" Geoff demanded. "What is the point in that? We're *leaving*."

"You're the one who left the loose end. You let that boy get away. I have to make sure neither the deputy or the rancher goes for help," Alex said as he reined his horse around. "Once we get out of the mountains, we disappear just like we planned. They will think we never made it out."

"You aren't planning to return Clete's horses," Tony said.

"That would kind of give it away that we got out, now wouldn't it?"

"You sure you can find the camp?" Geoff asked. "Don't you want me to come along?"

Alex shook his head. Just as he'd feared, even sick,

Geoff was catching on to what was going on. Tony wouldn't be able to get out of these mountains alone, and Geoff was in no shape. But both would try if Alex didn't come back.

"Load the horses," he ordered. "I won't be long."

He rode out of the ravine and followed the stone markers the old sheepherder had left behind. Geoff had failed to mention them—or hadn't paid any attention. Alex realized this venture had been doomed from the start.

The wind had blown the ridges clear. There were even a few frozen horseshoe tracks where two horses had gone this way during the first part of the storm.

He'd ridden quite a ways when he heard the sheep. Up over a rise, he looked down on the snow-filled meadow and the sheep all huddled together at the bottom of a rocky cliff. He could see tracks where someone had ridden out earlier.

Then he spotted the dog and knew he would have to move fast.

CHAPTER TWENTY-TWO

CLETE WAITED UNTIL Alex had ridden away before he moved closer to the downed plane. Both Tony and Geoff were busy loading duffel bags on the three remaining horses.

"He isn't coming back, is he," Tony was saying.

"You think he'd leave all this drug money for the two of us to split?" Geoff snapped. He looked ashen to Clete as he watched the man grimace in pain with each limping step.

"He won't really kill those people in that sheep camp?"

"They know about the coke since they found the plane before the storm started. Alex has no choice." Geoff sounded resigned.

Coke? That explained a lot, then, Clete thought. He figured the deputy and rancher over in the camp were a lot safer than he was right now since they would know the danger they were in. At least they were armed.

Tony stopped working and looked toward the western horizon. A patch of blue shone just over the trees as the snowstorm moved off to the east. "We could just ride out of here now with what we can carry. Or you can have it all. I don't even want it."

"So ride off. Go. I don't give a damn. Just don't be so stupid as to talk to anyone about this, you hear me?" Geoff moved to thrust a finger into Tony's face. "You ever talk and you're a dead man."

"He's planning to kill us anyway. He told me he was going to leave you here because he thinks your leg is infected."

Geoff let out a curse. "That's a lie."

"The hell it is. He told me last night. I think he plans to take all the dope and the money for himself."

Clete moved up behind Geoff. Neither man had heard him thanks to their raised voices and the skift of soft fresh snow under the trees. He'd picked up a broken branch, one he could use as a club.

As he moved up behind Geoff, he said, "Alex has left the two of you to take the fall, you fools. He's gone."

Geoff turned in surprise, and Clete nailed him in the head with the limb.

If it had been anyone but Geoff, he was sure the blow would have downed him like a fallen tree. But Geoff, even sick with the infection in his leg, was anything if not hardheaded. He staggered an instant before he lunged for him.

Clete swung again, but the glancing blow to Geoff's shoulder only elicited a curse. Geoff barreled into him, taking them both to the ground. Geoff was strong, but so was he, and while Geoff was injured and sick with fever, Clete wasn't. Also, he was fighting for his life.

"Shoot the bastard!" Geoff yelled to Tony. "Shoot him!"

Out of the corner of his eye, Clete saw Tony run for a gun. A moment later Tony came racing back, the pistol held out in front of him. He saw Tony fumble to work the safety, clearly not used to handling guns.

Tony raised the pistol and took aim. Clete, who had been on top of Geoff, rolled just as Tony pulled the trigger not once, but twice.

Geoff let out a scream as the first bullet caught him in the side and the second struck his back. Clete shoved the man off him and, moving quickly, charged the second man.

Tony was in a panic, fumbling with the gun, shocked that he'd shot the wrong man. The two grappled for the weapon, but Tony was strong and unlike Geoff hadn't been injured. He was bigger than he'd been in college. He twisted the gun away and staggered back from Clete, the barrel pointed at Clete's heart.

He thought of Bethany and the son he would never see as he waited to feel the bullet tear through his flesh.

But Tony didn't fire. He looked sick to his stomach and kept glancing over at Geoff and the blood in the snow. "Is he…?"

"Dead?" Clete nodded. "It was an accident. You didn't mean to shoot him. I'll testify to that in court. You just panicked."

Tony was shaking his head as if he couldn't believe this was happening.

"I heard you say you wanted to get out of here. Now's your chance. Go. Don't make this any worse. Make a run for it in case Alex does come back. You know he wasn't planning for either of you to leave here alive."

Tony narrowed his gaze at him. "What are *you* going to do?"

"I'm going after Alex to try to keep him from killing those people in the sheep camp."

Tony glanced toward the south and the way out.

"Go," Clete said and took a step toward him, then another until he gently removed the gun from Tony's trembling fingers. "I'm going to need my horse and some ammunition."

As JAMISON RODE, the falling snow began to let up. He could see farther ahead now, see the landmarks Maddie had given him to keep him on the right path back to civilization.

He couldn't get her off his mind. These days with her…then last night… Maddie was like no one he'd ever met. He felt as though they were equals, something he'd never felt with Lana. His ex-wife didn't have Maddie's backbone. She was stubborn, but not strong.

Jamison couldn't help but believe there was a reason he took the call from Fuzz Carpenter, that he was the one who'd come up here with Maddie Conner. He refused to let himself think about the future or his job back in New York. He loved being a homicide detective. But when he thought of Maddie, his heart soared and nothing else mattered.

He warned himself that it had all happened too fast.

They would need time and yet the way he was feeling? If this wasn't real, then he didn't know what was.

This feeling, he realized, was a new one. He and Lana had been friends. They'd shared the same background. Her parents had been delighted with the union. His parents had wholeheartedly approved.

"She's just what you need, son," his father had said. "Behind every successful man there is a woman just like Lana."

He hated to think now how much his father's approval had meant to him. But there were a lot of reasons he'd married her. Lana had been easy to get along with back then. The perfect pretty subservient wife. What more could a man ask for?

The night before their wedding, though, he'd gotten cold feet, but his father had assured him that friendship and similar backgrounds were more important in a marriage than passion. Passion burned out; the other didn't.

There hadn't been any passion to burn out with him and Lana and nothing strong enough in their common backgrounds to keep them together.

With Maddie… Heck, they were from totally different worlds. They certainly hadn't started as friends. Instead they were merely thrown together by circumstance and yet he had been intrigued by her from the first time he saw her. Her strength had drawn him like metal to magnet.

Now he felt like a schoolboy and warned himself that one night of passion didn't make a relationship. Who knew what would happen once they got out of these mountains. His heart ached at the thought. He wanted this. He wanted Maddie.

The sky cleared ahead. Snow still drifted down from the pine boughs, but it had stopped falling from the clouds. The visibility improved, and Jamison was making better time when he saw the tracks.

He brought his horse up short. A deep trough had been cut through the snow. In the shadows that had formed, he could see the tracks of what appeared to be more than a few horses.

He could see where the travelers had realized they were off course. They'd apparently gotten turned around in the storm. Had they kept going in the original direction they'd been headed, they would have run into the sheep camp.

Ultimately, they had turned to the southwest. He stared in the direction they'd gone, his heart in his throat.

Jamison didn't have to guess who they were. Worse, the tracks were only hours old. The drug runners had apparently traveled during the storm because there were a few inches of snow covering their tracks.

He still had miles to go to reach a ranch down in the Boulder River Valley and call for help. Then how long would it take for the sheriff's department to get a chopper up here? Too long.

The men on the horses would be armed. There was no doubt they were dangerous.

And determined. The fools had traveled through the storm. It would have been incredibly hard even using a global positioning device to find the plane again, not to mention how foolish it had been in a storm.

But the men had a lot to lose considering the amount of drugs on that plane and their value. He doubted they'd paid cash for them, which meant they had to retrieve them and get them sold to pay their supplier or face the consequences. Those consequences were much worse than being caught by the DEA.

Jamison felt the pistol at his hip. He was a deputy, which meant he was obligated to stop these men if possible. But his obligation to see that Maddie was safe was far more important to him right now.

He looked back, worried. If they had reached the plane last night, then did they see the tracks he and Maddie had left in the trees by the plane?

Jamison reined around. He couldn't take the chance. He had to go back. He just prayed he could reach Maddie before the drug runners did.

MADDIE HAD BEEN thinking about Jamison when she heard the dog bark. Last night seemed a fairy tale. The falling snow, the warmth of Jamison's body, the way he'd touched her and made love to her.

She'd thought she could never feel that way again about anyone. Jamison had proved her wrong. She shivered at the memory and hugged herself, wishing she was in his arms right now. Since she'd lost Hank, she'd had to be strong. She'd felt she couldn't show any sign of weakness or she might fall apart completely.

With Jamison she didn't have to pretend. He saw

her as she was. She had thought she could never put her trust in anyone. But she had. She trusted him with her life.

Just the thought of him made her ache. She'd already gone out and moved the sheep to lower ground where the snow was not so deep. The sun had come out once the storm passed. It now dazzled the countryside in blinding rays that turned the melting snow to tiny jewels.

She had come back to the tent to get her camera so she could assess how many lambs had been lost either in the storm or to a grizzly. With Lucy in the tent with them last night and the storm raging outside, she didn't doubt that a grizzly had gotten to the sheep undetected. She'd seen blood on the snow in several places and needed to follow the trail to find out what was left of her lambs.

She always hated losing even one, but right now she was more worried about Jamison. She couldn't help worrying about him riding out of the mountains alone. What if he ran into the drug smugglers? She shuddered at the thought because she could only assume he would be outnumbered.

Lucy barked again. This time the sound was high and sharp. Maddie cocked her head, listening. She'd left Lucy watching the sheep, but apparently she'd come back to camp.

Maddie picked up her camera, stuffed it into the pocket of her coat and reached for her rifle. Lucy's bark was closer as if she was headed for the tent at a run.

Her bark had gotten sharper, taking on a sound that was more than just a warning. There was fear in it. A grizzly? Her horse whinnied in the trees near the tent. *Something* was out there, something that had frightened the dog.

As she stepped through the tent flap, rifle in hand, she heard an answering whinny from a different horse. Had Jamison come back for some reason? But Lucy wouldn't be afraid of the deputy.

As Lucy came into view, she stopped just a few yards from the tent, the hair standing up on the back of her neck. Her gaze shot past Maddie as a low growl sounded in the dog's throat.

Maddie swung around but not quickly enough. The blow caught her on the side of her face and knocked her to the snowy ground. Her vision dimmed, drawing down to a pinpoint before she was able to focus again.

As Lucy dived for the man, Maddie realized she still had the rifle clutched in her hands. It was cumbersome, too long to turn easily, especially with the man so close.

She swung it, connecting with his hip. He let out a cry just an instant before the dog barreled into him. Lucy was growling and snapping at him. The man threw up his arms to fend off the dog while he screamed for her to call Lucy off.

"I'll kill the dog if you don't call her off," the man yelled as he managed to get hold of Lucy's throat. The dog was still trying to bite him. It was so unlike Lucy that Maddie was shocked speechless.

"I'll kill her!" the man yelled, and she heard Lucy whimper and quit snarling.

"Lucy," she called, then louder, "Lucy, no! Off! *Off!*"

Lucy went limp in his grip, and for a moment she thought he'd killed her. But when he set Lucy down, she leaped up and ran over to Maddie, who was still lying on the ground. It had all happened so fast she hadn't had a chance to get to her feet.

It wouldn't have mattered anyway. The man had pulled a gun and now pointed it at her heart.

"Put down the rifle and get up." The man was in his mid-thirties, she would guess, maybe a little older. Blond, blue-eyed, he had a privileged look about him, much like Jamison, she thought. Only there was a deadly coldness in this man's eyes that Jamison's could never have.

She stayed where she was for a moment, considering what to do. She had a pretty good idea who this man was. He had to be one of the men connected to the plane.

Knowing that, she also knew he had a fortune in drugs he desperately needed to get out of the mountains. Since she hadn't noticed a limp, she figured he was a friend of the man who'd been injured in the plane wreck. But that still made him an accessory to murder already.

"You really don't want to do anything stupid," the man warned her when she didn't move.

"No, I don't," she said and tossed the rifle away before she got to her feet. Lucy stood beside her, her teeth bared at the man.

"I don't like the look of that dog. Make it go away."

"Lucy, work," she ordered. The dog didn't move. "Lucy, *work*." As the dog slinked off toward the sheep, Maddie turned back to the man. "What is it you want?"

"Well," he said, glancing around. "For starters, tell me where the deputy is."

So he knew Jamison had been here with her. That meant he'd had contact with someone out of the mountains. "He went to get firewood. He'll be back soon."

The man laughed. "I don't think so." He cocked his head toward the pile of wood next to the tent. "Why don't we go in the tent? I could really use a cup of coffee and you look like the kind of woman who could get it for me."

She chuckled at that but opened the tent door. Out of the corner of her eye, she saw him pick up her rifle. He'd done nothing to hide his face. She could identify him in a lineup, which meant he had no intention of letting her live.

"I thought you might have some warm, dry clothing I could use, as well," he said.

She moved to the stove and grabbed the handle of the almost-empty coffeepot.

"Just in case you're thinking of throwing hot coffee on me or trying to knock me out with that, please know I will kill you."

"Oh, I suspect you will kill me either way," she said as she poured him a cup of coffee and gingerly handed it to him. "What's your name?"

He laughed as he took the cup. "Why would I tell you?"

"Why wouldn't you?"

He took a sip of the coffee, keeping his gaze and his gun trained on her. "Alex."

She nodded. "You look like an Alex."

He cocked his head. "I'm not sure I should take that as a compliment."

"Oh, is that why you're here? You're looking for compliments?"

"You're a real spitfire, aren't you? You didn't tell me *your* name."

"You already know my name."

He smiled at that. "Maddie Conner. Your reputation precedes you as a woman I was warned not to underestimate. I'm beginning to understand why I was warned."

He'd been warned by someone she knew? Or at least someone who had heard about her.

"So what are you doing here?" she asked as she considered what in the tent she could use as a weapon. She wasn't going to let this cocky bastard kill her without a fight.

He took another drink of his coffee. "Maybe I just wanted a place to warm up for a while, a cup of coffee and a change of clothing."

"You should have been more friendly. You might have gotten breakfast."

"Oh, I think I can have anything I want, don't you?"

CHAPTER TWENTY-THREE

ALEX GLANCED AT his watch. By now Tony and Geoff would have the horses loaded. They would be antsy and yet they would wait for him. He wondered how long before they realized he wasn't coming back?

Geoff would be so sick by now, his wounded leg so infected that he might not even be able to get on his horse. Tony would be terrified. The man had never done anything by himself. What would he do if he realized no one was going to lead him out of the mountains?

Eventually Tony would get scared and take off. Alex smiled to himself at the thought. Would the fool try to take the coke? Or would he just run? Didn't matter. Tony wouldn't get far, though. Even with a map and Geoff's GPS, he wouldn't be able to find his way out of the mountains. He'd panic and get lost for sure, and with supplies running low, he'd starve to death—if hypothermia didn't get him first.

Or whoever might be waiting down by Gardiner for the coke.

"You and your damned sheep," he said to the ranch woman. "What are you doing up here, anyway?"

"Sheep ranchers have always brought their sheep up here," she said. "I'm the last. Thanks to you."

"Oh, yeah. I should be on a horse right now with a string of packed horses behind me headed south of here with equivalent to enough money I could buy myself a small island."

"So why aren't you?"

He met her gaze. "Because of you and your damned sheep."

"So you messed up my life and I messed up yours," she said. "That sounds like we're even."

He laughed. "Not by a long shot."

The way Alex figured it, the deputy had ridden out for help—and not all that long ago. That meant he had plenty of time. He looked at the woman and smiled. This was going to be fun. He liked the idea of going out in a blaze of glory. But first he would get some satisfaction by making the woman pay.

"Deputy Jamison will be back any minute," Maddie Conner said. She didn't look scared of him, but Alex knew she'd be a fool if she wasn't. And Maddie was no fool, he thought. "He'll kill you if he finds you here."

His smile broadened. "I'm not worried since he hasn't gone to get wood. I saw your deputy's tracks. He left early this morning, no doubt to get help."

She met his smile with one of her own. "Why would he do that? He talked to the undersheriff yesterday. With the storm letting up, the feds should be here soon."

Alex laughed. "The feds? I don't think so. He wouldn't have left you here alone if he had gotten through to anyone off the mountain."

"I would think you'd be worried about getting the

drugs out of the plane and to your distributor before the feds get here."

"Do you think it's wise to show me how much you know about my...enterprises?"

"You wouldn't be here unless you saw our footprints at the plane."

"Good point."

"If you kill me, Jamison won't stop looking for you."

He cocked his head at her in surprise. "So it's like that, is it? Well, if I do get off this mountain it will be my word against...well, I guess it will just be my word. I merely came up here on a hike into Yellowstone Park, got caught in a snowstorm, stumbled onto your camp and found you..." He grimaced. "Horrible sight. So even if I'm caught running out of the Beartooths, I have good reason given the horror I've endured."

"Except for the drugs on you, you could probably pull that off."

"There aren't any drugs on me. Nor do I have any intention of getting caught. This is big country. You should know that. As far as anyone will know, I died up here."

He knew he was lying to her. He wouldn't be leaving these mountains, but then again, neither would she. He put down the empty coffee cup. "But you do have a point. I suppose we'd better get busy, don't you think?"

MADDIE FELT A COLD dread move through her. For the first time in her life, she found herself in the presence of pure evil. This man was capable of unspeakable things. One look in his empty eyes and she had known he planned to kill her. But before he did, he would hurt her. As he said, he blamed her. If she hadn't had sheep up here and Branch hadn't discovered the plane because of the sound the wind made…

He was just looking for someone to blame and she was it.

She promised herself that she would put up the fight of her life. It surprised her how badly she wanted to live. Just yesterday she'd been ready to quit. With Branch dead, she knew she couldn't keep the Diamond C going. For so long that had been upmost in her mind.

Then Jamison had come into her life. He'd promised her nothing and yet, he'd given her everything, including a will not to give up on herself. He'd given her hope, something she'd been short of after losing her husband and son.

And now this man wanted to take all of that and her life away from her.

Alex took a step toward her. She felt her heart drop as he pulled a switchblade and thumbed the button, the *snick* of the blade sounding loud in the tent.

Maddie stumbled back at the sight of the long deadly blade as it caught the light. But nothing was more frightening than the look in Alex's eyes.

"What? Nothing smart to say now?" he asked with a laugh.

She realized he had no intention of trying to get away with anything. He must realize he'd never get the drugs out of the mountains or get away. With Branch murdered by one of his associates, he would be going down. This was a man with nothing to lose.

Maddie could feel his anger. He planned to take it out on her.

As she stumbled back, her legs connected with the small supply box that sat between the two cots. She fell back on it, sitting down hard, and grabbed the sides of the box for support.

Alex's smile broadened. She was trapped with nowhere to run and had less of a chance to fight him since she was no longer on her feet.

Overconfident, he didn't see her right hand snake under the edge of the sleeping bag. She kept her gaze on his. She didn't have to fake the fear she knew was in her eyes or the trembling of her body as he advanced on her.

She would have one chance. Everything was riding on how quickly she could act, she thought, as her hand closed around the grip of the .357 Magnum pistol. She'd told Jamison she kept it handy and always in reach. She hadn't lied.

Unfortunately, she would never have time to draw the gun from under the sleeping bag, cock it and fire before Alex took it from her.

"I'm going to try to make this as fun as I can in the short time we have together," he said as he brandished the blade in front of her face. "At least fun for me."

She didn't move—pretended she couldn't as if struck by sheer terror—as he lowered the blade, dug the tip of it into the fabric of her shirt and cut a slice that exposed her bra beneath.

Maddie felt a trickle of blood from where the knife tip had cut her. As the blood made its way toward her belly, Alex spread her shirt open with his free hand and, sticking the knife between her breasts, cut her bra, exposing her large breasts.

He didn't even look at them, though. She saw not lust or even interest in his expression. He wanted to humiliate her, before he *really* hurt her.

But being a man, she knew he would eventually look at her nipples hardening in the chilly tent. The fire in the stove had burned out hours ago, the cold quickly moving in. She stared at his eyes, waiting.

The moment his gaze dropped to her breasts, she twisted her hand under the sleeping bag so the barrel was pointed at Alex, cocked the pistol and pulled the trigger.

JAMISON RODE HARD back toward the camp and Maddie. The sun ricocheted off the new fallen snow, blinding him. As his horse lunged through the drifts, snow showered over him, the brilliant crystals hanging in the air around him against a sky of deep blue.

He rode as if the hounds of hell were on his heels. He'd known the men would be back. No one just forgot about a plane full of drugs with a street value of more than five million dollars.

Jamison wondered about the buyer who would be waiting. Did he know about the downed plane? Surely he would be getting impatient. That meant the men who'd been running this load were in trouble. Soon they would have a drug cartel after them. That gave him little satisfaction if they were in the sheep camp right now.

He'd ridden back the way he'd originally come. It seemed farther than he remembered. He couldn't have been more anxious to get to Maddie. All his cop instincts told him he should have kept going toward the valley to notify law enforcement. But his heart thundered in his chest, demanding he go back. If Maddie was in trouble—

Ahead, he saw fresh tracks in the snow that crossed his own, the others coming up from the south and circling the camp. His stomach dropped at the sight of them. Only one rider, but he was headed straight for the sheep tent.

He knew better than to push the mare too hard, but he also feared what he would find back at camp if he didn't hurry.

Jamison had just dropped over the ridge when he heard the gunshot. It echoed across the mountainside. He could see the tent in the distance, the meadow of sheep blending into the snowy landscape.

The snow had drifted in bad once he left the ridgeline and started for the tent. The horse labored through it. It would be even slower if he tried to go on foot.

His heart hammered in his chest as a scream followed the first shot. Another shot echoed across the mountainside.

"Maddie!" Her name broke from his lips, a cry of pain and fear and prayer as he urged his horse on. "Maddie!"

That was when he heard it. The sound of a helicopter. As he raced toward the tent, he saw the chopper in the distance. It was headed toward camp. But Jamison feared neither of them would get there in time.

ALEX SCREAMED BOTH in pain and shock as the bullet tore through his right thigh. He lunged for Maddie and she fired again, but this time the bullet caught him in the side, barely grazing his skin.

Maddie managed to fall to the side as he came at her with the knife. The blade tore into the side of the tent, ripping down through the canvas and throwing Alex off balance.

She shoved him aside as she leaped to her feet. Her plan was to take a couple of steps and turn. She still had the .357 clutched in her hand and planned to empty it in him if she could just get far enough away from him to get a decent shot.

On her feet, she took a step—

Alex grabbed hold of her braid. He snapped her head with such force that she stumbled back into him hard. Her momentum threw them both off balance. His arm locked around her neck as he fell backward, she falling on top of him between the cots.

She struggled to lift the gun, even knowing she wouldn't be able to get a clear shot off. But he wasn't going to give her a chance to try. He threw his legs over her arms, pinning them at her sides and forcing her to drop the gun.

They lay like that, both breathing hard. She could

hear from his breathing that he was in pain. But neither wound was life-threatening.

"You're going to so wish you hadn't done that," he said through gritted teeth.

If she'd been scared before, now she was terrified. She'd wounded him. Anyone who lived in Montana knew how a wounded animal reacted. Alex was more deadly than any wounded grizzly. A grizzly would kill humanely. Alex wouldn't.

She'd expected him to stab her but apparently he'd dropped the knife when he'd cut down through the side of the tent and she'd shoved him away. She could feel the cold air rushing in from the slit in the canvas behind them. Alex's hot breath, though, was sickeningly moist against her neck.

"You're really going to wish you hadn't done that," he repeated. His words made it clear that whatever he'd planned to do to her before would be nothing compared to what he would do now.

She tried to free her hand to get the gun, but he only held her more tightly. The choke hold on her throat was so tight she could barely take a breath. She could feel wet blood from his wounds seeping into her clothing. Maybe there was a chance she had hit an artery and he would bleed to death. Unfortunately, she didn't think he was going to wait that long.

Maddie told herself that as long as they were locked together like this he couldn't hurt her. Unless he found the knife with his free hand. She shuddered at the thought as she heard him groping around behind him for it.

If he found the knife—

In the distance, Lucy began to bark. Someone was coming.

The sound of a helicopter filled the air. Alex heard it, too—just an instant before, closer, she heard the *snick* of the switchblade.

She screamed for help, but her scream turned to a shriek as Alex buried the knife in her thigh.

JAMISON WOULD NEVER forget the horrible shriek of pain that came from the tent as he rode up. And still he wasn't prepared for what he saw when he threw open the flap. He'd ridden into camp, jumping down from his horse and running breakneck to the tent. He'd seen the unfamiliar horse a few yards away. Common sense told him not to go busting in.

But common sense went out the window at the thought of Maddie being in such pain. Even with all his training, nothing could have kept him from getting into that tent.

The sight before him, though, brought him up short.

"Take another step and I will slice her from ear to ear," said the man with the knife at Maddie's throat. The two lay on the floor between the cots. The man had his back against the supply box and Maddie held down with one arm locked around her, the knife to her throat and her arms trapped against her sides with his legs.

Jamison took in the scene in a split second—especially

Maddie's expression. He couldn't tell how badly she was hurt—just that she was. Maddie's fingers were just inches from the .357 lying on the floor, useless because of the way he was holding her down.

They both appeared wounded. Maddie's jeans were soaked with blood on her right side. The man's were blood-soaked as well on the right thigh. His shirt was also dark with blood on the other side.

Clearly Maddie had put up one hell of a fight, but if the man moved that knife a quarter of an inch, that fight would have been for nothing.

He met Maddie's gaze. Beyond the pain in her expression, he'd seen relief and fear in her blue eyes as he'd burst in. She was fighting the pain, and the fear he saw was for him more than herself. There was steely determination in her expression even with a knife blade at her throat. If Jamison hadn't known how he felt about her before that moment, he did now. He would die trying to save her if that was what it took.

"Put down your gun," the man ordered. "Now!" He sounded as if he was injured enough that he couldn't stay in his awkward position much longer—but plenty long enough to cut Maddie's throat if only out of spite.

"Okay," Jamison said and took a step forward as he started to slowly lower the pistol to the floor. He kept his eyes locked with Maddie's.

"No," she cried. She tried to shake her head, but the knife was so close, she froze when she felt the bite of the blade. He saw her swallow and then seem to give up.

The man must have loosened his hold on her, because an instant later, she shifted a little to the right as if giving him permission for what he had planned and had tried to telegraph in his gaze.

She'd managed to move only a couple of inches. It wasn't much because of the way the man held her. As the attacker tried to get a better grip on her, the blade caught the light. Jamison saw the tip of the knife cut into her skin and had to steady his pulse.

He would get only one chance. He had to make it count. That he had no choice went without saying. Maddie had put up a fight for her life. Like him, she knew the man wouldn't have come here unless he planned to kill her. Kill them both, once Jamison put the gun on the tent floor.

He'd dealt with men like this one when he was a detective. He knew the look of a desperate man. For some macabre reason, when trapped and about to die, they always felt they needed to take as many people with them as they could.

Only an instant had passed. The sound of the helicopter grew louder. Outside the tent, a horse whinnied, then another. Jamison heard the jangle of tack as he continued to lean down slowly to put the gun on the floor.

Someone was approaching on a horse. The man heard it, as well. "Geoff?" he called out. "Is that you?" He sounded excited, more confident. "Tony?" Whoever had ridden up, they'd distracted the man and bought Jamison a few precious seconds.

He couldn't wait any longer. It was more risky than anything he'd ever done. He didn't dare think about how badly it could go wrong.

About to place the gun on the floor, he suddenly dropped to his knees and raised the pistol. He didn't have time to take perfect aim. All he could do was pray that his many hours on the shooting range didn't fail him now.

He fired.

CHAPTER TWENTY-FOUR

THE BULLET SEEMED suspended in air for those heart-stopping moments before it plowed into the man's head. Jamison saw Maddie close her eyes. Like him, she had to be praying.

The sound was incredibly loud within the walls of the canvas tent even with the noise of the helicopter as it approached.

Jamison must have blinked, because when he opened his eyes all he saw was blood. For a moment he thought Maddie had been hit. Or worse, that the man had cut her throat in that instant before the bullet entered his brain and stopped him dead.

He stumbled toward her. Her eyes were still closed. She lay a little to the side like a broken doll. A broken doll covered with blood.

Then her eyes opened, and he thought his heart would burst from his chest. She struggled to get free of the dead man and wipe away the blood that had splattered on her. He saw that her shirt was open, her breasts bare.

Jamison started to reach for her to cover her when he remembered the horse and rider they'd heard just before he took the kill shot. He swung around at the sound of someone approaching the tent. As he grabbed the corner of the tent flap and jerked it back, his weapon ready, he saw a man he recognized.

Clete Reynolds quickly lowered the gun he'd been holding as his gaze moved past Jamison to the dead man at the far end of the tent. "You got Alex. Good."

"Drop the gun," Jamison said to the man, not sure if he was one of the drug runners or one of the good guys. Nor did he have time to find out. "Get down!"

Clete did as he was told, lying flat in the snow, his hands behind him as Jamison picked up his gun and snapped on the cuffs.

Overhead the helicopter circled, whirling the fresh new snow into a blinding storm.

"Don't move," Jamison ordered and went back into the tent.

Maddie stood where he'd left her, looking stunned. He rushed to her, took her in his arms and lowered her gently to one of the cots. He could see where her blood-soaked jeans had a slit in them. He could see torn flesh beneath the fabric.

He took care of that first, taking a nearby towel and ripping off a strip to stop the bleeding. Fortunately, the blade hadn't hit a main artery. Then he removed his coat and put it around her. She was shivering uncontrollably.

As the helicopter engine shut off and the *whomp whomp* of the blades died down, he heard Undersheriff Dillon Lawson ordering Clete to stay down.

"We'll get you out of here to a doctor as soon as possible," Jamison told Maddie as he drew her into his arms, holding her and thanking God that he'd gotten back to camp when he had. He held her tightly, more grateful than she could know that his prayers had been answered.

"I'm all right." Her words sounded hollow. He'd seen the dazed look in her eyes as she'd struggled to her feet, struggled to wipe the man's blood from her face.

She had the .357 clutched in her right hand. He could hear the undersheriff calling his name. Jamison gently took the gun from her and, seeing that she was crying, wiped away the blood and her tears with his shirttail. With her dead husband's shirttail, he thought.

WHEN NETTIE CAME down to the store early that morning, she saw J.D. loading a suitcase into his pickup. She was still sore from her accident yesterday and not moving all that well. Last night, she'd had trouble getting to sleep and blamed both Frank and J.D. for that.

"Are you going on a trip?" she asked, even though she knew better.

He turned quickly as if startled. "I didn't hear you come up behind me."

"J.D.? What's going on?" She hated that her voice broke. As much as she didn't want to admit it, she'd miss him. She'd enjoyed his company and the attention he gave her. She hadn't realized how lonely she was.

But at the same time, she didn't trust him, knew she never could.

"I was going to drive up to your house before I left,"

he said as he closed his pickup door and came toward her. "I was going to say goodbye."

"So it's goodbye?" She wasn't surprised. He'd never been the type to stick around long. For all these years he hadn't needed Beartooth. She wondered if she would ever see him again.

"Where are you headed?"

"I have some business I need to take care of and it can't wait." He didn't seem to know what to do with his hands and finally stuffed them into the front pockets of his jeans.

He looked sheepish, and she wondered if it was from what had happened between them or because she'd caught him before he could escape. She didn't believe he'd planned to say goodbye to her. Unfortunately, J. D. West was also the kind of man who would rather sneak out of town than face any consequences.

"I didn't want you to think…"

"Think what, J.D.? That you sweet-talked your way into my bed? Or that I might think it meant more than it did?"

"Nettie, darlin'—"

"I'm not your darlin' and I'm not a fool. What happened between us meant the same thing to me that I suspect it did you. Just old friends comforting each other."

"Is that how it was for you?" he asked, his gaze searching hers.

She would never tell just what it had meant to her or how much she'd needed that reminder that she was still alive, still a healthy passionate woman who deserved better than she'd been getting.

"Still, I owe you my life," she said. "If it wasn't for you, I would have been killed by Frank's crazy ex-wife."

"I was just in the right place at the right time. Like I told you, I'm no hero, Nettie." He sounded sad about that, but it was probably the most sincere words the man had spoken to her.

"You won't be back, will you?"

He looked toward the Crazies. "I wish I could stay." His gaze came back to her. "I mean it, Nettie. If I could stay, I'd give Frank Curry a run for his money."

She shook her head. She'd never understand men. "That's why you sweet-talked your way into my bed? It was only to make him jealous?"

J.D. laughed. "I'm not saying I didn't enjoy the hell out of it, and if it made Frank jealous…" He looked behind her. "And it appears it worked like a charm." He stepped to her and lowered his voice. "Don't let Frank take you for granted anymore. You deserve a man who gives you what you need." His gaze met hers again and she felt the heat of his look. "If things were different…" He kissed her quickly then stepped back.

That was when Nettie saw Frank. "I need to speak with Nettie. *Alone*," Frank said through gritted teeth.

"Not a problem. I was just leaving town," J.D. said. "She's all yours." He winked at Nettie before he opened his pickup door and slid behind the wheel.

It wasn't until after J.D. had driven away that Frank demanded, "What the hell do you see in *him?*"

"Is that really what you wanted to talk to me about, Frank?"

He pulled off his Stetson and combed his fingers through his hair in obvious irritation. When he spoke his voice was soft and calm. "Is he really gone?"

"Looks that way."

He met her gaze. "Did you—"

"Like him? I did. Am I heartbroken to see him go? No. It was just nice to be with a man who liked me."

"*I* like you."

She raised a brow.

"Oh, come on, Lynette. You have to know the way I feel about you."

She stood firm. "Why don't you tell me, Frank."

He swallowed and turned the brim of his Stetson nervously in his fingers. "I'd do anything for you. I think the world of you. I… Wait a minute. Where are you going?"

"I have to open the store and I'm tired of hearing your platitudes," she said over her shoulder.

"Lynette!"

She kept walking.

"Lynette?"

She'd just reached the porch steps when he finally said the words she'd been waiting years to hear.

"Oh, hell, woman. I *love* you!"

She stopped, her back to him.

"I said 'I love you,'" he repeated more softly. She could hear him approaching but waited until he touched her shoulder before turning around. "I said I *love* you."

"Are you just saying this now because J.D.—"

"I've wanted to say it for a long time but I was afraid, and then Tiffany came to town and then Pam. I was worried if they knew how I felt, one of them would hurt you. As it was, Pam almost killed you."

"I take it she's long gone?"

"Every law-enforcement officer in the Northwest is looking for her. The truck she took from the Westfall ranch that she tried to run you down with was found in Williston, North Dakota, and a car was stolen there and later dropped in Minnesota. So we think she's gone. At least for the time being."

"So, Frank." She cupped his warm jaw. "Just tell me one thing, then. Are you going to kiss me or not?"

He smiled and pulled her to him. The kiss was just as she remembered from when they were young. It felt so right being in his arms. She felt as if she'd finally come home and assured herself there was still time for the two of them.

JAMISON LEFT HER in the tent, promising to come back and get her flown out as soon as he could. Maddie tried to stop shaking. The air in the tent had turned ice-cold, but nothing like the cold that had taken hold of her.

She knew she was in shock. No one could go through what she'd just experienced without coming out shell-shocked.

Once he'd gotten her leg to quit bleeding, he'd taken his coat back and wrapped her instead in a sleeping bag with specific orders not to move. She had turned her face away from what was left of the dead man. But out of the corner of her eye she'd seen the dark red splattered on the side of the tent and shuddered.

As much as she wanted to do as Jamison had said, she couldn't bear to have the man's blood on her. Getting up, she limped over to the stove. She barely felt her wounded leg, barely felt the other cuts and bruises on her body, the pain inside her was so intense.

The pot of water on the stovetop had gone cold, but she dipped the remainder of the towel Jamison had used to bind her wound into the icy water and began to wash her face. She felt numb, and not even the freezing water could make her colder. When she'd finished, she dried her face with the towel they'd been using to dry the dishes.

For the first time she felt as if she could breathe. Limping back to the cots and doing her best to ignore the body between them, she took off her cut flannel shirt and bra. The cold air in the tent skittered over her skin, dimpling it, as she drew out a fresh bra and shirt.

Her fingers were still shaking, giving her trouble with the snaps. She finally gave up and climbed back up on the cot, drawing the sleeping bags around her.

Outside the tent, she could hear Jamison filling the undersheriff in on everything, including the discovery of the downed plane and the load of drugs.

She was thankful for these few minutes to herself so she could get her emotions in check. Her chest hurt from keeping in the tears. She still couldn't cry, even when she thought about her relief at hearing the heli-copter and realizing at least part of her ordeal was over.

So much had happened. So much had changed, she thought. Before Jamison had left the tent, she'd watched him search Alex's body and pocket his cell phone, a set of keys and a map.

Now she listened to the undersheriff calling for backup, ordering a second chopper, paramedics and DEA agents. "We also are going to need to get at least three bodies out at this count. Maybe more. We have one injured citizen, as well."

Jamison stuck his head into the tent. She pretended to be asleep and didn't open her eyes. A few moments later she heard him being interviewed by the under-sheriff. Clete gave his statement, as well. She listened as he gave Dillon the drug runners' full names. Alex Branson. Tony Adams. Geoff Worthington.

Apparently he had known them at college, played football with them. It had been Clete who'd provided them with horses and brought them into the mountains under the men's ruse that they wanted to make the trip into Yellowstone Park just because it was something they'd always wanted to do.

Geoff Worthington was dead, Clete explained. He'd been shot during an altercation involving Clete and Tony Adams. Tony had apparently shot Geoff by acci-dent while attempting to kill Clete.

"And where is this Tony Adams?" the undersher-iff asked.

"The last I saw of him, he was on a horse loaded with the coke headed for Gardiner," Clete said.

Maddie heard the silence before Dillon barked, "We have another one out there somewhere. Let's find him."

"You might want to take a look at this," she heard Jamison say. "This is Alex's cell phone. There is one number he called numerous times."

"I suspect it is whoever Alex was getting his information from," Clete said. "He made a couple of calls that I saw. They would need someone to pick them up when they brought the drugs out and let them know if there was anything up here they needed to worry about."

"Like Deputy Jamison and Mrs. Conner," Dillon said.

Maddie heard Dillon contact his office. "Got it," he said a few minutes later. She listened as he made a call to Sheriff Frank Curry.

FRANK SWORE AS his cell phone rang. He released Lynette to glance at the screen and saw that Dillon was calling. After he'd turned in his resignation, gun and star, he couldn't imagine what the undersheriff would want. Unless...unless maybe Pam had been caught?

"I have to take this. Just give me a minute," he said to Lynette. He just prayed that this call would end the nightmare he'd been living.

"Frank?" Dillon said when he answered. He couldn't hear him well and figured he was still up on the mountain. "We've got one hell of a deal going up here in the

Beartooths. Every law-enforcement officer we can spare is on his way up here."

Dillon wasn't going to try to talk him into coming back to work, was he? He was wasting his breath.

He listened as the undersheriff told him about the crashed plane, the cocaine and what he'd found on the cell phone of one of the drug runner's.

"He made numerous calls to a cell-phone number. I had it run. The number belongs to J. D. West."

Frank didn't need Dillon to tell him what that meant. Now they knew what J.D. was doing in town—and why he'd just left.

He looked at Lynette. He wanted to tell her how right he was about her choosing the wrong men but held his tongue. She'd chosen *him* once. Maybe she was smarter than he thought by letting him go.

"Frank, the drug smugglers knew about Jamison and Maddie being up here. One of them had Maddie Conner. Jamison killed him. We're getting Maddie down to the hospital as soon as the other chopper gets here. She's hurt but not badly. I'm figuring J.D. told the drug smugglers that the two of them were up here. Who knows how J.D. found out."

Frank didn't need Dillon to draw him a picture. J.D. was involved. It came as no surprise. Nor did where J.D. had gotten all his information. Frank had wondered why J.D. had decided to stay with Nettie, why he'd wormed his way into her good graces and more. Everyone knew that if you wanted to know what was going on in the county, all you had to do was ask her.

"One of the men got away with about fifty pounds of coke according to Clete. The man's name is Tony Adams. We believe he's headed for Gardiner. I wouldn't have called you, but there was no one else—"

"I'm with Lynette right now. But I'll take care of it." He disconnected the call and looked at Lynette. "Did you tell J.D. about Deputy Jamison and Maddie Conner going up to the sheep camp?" He saw the answer in her expression.

"Are they all right?"

"They're bringing Maddie down to the hospital by chopper. It didn't sound like her injuries were life-threatening."

Lynette covered her mouth with her hand, her eyes wide. He could see her fighting the consequences of her gossiping.

"Did J.D. say where he was headed just now?"

"What did J.D. do?"

"Where was he going, Lynette?"

"I don't know. He said he was leaving for good, though." She frowned. "But a few days ago, I know he went to Gardiner. Maybe he's headed back there."

"I have to go." He reached into his coat pocket and pulled out a small pistol and a box of ammunition. "I want you to keep this loaded and with you at all times. If you see Pam—"

"I know what to do."

He kissed her and hurried out to his pickup. It was fairly new, with only a few miles on it since most of the time he was in one of the sheriff's-department vehicles.

He wished now he had a patrol SUV so he could use the siren and lights. But maybe it was better this way.

Dillon obviously hadn't turned in Frank's resignation. Not that he was worried about that right now. He was going after J.D. He needed to catch him with the drugs. This time J.D. was going away for a long while.

Frank didn't regret turning in his star, but he could have used his gun. Fortunately, he always carried a pistol under the seat of his pickup and a shotgun on the rack behind his head. Both were loaded.

Frank drove as fast as possible on the narrow paved road.

J. D. West hadn't been gone that long. Nor would he be driving as fast, Frank assured himself. Had he been thinking clearly, he would have followed the man sooner.

He didn't think clearly around Lynette.

Ahead, he spotted J.D.'s black pickup at the edge of Big Timber. Hanging back, he followed as the pickup got onto Interstate 90 and headed west. Nettie might be right, Frank thought. It appeared J.D. might be heading for Gardiner—just as suspected since one of the drug runners was headed in the same direction. He dropped back. The last thing he wanted was for J.D. to realize he was onto him.

NETTIE STARED AFTER FRANK, her heart in her throat. What had she done? Everyone knew about Deputy Jamison and Maddie Conner going up to the sheep camp, didn't they?

But she was the one who'd told J.D.

"Oh, Frank," she said, practically wringing her hands. Just moments before, they'd been kissing. And now he was gone again. Gone after J.D.

Her heart ached at the thought of losing him now, not after he'd told her he loved her. He'd finally broken down and said the words she'd been waiting years to hear.

"Don't you get yourself killed," she said to the empty room. "Please, Frank. You have to come back to me." She wiped at the tears and put through a call to the hospital. Maddie Conner hadn't arrived yet.

Nettie's friend didn't know what Maddie's injuries might be.

It quickly became apparent that her friend hadn't heard anything about what had happened up in the Beartooths.

"What's going on?" her friend asked.

Nettie wished she knew. But even if she had, she told herself she wouldn't have said a word to a soul. As she hung up, her gaze shifted to the café across the street. A young woman was getting out of a car in front of the café.

The slim, dark-haired woman stretched then pushed her sunglasses up on her head of long hair, glancing down the street of empty buildings before settling her gaze on the help-wanted sign in the lower café window.

Nettie watched with interest as the woman headed for the café. She wore denim capris, a red T-shirt and sandals. She couldn't have looked more out of place in Beartooth even if she'd tried.

Sure enough, Nettie saw that the license plates on the car were from Washington.

As the woman disappeared into the café, Nettie looked again down the empty highway. She was worried sick about Frank. Even more upset with herself for telling J.D. something she apparently shouldn't have. But what did her telling J.D. about Maddie Conner and Deputy Jamison have to do with the phone call Frank had received or why he'd taken off like he had after J.D.?

She thought of the bloody bandages J.D. had tried to hide in her Dumpster and was almost sick to her stomach.

Across the street, she saw Kate remove the waitress-wanted sign from the window.

CHAPTER TWENTY-FIVE

FRANK KNEW THE BARN where Branch Murdock's horse had been found. It was up a road out of Gardiner to the north and on the way to an old mining town called Jardine.

But first he looked around Gardiner for J.D.'s black pickup. As he recalled, the truck had California plates on it. He'd written down the number, a habit he had when he was suspicious.

Was that where J.D. had been living? He called the office and asked that the name James Dean West be run through the computer data searches.

"Call me back when you have something," he said and disconnected. Gardiner was a small tourist town on the edge of Yellowstone Park. What made it stand out from other such towns was the fact that it teetered on the edge of a deep gorge formed over the centuries by the Yellowstone River.

A bridge spanned the deep cut, dividing the town in two sections. There were the usual curio, pizza and gas-station shops along with several cafés and a few bars and motels. The old road went under a famous stone arch. The story was that Teddy Roosevelt had laid the first stone.

J. D. West's pickup was nowhere to be seen. Frank filled up his pickup with gas then took the road up the side of the hill overlooking the river gorge and headed for Jardine.

"I ran that name and plate number for you," his office told him when the call came through. "It was purchased in Banning, California, three weeks ago. The plates are new. Do you want last known address?"

"Why not?" Frank said, although he had no reason to think J.D. would be headed back to it.

"222 Mesquite Road, unit 4, Clovis, New Mexico."

Frank sat up a little. "New Mexico?" The last number he'd had for Pam was in New Mexico. "One more thing. Check the area code for me in Clovis." He held his breath, telling himself he was clutching at straws. Or worse, off his rocker.

"Clovis, New Mexico, is 575."

He hung up, shaken. It was just a coincidence that the number he'd reached his ex-wife at months ago had a 575 area code. Unless somehow Pam had met J.D. He could actually see how it might have happened. Some chance meeting, J.D. taking advantage of a woman who obviously was susceptible and one thing led to another. Maybe they got to talking about their pasts and realized they had something in common.

Hell, a whole lot in common. Not just Beartooth, Montana—but Sheriff Frank Curry.

J.D. was a good-looking guy—just the type Pam might let buy her a drink. What did Frank know of how she lived her life the past twenty years? He'd never known where she and Tiffany had lived or if they'd moved around a lot. Tiffany hadn't wanted to tell him and Pam sure as the devil hadn't given him a clue.

Or maybe it was pure coincidence that J. D. West had been in Clovis, New Mexico, and so had Pam.

The road toward the old mining town of Jardine narrowed. Frank concentrated on his driving. He had to be wrong about there being a connection between J. D. West and Pam Chandler. J.D. had been the one to save Nettie's life when Pam had tried to run her down.

They wouldn't have staged something like that. Or would they? What would have been the point? But he knew the answer to that. More of Pam's vengeful games. Nor had it hurt making J.D. look like a hero.

Ahead, the road turned into a near 4x4 trail. Frank slowed to pull the pistol from under his pickup seat. He couldn't wait to find J. D. West and get the truth out of him. If J.D. and Pam were somehow in on this together...

Then wasn't there a good chance J.D. would know where she was now?

DILLON INSISTED MADDIE be flown out of the mountains to the hospital as soon as the second chopper landed. Jamison had wanted to go with her, but they were short-handed and needed all the men they could get on the mountain. DEA officers were flying from Billings, but local law enforcement was needed to secure the plane.

"Don't worry about your sheep," Dillon told her. "Your neighbor Fuzz Carpenter and his son have offered to come up and take care of things until you are able to make other arrangements. They are on their way."

"Fuzz is doing that for me?" She was touched. After Hank had been killed, Fuzz had made an offer on her ranch. She hadn't taken it in the vein it was probably offered. Instead she saw it as another rancher telling her she had no business running a sheep ranch because she was a woman.

Now she merely accepted Fuzz's help graciously. Her leg hurt too badly to argue. Her throat also ached and felt bruised from where Alex had choked her. Fortunately, her other cuts were superficial.

She wondered if the undersheriff's determination to rush her to the hospital had less to do with her injuries and more to do with getting her off the mountain and to safety.

Tony Adams still hadn't turned up, but all available local law enforcement that could be flown into the mountains were looking for him. Meanwhile, the bodies of Alex Branson and Geoff Worthington as well as Branch Murdock were to be brought out as soon as possible, Dillon had informed her.

"Don't worry about me," she'd told him. She looked around for Jamison, hoping to see him as she was led to the chopper.

"Bentley is briefing the others on the location of the plane," Dillon said. "Is there anything you'd like me to tell him?"

Bentley. She smiled, finally remembering his first name. "No," she said. "There isn't anything."

The chopper ride to the hospital was short. It amazed her the hours she'd spent on horseback riding up into these mountains. She could have saved herself another lifetime by taking a helicopter.

Maddie knew then that she wasn't holding up as well as she thought. Tears stung her eyes, but she willed herself not to cry. She wished Bentley Jamison was by her side, but he was a deputy foremost and he was needed back in the Beartooths, and it was time she learned what it was like to truly be alone.

The doctor insisted Maddie stay in the hospital overnight because of fear of infection in her leg. He'd cleaned the deep wound, taped the cut closed and seen that she got antibiotics. Then he'd left her alone in the small room.

Outside her window she saw that the sun had sunk behind the Crazies. It was hard for her to believe that just that morning she'd awakened in Jamison's arms. She knew she was lucky to be alive and lying in this bed with only a knife wound to her leg.

As she lay there, she told herself she had some decisions to make. But all she could think about was Jamison still up on that mountain with a killer. Her last thought was a prayer for him before she fell into an emotionally exhausted sleep.

BETHANY LOOKED UP as her husband came through the hospital-room door. She'd never been so happy to see him.

But as he rushed to her, she saw the bruises on his face.

"What happened to you?" she cried as she tenderly touched his discolored cheek and surveyed the cut lip and black eye.

"It's a long story," he said. "But I'm fine."

His eyes were bright, and he seemed better than he'd been in a long time.

"I was so worried about you."

"I was the one worried about you," he said. "Oh, Bethany, I should never have taken the job."

"That's all over now," she said, cupping his strong jaw and drawing him down for a kiss. "Have you seen our son?"

"He's beautiful."

Tears filled her eyes. "He looks like you."

Clete put his arms around his wife. "I'm so sorry I wasn't here."

"You're here now," she said as she hugged him.

"I thought you might like to hold your son," the nurse said, coming into the room from the nursery down the hall.

Clete turned, his gaze going to the bundle in the nurse's arms. He stepped to her, and she gently placed his son in his arms. Bethany witnessed the expression on his face when he turned to her. It was a moment she would never forget. There was such a sense of wonder in Clete's eyes.

He looked from the baby to her. "*We* did this?"

She laughed, unable to hold back the tears any longer. "We sure did."

Drawing back the blanket the baby was wrapped in,

he turned their son so she could see him. "That's your mama," Clete said then looked up at Bethany in alarm. "He doesn't have a name."

"I thought we could name him after his father and call him C.J. for short."

Pride and gratitude welled in her husband's eyes. "You have made me the happiest man in the world."

She smiled as he handed her their son and climbed up on the bed next to her. "Tell me what happened," she said as they watched their son sleep.

Clete began to talk, pouring out the horrible story. She gasped when he told her about being drugged and, worse, that at least one of the men had wanted to kill him.

"You're a hero," she said when he'd finished.

He let out a humorless laugh. "Yeah, that's me. I left my pregnant wife."

She shook her head. "If you hadn't gone up there, they would have gotten someone else to take them back into the Beartooths. They didn't kill you because they knew you, it sounds like. Whoever else they might have gotten to take them wouldn't have faired as well."

He turned to kiss her. "They are why my football career ended," he said and told her what he'd overheard.

"I'm so sorry." She heard the pain in his voice and worried that he would always regret coming back to Beartooth.

"It was a long time ago," he said after a moment. "Who knows? If I hadn't come back, maybe you and I would never have married and had a son. I'm not sorry.

I'm just glad I know the truth now." He looked over at her. "You are so beautiful," he said with a sigh. "When do we get to take our son home?"

Bethany felt all her worries dissolve like water vapor. They were both just learning about marriage and their commitment and each other. They had time to figure it out. All she knew at this moment was that they were going to be all right. Oh, yes, they were going to be just fine.

FRANK PASSED A FEW HOUSES, most looking as if they'd been there for years. Montana's new prosperity of fancy houses owned by out-of-staters hadn't hit Gardiner like it had other parts of the state.

Farther up the road, in a wide ravine, he caught sight of what was left of the old mine. A large metal structure rusted in the waning light. The long-abandoned equipment cast a tall shadow against the hillside. Not far after that, he passed the barn where Branch Murdock's horse had turned up and the small ranch house next to it.

The road got worse shortly after that. Frank found a place in a stand of pines off the road and hid his pickup. He would go the rest of the way on foot. Taking the pistol and the shotgun he worked his way up the tight canyon.

He found J.D.'s black pickup parked off the road in the trees a little way up the road. Sneaking through the pines, he approached the truck. He found it empty, but he knew J.D. couldn't have gone far. His suitcase was in the back, and Frank was betting he hadn't gotten what he'd driven up here for yet.

Frank worked his way toward the spot where he figured the trail over the Beartooths came out. Had he not been going slow, he might have stumbled over J. D. West.

His body lay in the shadow of a large pine, curled slightly forward as if at one point he had been leaning against the pine trunk—until he'd been shot.

The bullet had entered his chest and come out his back, which led Frank to believe J.D. had trusted whoever had killed him. Trusted them to the extent that he hadn't gotten up when the killer had walked up to him and, standing within a few feet, had fired directly at his heart.

Frank hurriedly began to go through J.D.'s pockets when he heard something whiz by his ear before making a *thunk* sound in the tree trunk behind him. The shooter was using a silencer. He definitely hadn't heard a shot.

He quickly threw himself behind the tree as another bullet blew past to kick up dried pine needles just feet away from him.

He squatted down, keeping as much of his body behind the tree as possible, and pulled J.D.'s body toward him to go through the man's pockets. He found a wallet, a cell phone and a set of keys. He stuffed all three into his pocket. He found nothing else. J.D. was apparently traveling light.

Pulling his pistol, he peered around the tree trunk. He had an idea where the shots had come from based on the trajectory of the bullets. The canyon was lined with large boulders. From behind any one of them the shooter would have the advantage. It was like shooting fish in a barrel. Worse, the killer had him pinned down.

Frank tried to remember if he'd seen another vehicle parked below. He hadn't passed one on the way up this ravine. The killer could have parked down by the mine or even by one of the old houses along the road up here. Frank hadn't noticed because he was only looking for the black pickup J.D. was driving.

Was the killer still up there watching him, waiting for him to step out in the open before taking another shot? He couldn't even be sure how many were up there. No doubt waiting for the drugs that they thought would be coming out of the mountains.

The eerie silence that fell over the trees made him hold his breath, his senses keen. It was growing darker in the canyon, the waning light casting long shadows through the pines.

Off in the distance, a squirrel chatted. Closer, a horse whinnied, making Frank start. He moved around the tree to look up the trail. A large man on a horse came slowly down the trail. The man looked so fatigued that he could barely stay in the saddle.

The drug smuggler Dillon had told him about, Tony Adams, Frank thought, spotting two duffel bags tied on each side behind the saddle. That explained what J.D. had been doing here—and no doubt the shooter, as well.

Frank stayed where he was, letting the rider continue down the trail, planning to wait until he came alongside him.

Tony's head suddenly came up; surprise and something worse crossed his expression. Had he seen J. D. West's body? Or had he heard something?

The man shuddered and fell forward. Frank looked to the rocks that lined the canyon wall as the drug runner tumbled from his horse.

He could see two gunshot wounds in the man's back as he fell. Frank swore under his breath and tried to work his way to the man.

He heard what sounded like a whine next to his ear. An instant later a bullet ripped into the bark of a tree behind him. He ducked behind another tree. "Tony?"

No answer.

He glanced around the tree, hoping he could spot the shooter. "Tony?"

Still nothing.

He had to assume the man was dead. With J.D. gone as well, there was only him left. Frank was debating what to do when the horse Tony had been riding took a step toward him.

"Come on," Frank said to the horse. "Come on." The horse took a few more steps in his direction. Just a couple more and he would be able to get a boot in the stirrup. He could stay hunkered down on one side of the horse, narrowing down the shooter's window of opportunity.

The horse took another step, then another. Frank reached for the reins. A bullet whizzed past. He grabbed the saddle horn and threw a boot into the stirrup. He clung to the saddle as he kicked the horse into motion.

Frank could see that the trail turned within a few yards. If he could just reach there, the trees would shelter him from the shooter.

The dirt next to him flew up as a bullet ripped through it. Frank urged the horse to keep going. As he reached the bend in the trail, another bullet sliced off bark in the tree next to him. And then he was in the trees. He swung up in the saddle and, keeping down, rode like hell.

Frank rode the horse down the road, put in a call to Dillon then waited. No one came down the road. It gave him a lot of time to think. Tony and J.D. were dead. Everyone connected with this failed drug deal was dead—except for the shooter and whoever else might be up in those mountains.

On a hunch, he checked the duffel bags on the horse. He shouldn't have been surprised to find them full of rocks. No coke. What the hell?

Tony had met someone along the trail who'd taken the drugs? Or had Tony suspected a double-cross and hid the drugs back in the mountains? It was no longer Frank's problem.

He waited until a DEA agent showed up to take over, gave him his statement and drove into Gardiner.

It wasn't his nature to leave this for the DEA and local law enforcement to figure out. But he had a thread, a tenuous one at best, to Pam. Two people who happened to be in the same New Mexico town at possibly the same time. It was all he had.

If Pam had known J.D.... He knew it was a long shot.

After the long day he'd had, he checked into a motel.

He pulled out J.D.'s cell phone. He'd given everything else to the DEA agent. The wallet had been new, with only a couple hundred dollars in it and nothing else. The key ring only had a key to the truck on it.

He would mail the phone to Dillon tomorrow. But tonight he wanted to see who the man had called.

He touched the cell phone's screen, bringing it to life. He could tell by looking at the phone that it was new, so he didn't expect to see many numbers on it.

But when he checked the calls sent, he got a surprise. There was a half dozen, all to the same number except for one.

It was that one number that jumped out at him.

J. D. West had called the Westfall ranch.

Frank stared at the number. He'd been right. There had been some connection between Pam and J.D.

The realization gave him little satisfaction. J.D. was dead and Pam was still missing.

CHAPTER TWENTY-SIX

AS THE FUNERAL limo neared the cemetery, Maddie closed her eyes, fighting tears. The week since she'd returned to the ranch was a string of endless sleepless nights and empty hours of walking around the house in a state of grief.

Jamison had called every chance he got to check on her. She'd told him she was doing fine. "As well as could be expected," her mother would have said.

He had sounded as exhausted as she felt since he'd stayed back in the Beartooths to "mop up."

"The drugs weren't in the plane when we reached it," the deputy told her.

"How is that possible?" she'd asked and shuddered at the memory of the plane and the smell of death that permeated the dense stand of pines. "Tony couldn't have carried all of the drugs out even with two horses, right?"

"The DEA officers think he hid them."

The Sweetgrass County grapevine had been abuzz with nothing else all week. Even Maddie, who'd done her best to stay clear of it, had heard.

"Why would he put rocks in the two duffels he brought out?"

"Another theory is that he was the decoy while the drugs were taken out another trail."

"So there might have been other drug runners who came into the mountains from the Yellowstone Park side?"

"Like I said, it's just a theory. It could have been a double cross, someone who found out about the downed plane and the plan to take the drugs out through Gardiner. Fuzz and his son are taking good care of your sheep." Silence, and then he said, "I want to see you. We'll be coming down soon."

She'd made an excuse to get off the phone, but he'd called again the next day and the next. Each call became a little shorter until the past couple of days there hadn't been any.

Maddie wasn't surprised. As the ordeal on the mountain began to dim, so did the feelings. At least she assumed that was the case for Jamison. He had planned to stay here only a year. His job was waiting for him back in New York. By now, she was sure he'd had his fill of Montana. Maybe he would go even sooner.

The thought made her sad, but then everything did. At night when she trolled through the house, she couldn't bear her life. She'd been told that she shouldn't make any big decisions for a year. Easy for everyone else to say, but she was the one left alone in this house with all its past. The memories gave her no comfort.

Her third day home she'd called a Realtor friend. "I want to sell the ranch. How quickly can you do that?"

Bob Burns had sounded surprised. "Maddie, I would

strongly advise against that. Give it some time. I'm sure—"

"I won't change my mind. Please, list it. Let me know when you have a buyer."

"Won't you want to at least keep the house and some of the property?"

"No. Sell it all. Lock, stock and barrel."

"I'll have to run some numbers and get back to you. How soon do you want—"

"As soon as possible." Then what? she asked herself after she'd hung up. She didn't know. Didn't care.

She'd expected to feel a deep sense of sadness. Instead, she'd felt lighter as if a huge weight had been lifted from her shoulders.

As she'd walked around the house, she'd realized she hadn't really looked at it in years.

"This is my mother's house." It had shocked her to realize that. When she and Hank had gotten married her parents had moved to Arizona and given the newlyweds the house and sheep ranch. They'd been so busy working that they hadn't made any changes. When Matthew had come along, she'd painted one of the spare rooms for him. It was still a pale blue that had faded with the years.

Her parents had come home the summer her father took ill. Her mother had been gone within weeks after her father. Both were buried up on the hill along with her grandparents, and Hank and Matthew, and an assortment of faithful dogs.

That day, hot tears had streamed down her face and

Lucy had come over to her. The dog hadn't left her side since Jamison had seen that Lucy was returned to her. She'd petted the dog, knowing how much Lucy missed Branch.

Just the thought of Branch's death had brought back Hank's and Matthew's. It was as if she had finally grieved for them since there hadn't been time back when they'd died. She'd hugged the dog and cried. Lucy had licked her hand, making her cry even harder.

Everywhere she'd looked that day she'd seen painful memories. The house had filled with memories leaving no room for air to breathe. She had known that if she stayed there a moment longer—

But as she'd looked around the house she'd spent forty-five years of her life in, she also thought of the memories she couldn't bear to part with. It was there her son had taken his first steps. In a bedroom down the hall was where he was conceived.

There were so many precious memories in that house, she thought now. How could she just walk away?

Maddie felt the funeral limo come to a stop. She'd always been able to pull herself up by her bootstraps. Today she needed that inner strength more than she ever had in her life. "Just let me get through this," she prayed in a whisper as the driver opened her door.

As she stepped out, she was taken aback. There were pickups everywhere and people. For a moment she thought there must be another funeral today. But as she moved toward the open grave, she saw that they had come for Branch.

Her heart lodged in her throat. She shook her head in disbelief. They had come to pay their respects. They'd come for her. Her heart swelled, her eyes welling with tears, as she was suddenly surrounded by ranchers and county residents she hadn't seen since Hank and Matthew's funeral.

She couldn't blame any of them for leaving her alone the past four years. She'd made her ranch the prison it had become. Bitter and hurting, she hadn't wanted their sympathy. Nor their pity. She'd been so filled with pride and determination to prove that she could do it herself without anyone but Branch. A part of her had felt that she would have fallen completely apart if she had let anyone else in. She had needed to be strong to keep the ranch going.

Now she couldn't have been more touched that they had shown up for Branch's graveside service. She'd kept it simple, skipping a church service because she knew Branch wouldn't have wanted it.

Maddie fought her tears, overwhelmed at this kind of turnout. Branch would have hated it, she thought, and couldn't help but smile to herself. But she was touched to see them all here.

As she moved to the grave, she straightened her back, willing herself not to fall apart. And yet nearing the open grave, she felt the last of her resolve waning. Any moment she would be sobbing her heart out.

Branch had been the one person in her life she knew without a doubt that she could depend on. He'd been her family, her friend, her steadying rock in the threatening storm that had been her life.

Then, just when she felt herself crumbling, she saw him. Jamison stepped to her. He looked nothing like the deputy who had driven up in front of her house only two weeks ago.

The stubble she remembered only too well from her night of passion with him in the wall tent at sheep camp had grown into a short beard. His hair was longer, too, and the fact that he'd made no attempt to chop it off, she thought, meant he'd left it like that on purpose.

Like most everyone around Branch's casket, Jamison wore jeans, boots, a dress Western shirt and his Stetson, which he now removed.

He seemed so different and yet when she looked into those gray eyes she saw the man she'd fallen in love with up in the Beartooth Mountains. The thought came as a small shock. Not that she'd fallen in love with him, but that she was now admitting it.

He gave her a smile and offered his arm. She took it, gripping his strong forearm and feeling stronger herself.

"You will get through this," he whispered to her.

She looked around at all her neighbors as the preacher said a few words over Branch's casket. She'd told him to keep it short and sweet. Branch, as much as he believed in a higher power, didn't hold much stock in churches or preachers, for that matter. He always said he spoke to God up in the mountains.

It was one reason she'd picked this gravesite for him.

It had a great view of the Beartooths, got a lot of sun and still had a few pine trees to protect it in the winter.

The service over, Maddie knelt down and picked up a handful of dirt. It felt warm in her fingers. She could feel the sun on her back. Summer really was coming, she thought as she slowly let the earth fall to the top of the casket.

"Goodbye, Branch. Sleep well," she whispered and stood, glad to feel Jamison's arm around her as a crow cawed from a high branch and then flew out across the vast Montana sky.

JAMISON FELT LIKE a teenage boy as he drove up the Boulder River Valley. He'd called Maddie every day since the funeral, but she'd put him off. He'd heard that she'd sold the Diamond C to Fuzz Carpenter and that he'd made her a good offer.

So now what was she planning to do? Jamison had no idea. When he'd called, she would get him off the phone as quickly as possible. He was worried about her being out there alone. But every time he suggested they have dinner or he come out, she'd have an excuse.

Not today, though, he thought as he turned onto the road into her ranch. He couldn't help but remember the first time he'd driven in here. The wind had been howling that day, gently rocking his patrol SUV. It was no different today.

Today there were no freshly washed sheets on the line, but that old weathered rocker was still on the porch, teetering back and forth in the gale.

He was relieved to see her pickup parked in front of the house. He'd called and they'd spoken for only a moment. He hadn't told her he was driving out. He'd had the feeling she might have left to avoid him.

He parked, got out and stood for a moment, thinking about the first time he'd seen her. There'd been such a self-assuredness about her as she'd come out on the porch and leaned against one of the posts. He recalled the way she'd squinted into the sun, those cornflower-blue eyes looking steely and yet wary.

Jamison was a little worried about what kind of reception he was going to get. But he wasn't leaving until she told him why she'd been avoiding him.

Before he could reach the bottom porch step, the front door opened.

He hadn't seen her since he'd been forced to leave her after the funeral. That day she'd worn dress boots, black jeans and a black jean jacket. He'd known that she wouldn't wear a dress. She was a sheep rancher and he suspected Branch would have wanted her to remember that at his funeral.

Today she was wearing a cotton shirt and jeans. Her feet were bare, and he got the feeling from the smudge of dirt on her cheek and her disarrayed hair that had come loose from her braid that she'd been busy. Probably packing. He hadn't heard when she was supposed to be out of the house, but he suspected it would be soon.

"You should have warned me you were coming out," she said.

"And give you a chance to dodge me?" He shook his head as he climbed the steps. "Not a chance."

"We don't have anything to say to each other. I'm sure you've heard that I sold the ranch to Fuzz Carpenter."

"I did. What will you do now?"

She shrugged. "Like I told you before, anything I want to."

"You won't leave the area, will you?" He hated the emotion he heard in his voice. But he didn't want to lose her.

"Why would it matter? You'll be going back to New York before long."

"I'm staying."

She lifted an eyebrow. "Since when?"

He met her gaze and held it. "Maybe this place is growing on me. Maddie, you know damned well why I want to stay." He was just inches from her. He wanted to take her in his arms, but the look in her eye warned him not to try. There were things that needed to be said between them first.

"I know you have a pot of coffee on. I suppose it is too much to hope you baked a cake."

She gave him an unamused look, but she stepped back to let him enter the house. Just as he'd thought, she was packing.

"When do you have to be out?"

"The last of the month," she said as she led the way into the kitchen.

"I've missed you."

She had been in the process of getting two mugs from the kitchen cabinet but slowed at his words. "Jamison—"

"My first name is Bentley."

She turned with a mug in each hand. "I know." As she turned her back again to fill the mugs, she said, "What happened up in the mountains—"

"Don't try to reduce it to something it wasn't."

He saw her shoulders sag as she came around to face him. He took one of the mugs from her hand. "I'm not going to let you just write us off without even giving us a chance."

"I'm selling the ranch. I'm thinking I might want to travel."

"Really?" He couldn't help but notice the sun coming in the kitchen window. It lit up her face. She'd never been more beautiful, he thought, but wisely didn't voice it.

"Maybe I want to cut loose of my roots and see the world."

"Sounds like fun. I'll pack my bag. When do we leave?"

She shook her head. "You aren't going to quit your job and travel the world."

"Try me."

"What about your job back in New York City? You said you loved being a detective."

"I did love it, but I realized something up on that mountain with you. I was hanging on to that job, keeping one foot in the past, afraid to make a real commitment to the future."

She took a sip of her coffee and leaned back against the counter. "And now?"

"I want to stay here. But I don't want you feeling as if you're the only reason I've decided to stay. I love it out here. I want to make it my home." He met her gaze. "But I won't kid you. I want you, too."

Maddie shook her head. He made it all sound so simple.

"No more living in the past for me, Maddie. I called my old boss and told him to fill the position. I'm not sure where I might end up, but I'm not going back no matter what happens with you and me." He raised his coffee mug. "To new beginnings."

A comfortable silence seemed to fill the kitchen. The sun warmed it, making everything glow. The aroma of coffee hung in the air while just outside the open window, a meadowlark sang from a fence post.

"Can we talk about what is really going on?" he asked after a moment.

"You already know. I'm packing." Her voice warbled a little. "Like you, I'm leaving the past behind."

"I was by Branch's grave earlier. I saw the tombstone you bought him. It had a lamb and sagebrush on it. He would have liked it."

She shook her head even as tears filled her eyes.

Jamison stepped to her, took the coffee mug from her hand and pulled her into his arms as she began to cry.

"He was murdered because of me," she sobbed.

"He died because some drug runner killed him."

"If he hadn't been up in those mountains—"

He drew back to meet her gaze. "We all have a choice. Branch chose to herd your sheep to the high country each summer. You chose to hang on to this ranch come hell or high water. Either of you could have chosen differently."

"Could we have?" She reached for a paper towel and wiped her tears. "I feel as if my destiny was already written and there wasn't a damned thing I could do about it."

He shoved back his Stetson. "Destiny? Like my meeting you?"

She started to say that was different.

"You can't have it both ways, Maddie. The future is in your hands. You're going to have to choose. Just like Branch chose not only to take your sheep up into the Beartooths, but also to leave markers so we could find the plane filled with cocaine. You can choose to be happy, Maddie."

"It's not that easy."

"What are you so afraid of?"

"I'm not afraid," she said, bristling. "But just because we were thrown together up there on the mountain… We needed each other up there. But life is…different down here."

He shook his head. "I'm sorry to hear you say that. I thought nothing could scare you. Clearly I was wrong." He let out a sigh and stepped back. "You decide to take a chance on happiness, you give me a call."

He started for the door, fearing she would let him walk through it.

"Bentley."

He stopped, closing his eyes and saying a little prayer of thanks, before he turned back to her.

"I can't do this anymore," she said with a sweep of her arm that took in more than the room. It took in the whole sheep ranch.

"You don't have to," he said quietly.

She looked around the room, tears in her eyes. "Fuzz Carpenter has wanted to buy the place since Hank died. I just dug my heels in because…" She looked up at him.

"Because it's your nature?"

She smiled at that.

"If this is really what you want to do, then why not?"

She looked around for a moment then settled her gaze on him. "I feel like I've failed."

"You know better than that."

"I needed this place after I lost Hank and Matthew. It distracted me from the grief. It was my lifeline."

"And now?"

"You asked me up on the mountain what I would do if I didn't sheep ranch."

"I remember."

"I hadn't even thought about it. But I have now. I want to help boys like Dewey."

"What, not travel the world?"

She turned to smile at him. "You knew that wasn't me, didn't you."

He nodded. "But I would have quit my job and gone with you. I want to be with you."

"I find that hard to believe as contrary as I am."

He smiled. "You are one contrary woman, no doubt about that. But I'll take you as you are. If traveling the world comes with it, then count me in. Same if it's starting some kind of way station for troubled kids."

"Do you know what you're saying?"

He laughed. "Maddie, I want to date you. Court you. Whatever you want to call it. And when the time comes, I'm going to marry you."

"Jamison, we hardly know each other."

"Oh, we know each other," he said. He stepped to her and slipped his hand around her slim throat to cup the back of her neck. He pulled her to him and kissed her on the mouth. "Oh, we know each other just fine." And he kissed her again.

When he drew back, he said, "I'm falling for you, Maddie Conner. Given time, I think you might fall for me."

"You're pretty sure of yourself, Deputy."

He grinned. "I'm sure of us," he said, his gaze locking with hers. He slowly lowered his lips until they brushed across hers. He felt her tremble and gathered her closer. "Let's start with dinner tonight." He let go of her. "I'll pick you up at eight."

MADDIE STOOD IN front of the mirror, entranced by the woman she saw there. She ran her hands over her hips, lost in the silky feel of the dress. It was new. For new beginnings, she'd told herself when she'd bought it, feeling extravagant and giddy with excitement.

She touched her finger to her lips. They still tingled from Jamison's kiss earlier. Her gaze took in the flush of her cheeks, the brightness of her blue eyes. She smiled at the woman in the mirror.

A date?

She shook her head. She hadn't dated since high school—and only then with Hank.

She thought of Bentley and told herself there was no reason to be nervous. She knew this man. She pictured him with his shirt off, standing at the edge of the creek that first morning on the way to sheep camp, and felt that shiver of desire. He'd ignited something in her, a passion she hadn't known she possessed.

Was it any wonder she'd pushed him away, afraid on so many levels. But he was right. They did deserve a chance.

She looked again at the woman in the mirror, surprised to see her body. It wasn't bad for a woman forty-five. She'd kept in shape working the ranch. It hadn't been something she'd thought about. Just as she hadn't looked at her body in years.

Now she could admit that she'd hidden it, thinking she could put her sensuality on a shelf—just like she had her life. Or that she could hide it by wearing jeans and Hank's old flannel shirts for so long.

She had legs, she thought with a laugh as she admired them and the heels she'd bought to go with the dress.

The dress fit perfectly, cupping her full breasts and skimming over her hips. She stared for a moment longer at herself. It had been so long since she'd looked at herself that it felt as if she was looking at a stranger.

Maddie felt a flutter of excitement as she began to pull her hair up. No braid tonight. This was going to be a whole new her.

She thought about the money she would get for the ranch. It would be plenty enough to buy a small place, preferably with a large old farmhouse, and some land so she could start her home for boys like Dewey.

She thought of her own son, Matthew, and felt a lump in her throat. She would need a place big enough to have horses and maybe even a few cows. She smiled, knowing Matthew would have approved. She would start looking for a place tomorrow.

At the sound of a vehicle driving up in the yard, she left her bedroom and walked toward the front door.

Her heels clicked on the old hardwood floors. It made a nice sound. She heard music coming from the car that had pulled up in front of her house. She recognized the song, a catchy, summery tune. It lifted her heart as if attached to a helium balloon—as did the sight of the man who climbed out from behind the wheel.

Bentley Jamison couldn't have looked more handsome in his dark suit. If she hadn't already fallen in love with him, she thought she would have all over again as he made his way up the steps.

He let out a long whistle. "You look…" For a moment he seemed at a loss for words. "…beautiful."

She felt beautiful as she saw herself reflected in his eyes.

He held a bouquet of white daisies in his one fist and a box of candy in the other.

She laughed as he handed her both. "You shouldn't have."

"I wasn't sure how courtin' out West worked, but I wanted to cover all my bases." He looked down at the suit he was wearing. "Is it too much for Big Timber?"

She smiled. "It's perfect. But I don't need flowers or candy. All I need is you," she said, meeting his silver gaze.

Jamison pulled her close to cup her cheek in one of his large hands. He brushed his thumb pad over her lower lip. His thumb pad felt rough, and she had to smile as she remembered the greenhorn who'd stood on this porch not all that long ago.

Welcome to Montana, Deputy, she thought as he kissed her, sending a shiver of expectation through her. Whatever the future held, Maddie knew Bentley Jamison was going to be part of it.

* * * * *

Start your holidays with a bang!
Read on for an excerpt from
CHRISTMAS AT CARDWELL RANCH
by USA TODAY *bestselling author*

B.J. Daniels

"Lily, I have a bad feeling that the reason Mia's condo was ransacked and my father's too was that they were looking for this thumb drive."

"Then you should take it to the marshal," she said, handing it to him. "I have a copy of the letters on my computer, so I can keep working on the code."

He nodded, although he had no intention of taking it to the marshal. Not until he knew which side of the fence Hud Savage was on.

"Until we know what's really on this," he said, "I wouldn't mention it to anyone, all right?"

She nodded.

"I need to get to the hospital and see my father, but I don't like leaving you here snowed in alone."

She waved him off.

"I'll keep working on the code and let you know when I get it finished."

She sounded as if she would be glad when he left her at it. He was reminded that she also had plans to talk to her former fiancé today. He felt a hard knot form in his stomach. Jealousy? Heck yes.

Except he had nothing to be jealous about, right? Last night hadn't happened. At least that was the way Lily wanted it.

"I want you to have this." He held out the pistol he'd taken from his father's. "I need to know that you are safe."

Lily held up both hands. "I don't want it. I could never…"

"Just in case," Tag said as he laid it on the table, telling himself that if someone broke into her house and tried to hurt her, she would get over her fear of guns quickly. At least he hoped that was true.

Available October 22, only from Harlequin® Intrigue®
wherever books and ebooks are sold.

HIEXPBJD1113

JILL SORENSON

He's her only hope...

Park ranger Hope Banning's plans for a little R & R are put on hold when a plane crashes at the top of a remote mountain. Hope will have to climb the summit and assess the situation. And the only climbing partner available is Sam Rutherford—the enigmatic man she spent a night with six months ago.

Ever since Sam lost his girlfriend in a falling accident, he insists on climbing solo. But Hope and any potential survivors need his help. As Sam and Hope set out on an emergency search-and-rescue mission, he realizes the sparks still sizzle between them. And when they learn a killer is among the survivors, they must place their trust in each other for a chance at happiness.

Available wherever books are sold!

Be sure to connect with us at:
Harlequin.com/Newsletters
Facebook.com/HarlequinBooks
Twitter.com/HarlequinBooks

HARLEQUIN® HQN™
www.Harlequin.com

PHJS795

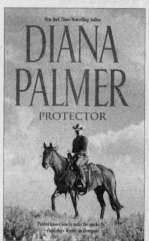

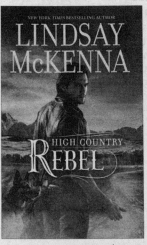

REQUEST YOUR FREE BOOKS!

2 FREE NOVELS
FROM THE SUSPENSE COLLECTION
PLUS 2 FREE GIFTS!

YES! Please send me 2 FREE novels from the Suspense Collection and my 2 FREE gifts (gifts are worth about $10). After receiving them, if I don't wish to receive any more books, I can return the shipping statement marked "cancel." If I don't cancel, I will receive 4 brand-new novels every month and be billed just $6.24 per book in the U.S. or $6.74 per book in Canada. That's a savings of at least 22% off the cover price. It's quite a bargain! Shipping and handling is just 50¢ per book in the U.S. and 75¢ per book in Canada.* I understand that accepting the 2 free books and gifts places me under no obligation to buy anything. I can always return a shipment and cancel at any time. Even if I never buy another book, the two free books and gifts are mine to keep forever.

191/391 MDN F4XN

Name _____ (PLEASE PRINT)

Address _____ Apt. #

City _____ State/Prov. _____ Zip/Postal Code

Signature (if under 18, a parent or guardian must sign)

Mail to the **Harlequin® Reader Service:**
IN U.S.A.: P.O. Box 1867, Buffalo, NY 14240-1867
IN CANADA: P.O. Box 609, Fort Erie, Ontario L2A 5X3

Want to try two free books from another line?
Call 1-800-873-8635 or visit www.ReaderService.com

* Terms and prices subject to change without notice. Prices do not include applicable taxes. Sales tax applicable in N.Y. Canadian residents will be charged applicable taxes. Offer not valid in Quebec. This offer is limited to one order per household. Not valid for current subscribers to the Suspense Collection or the Romance/Suspense Collection. All orders subject to credit approval. Credit or debit balances in a customer's account(s) may be offset by any other outstanding balance owed by or to the customer. Please allow 4 to 6 weeks for delivery. Offer available while quantities last.

Your Privacy—The Harlequin® Reader Service is committed to protecting your privacy. Our Privacy Policy is available online at www.ReaderService.com or upon request from the Harlequin Reader Service.

We make a portion of our mailing list available to reputable third parties that offer products we believe may interest you. If you prefer that we not exchange your name with third parties, or if you wish to clarify or modify your communication preferences, please visit us at www.ReaderService.com/consumerschoice or write to us at Harlequin Reader Service Preference Service, P.O. Box 9062, Buffalo, NY 14269. Include your complete name and address.

SUS13R

Under Montana's big sky, two lovers will find
their way back to one another...if an unsolved
murder doesn't pull them apart forever....

A gripping romantic suspense from
USA TODAY bestselling author

B.J. DANIELS

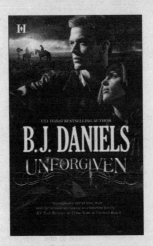

UNFORGIVEN

Available in stores now.

B.J. DANIELS

83793	CARDWELL RANCH TRESPASSER & BIG SKY STANDOFF	___ $6.99 U.S.	___ $7.99 CAN.	
83787	JUSTICE AT CARDWELL RANCH	___ $5.99 U.S.	___ $6.99 CAN.	
77757	REDEMPTION	___ $7.99 U.S.	___ $9.99 CAN.	
77673	UNFORGIVEN	___ $7.99 U.S.	___ $9.99 CAN.	
69680	CARDWELL RANCH TRESPASSER	___ $5.50 U.S.	___ $6.25 CAN.	
69602	CORRALLED	___ $5.25 U.S.	___ $6.25 CAN.	

(limited quantities available)

TOTAL AMOUNT	$ _____
POSTAGE & HANDLING	$ _____
($1.00 FOR 1 BOOK, 50¢ for each additional)	
APPLICABLE TAXES*	$ _____
TOTAL PAYABLE	$ _____

(check or money order—please do not send cash)

To order, complete this form and send it, along with a check or money order for the total above, payable to Harlequin HQN, to: **In the U.S.:** 3010 Walden Avenue, P.O. Box 9077, Buffalo, NY 14269-9077; **In Canada:** P.O. Box 636, Fort Erie, Ontario, L2A 5X3.

Name: _____
Address: _____ City: _____
State/Prov.: _____ Zip/Postal Code: _____
Account Number (if applicable): _____
075 CSAS

*New York residents remit applicable sales taxes.
*Canadian residents remit applicable GST and provincial taxes.